RETURN 20,000 LEAGUES UNDER THE SEA

STEVE BARLOW & STEVE SKIDMORE

USBORNE

First published in the UK in 2011 by Usborne Publishing Ltd., Usborne House,
83-85 Saffron Hill, London EC1N 8RT, England. www.usborne.com

Cover illustration by Sam Hadley.

A CIP catalogue record for this book is available from the British Library.

ISBN 9781409521426 J MAMJJASOND/11 02483/1

Printed in Reading, Berkshire, UK.

In 1934, the international crisis caused by the rise of totalitarian governments in many parts of the world is growing more serious by the day. New discoveries in science and medicine promise a bright future; at the same time, new weapons threaten global disaster. This is the new Scientific Age: an age of invention, adventure – and deadly danger...

1 RECORD...

"**A**re you absolutely sure you want to do this?"

Luke Challenger's question was kindly meant, but Nick Malone greeted it with indignation. "Of course I am! I know what I did wrong last run – I'll be fine, you'll see."

Luke gave a resigned nod and signalled to the speedboat driver, who motored gently ahead until the rope trailing behind the boat tightened. Nick, grasping the handle at the rope's end and crouched with his waterskis raised almost vertically in front of him, began to move through the water. Luke gave the driver another signal, and the boat surged forward, sweeping over the smooth surface of Lake Windermere as Nick rose on his skis. He swept across the boat's wake from side to side, increasing speed in preparation for his jump.

As they approached the ramp, Luke found himself muttering encouragement: "Come on, Nick, keep your knees flexible, be prepared for the shock... Go for control, not distance..." He broke off. Nick couldn't hear his instructions, even if he shouted – and anyway, it was too late.

Nick hit the ramp travelling at about seventy miles per hour. For a split second, all seemed well...then he veered off to the left, lifting one ski in an attempt to keep his balance – and by the time he shot from the top of the ramp, he had let go of the rope and lost a ski. With a yell of despair and a confusion of flailing limbs, he hurtled through the air and plummeted into the lake with an almighty splash that echoed mockingly from the surrounding fells. Luke winced.

The boat circled round and Luke hauled his luckless cousin over the side. Nick lay gasping like a stranded fish and rubbing at sore spots (seemingly every part of his body he could reach). In between gasps, he said, "I almost had it that time." At length, he sat up and eyed the ramp as if it had done him a personal injury. "All right, let's try it again."

Luke ran his fingers through his wet hair and eyed his cousin with concern. Both of them were reasonably proficient waterskiers; but whereas Luke had mastered the ramp on his third attempt, Nick had been struggling all morning. Unhappily, once his mind was set on something, Nick never gave up: he would make a successful jump or kill himself trying. At the moment, the second possibility seemed the most likely, so Luke forced his expression into an apologetic grimace. "Would you mind...? I think I've jarred my back a bit. I wouldn't mind a rest."

"Can't take it, eh?" said Nick breezily. Luke's spade-shaped Challenger jaw tightened as he bit back an angry response, which would have been along the lines of, *I only said that to give you an excuse to stop before you break your stupid neck!* Fortunately, the words remained unsaid and Nick, looking the other way, failed to notice his friend's thunderous expression. "Ah, well," Nick continued while Luke mastered his temper, "I suppose it won't do us any harm to have a break. We can always come back this afternoon."

Hoping that if they did, the local hospital would turn out to have a good fracture clinic, Luke signalled to their driver. The boat's engine whined as they left the waterskiing area. Barely a minute later, they were stepping onto the landing stage and making for the changing rooms to recover their clothes.

"Pretty fast, that boat," said Nick conversationally. "Nothing like as fast as your da's pride and joy, of course." He gave Luke a conspiratorial wink. "Why don't we go down to the Challenger boathouse and see how they're getting on?"

"Because," Luke told him, "my father said that if he caught me anywhere near his precious boat, he would tear me into little pieces with his bare hands."

"Ah, now that's a remark that could be interpreted in several ways."

"Really?" said Luke sceptically. "I can only think of one. I'm already in his bad books over what I did to his car."

"You mean, when you used nitroglycerine as a fuel additive?"

"He wasn't using the car at the time. It was an experiment," said Luke defensively. "And it was only a small amount of nitroglycerine."

"It was still enough to blow the cylinder head into the next county."

"Well, anyway, he made it clear that one more stunt like that and he'd have my guts for garters."

Nick struggled into his shirt; as his head emerged,

his dark curls fanned out like the fronds of a sea anemone. His mouth curved into his trademark good-natured grin. "Sure, he says these things, but he doesn't mean them."

"I'm not sure I want to test that theory." Luke towelled his mane of fair hair. "I had enough of a struggle persuading him to let us come up here at all. He only agreed because Mother's digging up fossils in Colorado and he's running out of relatives to palm us off on..." Luke broke off and bit his lip. In previous summers, while his mother had been away on some expedition or other, Luke and Nick had taken their holidays with Nick's father. But Edward Malone had died almost exactly a year ago in a blazing Zeppelin over a remote South American plateau; the last thing Luke wanted was to remind Nick of that.

But Nick didn't seem to have caught the remark. "I thought it was so the security men he brought here to protect the boat could protect us, too."

Luke snorted derisively. "Waste of time if you ask me. My father's security is like elephant repellent."

"Elephant repellent? What does that do?"

"Repels elephants. I sprayed some on this morning. Look around you – see any elephants?"

"No."

"Good stuff, isn't it? Dad's security is like that. It's

'protecting' us from something that isn't there in the first place."

Nick struggled with a sock. "Are you sure about that? I seem to recall a Japanese colonel – that Mochizuki woman – who followed us across the Atlantic and half of South America last year, shooting all the way."

"Yes, but she's dead. The Sons of Destiny were wiped out a year ago, remember."

"I guess so. Personally, I'm quite glad that no one has tried to kill us lately. It's relaxing."

Luke finished tying his shoelaces and led the way from the changing room, along the lakeside path to the boathouse where the Challenger Industries powerboat was moored.

Britain and America had been locked in a struggle for the world water speed record for several years. Kaye Don, driving *Miss England III*, had set a target of 119 mph on Loch Lomond in July 1932. Not to be outdone, his American rival, Gar Wood, had built *Miss America X* and in September of the same year had set a new record of 124 mph, making it clear that in terms of money and know-how, the USA was unbeatable. Don had given up in despair and *Miss England III* had gone to a museum. Now Sir Andrew Challenger, Luke's father, planned to steal the Americans' thunder with a new record attempt. The boat he hoped would be a world-beater was being prepared, under heavy security, a few yards away from where Luke and Nick were walking.

Sir Andrew had named his boat *Enid II* in memory of his sister. Enid Challenger had married Edward Malone; Nick was their only son. Unhappily, she had died several years before. Perhaps, thought Luke, it was the fact that the Challenger boat bore Nick's mother's name that explained why Nick was so determined to get as close to it as possible. Or perhaps, he reflected, it was sheer devilment.

Nick pointed at a group of figures in white overalls walking away from the boathouse. "Look – that's your da's people going for lunch." He eyed the long, whitewashed building hungrily. "It all seems quiet over there. Sure, one little peek won't cause anybody any trouble at all." Sticking his hands in his pockets and whistling with studied nonchalance, he sauntered towards the door. Luke glanced around, but, surprisingly, none of his father's security team seemed to be about at the moment. With a mental shrug, he turned from the path to follow Nick.

The boathouse was dark after the bright sunlight outside. The sleek shape of *Enid II* floated serenely in the small dock that fitted it like a glove. The long shed seemed to be deserted – but a rhythmic tapping indicated that someone was still at work, and after a few moments a white-overalled figure appeared from behind the boat's engine cowling. He gave the boys an owlish stare. "You shouldn't be in here, you know."

"It's all right," said Nick quickly. "He's Luke Challenger. That's his da's boat you're working on. I'm his cousin Nick, so it's all family, d'you see?" He gave the man a closer look. "You're new, aren't you?"

"That's right – standing in for Mr. Parker. Tummy trouble." The man shrugged and wiped his hands on a cloth. "Look around if you want. I'm a mechanic, not security. It's all the same to me."

Luke and Nick exchanged glances. They knew that the chief mechanic, Hargreaves, had been warned to keep them away from *Enid II* – but, by some stroke of luck, the message didn't seem to have got through to Parker's replacement. Encouraged, Nick stepped forward and looked around. "You on your own?"

The mechanic gave a mournful nod. "That's right. The rest of them have gone to the pub. Suppose I might as well have gone with them – we've been having engine trouble all morning and I'm blessed if I can see what's wrong."

With a casual air that completely failed to disguise his eagerness, Nick said, "Would you like me to take a look? I'm pretty good with engines."

The mechanic looked from Luke to Nick and back again. Luke nodded. "He's a genius."

"Well, I shouldn't by rights…" The man sighed. "Oh well, I don't suppose it can do any harm. I'm off for a cuppa. If anyone asks, I haven't seen anything." Shaking his head, he pottered off towards the shadowy end of the boathouse. Moments later, the sounds of a kettle being filled wafted from the gloom.

Nick was beside himself with glee. "That's a stroke of luck!" He dived head first into the engine compartment.

Luke addressed his friend's protruding backside. "I'm not sure this is such a good idea. I'm in enough trouble with my dad already, remember. What if the others come back?"

"What if they do? We're helping, aren't we?" Nick's voice was muffled. He wriggled into a new position. "Ah!"

"Ah, what?"

Nick emerged, grinning. "Try the starter."

"Start the engines? You're joking! We'll be lynched."

"D'you want to live for ever? Go on, give it a try."

Muttering darkly under his breath, Luke jumped into the driver's seat and pressed the starter. Immediately, the two Rolls-Royce engines roared into life. Nick wiped his hands with a modest air.

The mechanic came scurrying from the back of the

boathouse, a steaming kettle in his hand. "How did you do that?"

Nick examined his fingernails. "Oh, the master's touch, you know." His voice became wistful. "I don't suppose we could…test it out?"

The mechanic scratched his head. Unfortunately, in his astonishment he forgot that the hand he chose to do this with was the one holding the kettle. "Well, I – ouch!" He put the kettle down hurriedly and rubbed his scalded ear.

"You should put something on that," said Nick quickly. "Butter's good for burns." As the mechanic retired, rubbing his ear and groaning, Nick started casting off mooring lines. "Come on," he hissed. "I asked if we could take her out, you heard me!"

Luke gawped at him. "He didn't say 'yes'!"

"He didn't say 'no', either!" Nick clambered into the co-driver's seat. "Let's go! We'll never get another chance like this!"

"This is a very, very bad idea." Scowling ferociously, Luke selected reverse gear. Its engines rumbling softly, the boat pulled out of the shed and into open water. As the bows cleared the short jetty, he swung the stern to the side, selected forward gear and began to open the throttles.

Nick threw back his head and gave an exultant whoop. "Ah, that's grand!"

"We are going to be strangled for this," said Luke. "You know that, don't you?"

Nick gave him a reckless grin. "It'll be worth it."

After a moment, Luke returned the grin. "Maybe it will."

"All right then." Nick rubbed his hands. "Let's see what she'll do."

Luke opened the throttles further and headed for Newby Bridge at the south end of the lake. "What was wrong with the engines, anyway?"

"Just a bad electrical connection to the ignition. I'm amazed they didn't spot it."

"You wouldn't be if you'd seen half a dozen of Dad's boffins stripping down an FM radio to find out why it wasn't working, and not one of them noticing they'd forgotten to plug it into the mains." As the lake narrowed, Luke swung the craft around and reduced the throttle to idling speed.

"Come on!" Nick was jiggling in his seat, impatient to be off.

"Calm down." Luke rummaged under his seat and found a helmet and goggles, which he strapped on. Nick followed his lead. "I'm waiting for our wash to die down," Luke explained. "If we hit our own wake at speed, it could damage the boat." He watched as the last of the waves generated by their passage rippled along the lakeshore and disappeared. "Fasten your seat belt," he said. Grinning, Nick buckled up the safety harness to hold him in his seat. "All right. Here we go." Luke eased the throttle levers forward.

The engines thundered. *Enid II* shot across the calm blue water, leaving a fantail of spray and white foam behind her. Luke and Nick were thrust back in their seats. Nick's mouth opened wide in an exultant yell, but the sound was snatched by the wind and lost behind the speeding boat. Luke gripped the wheel tightly, scanning the water ahead for hazards. The boat bucked and skittered like a living thing over the wavelets, but Luke held his course in a long curve, following the centre line of the lake as it swept up the wooded valley.

Far too soon, they were approaching the island chain off Bowness. Luke eased back on the throttles and the speedboat's bows settled back into the water with the grace of an alighting swan.

Nick let out his breath in a long whistle. "Amazing! Just amazing."

Luke swung the boat around, back the way they'd come. "One more run, then we'll have to take her back."

"Oh, come on!"

"We're in enough trouble as it is. Anyway, we'll have to wait for the wash again. We've got a few more minutes."

Nick folded his arms and sulked.

Seeking something to distract his disappointed friend, Luke pointed skywards. "See that?" A sleek silver biplane was banking around, its wings flashing in the sun. "RAF – a Hawker Hart, I think. Wonder what he's doing over here? Probably training." Luke watched as the aircraft made a turn and dived towards them. "He's really low," he observed. "I suppose—" He broke off as a series of bright flashes appeared above the propeller boss. A split second later, white splashes appeared on the water in a neat, regular line, heading straight for *Enid II*.

Luke stared at Nick in stunned disbelief. "He's shooting at us!"

2 ...ATTEMPT

Luke's stupefaction lasted less than a second. With a violent oath, he shoved the throttle levers all the way forward, simultaneously swinging the wheel.

Engines screaming, *Enid II* took off like a rocket, curving away to the right. Machine gun rounds stitched the placid water where the boat had been lying.

"Missed!" Nick made a rude gesture at the aircraft as it roared overhead. Then he turned a pale face to Luke. "Zigzag! The Hart's a two-seater – there'll be an observer with another machine gun!"

"I know." Luke spun the wheel again, just as the observer fired a burst from his Lewis gun. Unlike the pilot's fixed guns, which he could only line up on a target by aiming the whole plane at it, the observer's gun was on a swivel and could be swung to fire in any direction that didn't actually involve hitting the aircraft's wings or tail. It was only thanks to Luke's violent manoeuvre that the bullets flew wide. The boat skittered wildly across the water until the chines of the hull bit, and *Enid II* steadied and tore off down the lake at full speed.

Nick stared at Luke. "What on earth have we done to annoy the RAF?"

"You don't suppose that's really the RAF? That plane's been hijacked!"

"Who by?"

"By people who're trying to kill us!"

Nick gave his cousin an accusing look. "You said your da's security was a waste of time…"

"Forget what I said!" Luke throttled back the engines.

"What are you doing?" Nick was appalled. "We can't afford to lose speed – that plane'll be after us again in a minute." He craned his neck to watch the distant silver aircraft perform a banked turn over the north end of the lake.

"Yes, and it can do 185 miles per hour. This boat's maximum speed is under 150, and so far it's never been tested above 100. We're not going to avoid that plane by outrunning it. Anyway, we're going to run out of lake before it runs out of sky."

"So what do we do?"

"Outmanoeuvre it. We can turn faster than he can."

"We can't keep doing that for ever..." Nick's face paled. "Watch out! Here he comes again!"

Luke opened the throttles and once again, *Enid II* leaped forward. He swung the wheel violently from left to right as the roar of the aero-engine grew louder. The bullets from the pilot's Vickers machine guns went wide as the boat's zigzag course frustrated his aim, but as the biplane roared past, the observer again brought his swivel-mounted gun to bear. Nick and Luke ducked as several metallic pings indicated that shots had struck the engine, and two splintered holes appeared in the side-deck.

The lake was narrowing. His mouth set in a thin, hard line, Luke steered for the nearer bank. He set the control levers to half-throttle and steered the boat into a sweeping turn that sent up a glistening fan of spray. The opposite bank loomed as the boat struggled to complete the turn. Nick gasped as the hull brushed the reeds barely two yards from the shore, and breathed a sigh of relief as Luke gunned the engines to send *Enid II* back the way she had come.

"What about our wake?" demanded Nick feebly.

"Forget the wake!" The words were hardly out of Luke's mouth when the boat hit the wash of its previous passage. *Enid II* bucked like a nervous filly and almost turned over – for a moment, Nick was treated to the sight of a vertical horizon as the boat tipped on its side and the engines, with their propellers completely out of the water, screamed in protest. Then the hull smacked back onto the surface of the lake.

Nick gulped. "That was close. If the plane doesn't get us, your driving will."

"Never mind my driving! We wouldn't even be in this mess if you hadn't been so keen to get a look at this boat."

The injustice of this stung Nick. "How was I to know some madmen in a stolen plane would start shooting at us?"

Luke shook his head in angry frustration. "I'm not blaming you. I should have known that something was wrong. No security…and that mechanic in the boathouse – a 'late replacement' was he? Odd, the way he let us take the boat just like that, don't you think?"

"You mean…?"

"I mean, it'd be easy enough, when he saw us coming,

to biff one of Dad's security men, nip into the boathouse when everybody went for lunch and put on a white overall. The whole thing's a set-up. Happy-face back there must have been on the phone to his cronies as soon as we left the jetty."

Nick was switching his glance from the scene in front of the boat to that behind it in growing alarm. "Changing the subject – that plane's coming back and we're getting awfully close to those islands. Are you planning on doing a turn any time soon?"

Luke's mouth twisted in a ferocious grin. "No."

"But the islands!"

"We're going between them."

Sliding down in his seat, Nick slowly and deliberately closed his eyes.

Marjorie Bassenthwaite was feeling quietly pleased with herself. The floating restaurant she had booked for her little gathering had been an inspired choice. She had spent weeks worrying about what the weather might do to her carefully-laid plans; but in the event it was a glorious day, and a perfect setting. This was the moment she would make her mark on local society. It would be even better if Charlie Ennerdale chose to mark the occasion by proposing to her daughter Honoria.

The perfect make-up of Marjorie's brow furrowed in a brief frown. Even with a mother's compassionate eye, she had to concede that Honoria wasn't much of a catch; but then, Charlie, though as rich as turtle soup, had the brains of a trout and a face like a horse, so it would probably work out all right.

Marjorie thrust the thought to the back of her mind – nothing must be allowed to spoil her perfect day. She eyed with approval the bright awnings, the crisp white tablecloths, the fluttering bunting and the colourful flower arrangements. Her indulgent gaze travelled over the elegant guests wearing summer dresses and flannels, fashionable hats and jaunty straw boaters. Then she frowned again as the distant hum of powerful engines grew into a full-throated roar that threatened to drown out the palm court orchestra she had hired for the occasion. Some people, she told herself, have no consideration...

Luke grabbed Nick by the shoulder and hauled him upright. "I need you to spot for me! Keep an eye on that plane. Let me know as soon as it fires."

Nick nodded, and turned his head to stare over the boat's stern while Luke headed for the gap between Bowness, with its expensive waterfront houses, jetties and moorings, and the wooded shore of Belle Isle. "He's completed his turn…lining up behind us…" Nick grabbed for the cockpit combing to avoid being thrown out of the boat as Luke jinked to avoid a small, buoyed islet. "He's coming in…and firing…NOW!"

Luke hauled at the wheel, sending *Enid II* careering towards the Bowness shore.

Marjorie Bassenthwaite's eyes opened wide in horror as the motorboat that was tearing down the lake like a mad thing suddenly turned in a fountain of spray and headed straight for her immaculate social gathering. The orchestra faltered. Guests sprang to their feet, scattering tables and chairs, china plates and teacups, and tiny triangular cucumber sandwiches. Waiters dropped their napkins. There were hoarse cries and screams. A few hopeful souls waved their arms as though by doing so they could steer the aquatic juggernaut from its course. Marjorie looked up, aghast, as a silver biplane, guns chattering, flew by at treetop height. She turned her gaze back to the lake and gave a low moan.

At the last possible moment, Luke steered the boat aside. It hit the floating restaurant a glancing blow, throwing several people into the water. The spray of its passage hit the guests like a tidal wave, instantly drenching them. Members of the orchestra stared in dismay at their sodden instruments. Then the boat's wash hit, sending the pontoons on which the restaurant floated tilting and swaying in a crazy dance. More guests went into the lake; those that remained lost their footing and tumbled to join the chaos of upended furniture and ruined sandwiches sliding around the deck, while the awnings and bunting collapsed over the whole kicking and screaming crowd.

Marjorie surveyed the chaos with a sinking heart. One thing was clear: Honoria wasn't going to be proposed to today. "Oh…*bother!*"

As the biplane swept overhead, Luke swung the boat around the end of Belle Isle to head between the island and the lake's western shore.

"I hate to worry you," said Nick, "what with you being so busy and all, but I can smell petrol." He glanced over his shoulder. "Yep – they hit a fuel tank that time. We're going to run out of juice very shortly."

"Right." Luke cut the throttle. The engines subsided to little more than tickover; *Enid II* bobbed on the waves.

Nick gave him a nervous look. "So what do we do? Beach the boat? Swim for it?"

"Either way, we'd be sitting ducks." Luke turned his head to watch as the plane banked lazily, turning for another run. "We can't keep dodging them. Did you notice he was going more slowly when he went over us that last time?"

"Funnily enough, no! All I saw was that tea party we nearly ran into."

"Well, he was – probably to give his observer more time to get a decent shot in. That could work in our favour. I'm going to try something, but I have to get the timing exactly right."

Nick threw him a glance. "Oh, no," he said, "I know that look. You've got some crazy idea in mind, haven't you?"

Luke gave him the sort of grin usually associated with skulls on pirate flags. "Could be."

Nick sighed. "Well, it can't be any worse than just sitting here waiting to be shot at."

"Couldn't it?" Luke switched his attention back to the plane, which was now lining up for another run. He waited, eyes narrowed, judging speed and distance. Nick watched his friend with a mixture of hope and apprehension. He trusted Luke's judgement, and that had worked out so far: the evidence being, they weren't dead yet...

Then Luke yelled, "Here goes!" and opened the throttles once more. The boat leaped forward, and Nick forgot everything except the need to hold on. He twisted his head, just as the first flashes appeared through the spinning blades of the propeller, and yelled, "He's firing…!" A split second later his head snapped forward, banging his nose against the dashboard, and his body strained against the safety harness as Luke abruptly cut the throttles. The boat tried to nosedive into the lake. Water swept over the foredeck and splashed into the cockpit.

Startled by the boat's suddenly coming to what amounted to a dead stop, the pilot of the plane ceased firing. The few rounds he had shot off pattered harmlessly into the lake well ahead of the boat.

As the aircraft loomed overhead, Luke opened the throttles and once more *Enid II* was charging over the ruffled water. This time, Luke held a steady course, keeping the boat under the belly of the plane.

Nick looked up at the undercarriage, the fuselage – and the two neat racks of cigar-shaped objects nestling beneath the wings. He prodded Luke fiercely in the arm. "You do know this plane is a bomber, don't you?"

Luke didn't glance up. "Yes."

Nick gripped the cockpit sides as bombs began to detach from the aircraft and fall gracefully towards them. "Oh, nooooo…"

Water erupted around the speeding boat as the bombs struck. Luke and Nick were blinded by plumes of stinging spray as the boat weaved drunkenly from side to side with the force of the blasts. But Luke held his course, and his nerve. As the last of the bombs fell without striking the boat, the plane drew ahead slightly. Nick wiped water from his eyes, and saw where they were heading. He turned to Luke with an expression of horror. "You have got to be joking!"

Luke made no reply. He steadied the boat and gunned the thundering engines for one final effort...

The thrust of power set the boat moving slightly faster than its attacker. *Enid II* hit the ramp of the ski jump that Luke and Nick had been struggling to master all morning and leaped like a salmon. Nick caught one brief glimpse of the observer's appalled expression before the prow of the boat slammed into the biplane's tail assembly, demolishing it completely. Then the boat fell back to the lake, hitting the surface with a jarring shock that made Nick feel as though his spine had burst up through the back of his neck. At the same moment, the aircraft, engine screaming, spinning hopelessly out of control, dived into the lake with a thunderous splash.

Dazed, Luke throttled back. He circled the foaming, oil-streaked water where the plane had gone down for several minutes...but there seemed to be no survivors.

* * *

By the time Luke steered *Enid II* back to her jetty, the mechanics and drivers – with the notable exception of "Mr. Parker's replacement", of whom there was no sign – had returned from lunch. They watched the boat's approach in horrified silence.

Enid II had a huge gash in her bows. Her wooden decks were pocked with jagged bullet holes. She was low in the water, and settling more with every passing moment. One of the engines was completely dead; the other was coughing badly and its exhausts were throwing out clouds of oily black smoke.

Luke brought the battered speedboat alongside the jetty. He clambered out of the flooded cockpit and shook one leg experimentally – water showered from his sodden trousers.

He looked up into the horrified gaze of the Challenger team, and gave an apologetic shrug. "I'm afraid she's going to need a bit more work..."

3 NANNY

Kingshome Abbey, Wiltshire, England:
Headquarters of Challenger Industries

Good morning, Master Luke, Master Nick."
Bateman's bulldog face was expressionless, as usual.

"Good morning, Bateman." Luke's reply was equally non-committal. His father's major-domo was not a man to inspire confidences. If they had been met by any other member of Sir Andrew Challenger's staff, Luke could have counted on some degree of sympathy and done a bit of digging to find out exactly how much trouble he and Nick were in. With Bateman, he knew from long experience, it was hopeless. The man was about as sympathetic as a brick, and rather less forthcoming.

Bateman held out a letter on a silver tray. "For you, Master Nick." Looking startled, Nick took it. "Wait here, please." Bateman knocked on the door of Sir Andrew's study and, without waiting for a reply, went in.

Luke took a seat on an uncomfortable chair and glanced around the familiar hallway: the stained glass windows, the dark, heavy oak panelling and the slightly knock-kneed suit of armour beside the foot of the stairs did nothing to lighten his mood. His feeling of gloom continued to deepen until a whoop of excitement from Nick caught his attention. "Who's the letter from?"

"Mercedes." Nick flashed him a grin and scanned half a dozen lines. His face fell. "Oh, no!"

"When's she arriving?"

Nick looked stricken. "She isn't!"

"But it was all arranged – she was supposed to be coming here next week. Don't tell me she tried to escape again."

Still reading, Nick nodded glumly and Luke groaned. Mercedes had been their guide when they rescued Luke's mother Harriet from the Lost World the previous year, an episode in which Mercedes' father had lost his life. For his sake Harriet Challenger had decided to take the mercurial Brazilian girl in hand. Unfortunately for all concerned, she was convinced that it was in Mercedes' best interests to be given the finest education that money could buy. Mercedes had so entirely disagreed with this plan that she had now broken out of three expensive English public schools, leaving a trail of confusion and (in at least one case) outright rebellion in her wake.

"This time she got as far as Southampton before they picked her up." Nick, who had a soft spot for Mercedes, sounded proud, rueful and a little envious of her exploits. "She says she was trying to stow away on a steamer for Rio de Janeiro when she was spotted, and now your ma's decided to pack her off to a maximum-security Carmelite nunnery on a mountain in the Pyrenees. Apparently, the only way you can reach the place is by some sort of crane."

"I still wouldn't bet against her getting out of there."

"Nor would I. The main point is, she won't be coming here." Nick was distraught. "A whole summer in this dump, and no Mercedes! It's enough to drive you to despair."

Luke's reply was forestalled by the reappearance of Bateman, who gravely announced, "Nanny will see you now."

Luke stared at him. "Who on earth is Nanny? I thought my father had called us in."

"Sir Andrew is otherwise engaged at the moment."

Bateman held the study door open. Exchanging a puzzled glance, Luke and Nick went through it.

The study was the same as ever, except for the addition of what looked like a radio loudspeaker in a handsome walnut cabinet, sitting on the right-hand side of Sir Andrew's desk. As Bateman closed the door behind them, a voice issued from the device. "Luke and Nick. How good of you to come. Do sit down."

"Nanny?" Luke was thoroughly perplexed. He hadn't had a nanny since he'd been packed off to his first prep school at the age of seven.

"That's right, dear." The voice was female; calm, and as plummy as Christmas pudding.

"Whose nanny?" demanded Nick.

"Everyone's nanny, Nick dear." The voice gave an apologetic cough. "Perhaps I'd better explain. Following the sad loss of your father last year, Challenger Industries needed a new Head of Security. You see that, don't you?"

Luke avoided Nick's eye. He knew that Nanny was being careful not to remind them that Edward Malone had been revealed as a traitor who had been working for their shadowy enemies all along. "Go on."

"Well, Sir Andrew decided it would be best if Mr. Malone's successor were more…anonymous, and therefore less vulnerable to pressure."

Nick remained angrily silent. Luke said, "So 'Nanny' is a sort of code name."

Nanny's disembodied voice sounded pleased by Luke's ready grasp of the situation. "Precisely, dear."

"But a code name for what?" demanded Luke. "Are you my father's new Head of Security, or just someone who speaks for her – or him – or them? Are we really talking to a person, or an organization – MI5, say, or the Secret Intelligence Service? Who are you, exactly?"

"That," said Nanny primly, "would be telling." Nick gave a snort of disgust.

"All right." Luke sat in an overstuffed leather chair and crossed his legs. "I suppose you know all about the Windermere attack."

"Oh, yes, dear." Nanny sounded disapproving. "Deplorable. Quite shocking."

"How was it worked?"

"What we should be asking is, who was behind it?"

"We know who was behind it," said Luke impatiently. "The Sons of Destiny."

"Do you think so, dear?" Nanny's voice was infuriatingly calm. "I wonder why, if that's the case, they went to all the trouble of luring you out onto the lake."

Luke shrugged. "They had a plane and people to fly it, and my dad's boat was a target they couldn't miss."

"Though as it turned out, fortunately, they did. It

doesn't prove the attack was made by the Sons of Destiny."

"Well, it should be easy enough to check!" snapped Luke. "They all have a snake coiled round a spear tattooed on the inside of their left wrists."

"I'm afraid I don't know what the gentlemen from the aeroplane may have had tattooed on their wrists," said Nanny reproachfully, "or anywhere else for that matter. The lake is rather deep where they crashed. Recovering the bodies is proving to be a *teensy* bit difficult."

Luke threw up his hands in disgust. "Is there anything you *do* know?"

"Oh, yes, dear. We know the mechanic was an imposter."

"I think," said Luke with heavy irony, "we'd managed to work that out for ourselves."

Choosing to ignore this, Nanny went on. "He must have waited days for his opportunity. When he saw you out on the lake, he disposed of your father's security guard by offering him a cup of tea absolutely brimming with knockout drops. It was foolish of the guard to be caught out so easily." The plummy voice was stern and unforgiving. "Nanny had to be very cross with him.

"Then the fake mechanic sabotaged the boat's engines in such a way that Nick would easily be able to spot the problem. And, yes, the local switchboard confirms that he telephoned the air base as soon as you'd cast off – and just before he disappeared into thin air. But you were wrong about the aeroplane being hijacked. I'm afraid the pilot and observer were genuine RAF – the pilot was a Squadron Leader, no less."

Luke was outraged. "And nobody spotted they were also members of the Sons of Destiny?"

"We don't know that for certain, do we, dear? Though I agree it seems very likely. The Sons of Destiny are a secret organization, after all. Its members don't go around telling people they're really working towards global war and the destruction of all democratic government so that they can rise from the ashes and take over the world. They pretend to be like everyone else. That's rather the point of a secret organization, you see."

"I thought we'd seen the last of those lunatics!" said Luke harshly. "Weren't their whole High Command wiped out in Brazil last year?"

"Really, dear!" Nanny's voice was gently reproving. "You should know better than that! Yes, their tame assassin, Colonel Mochizuki, certainly came to a sticky end. A pity, really."

Luke spluttered. "A pity?"

"Well, she was only the second female to be accepted for training as a samurai in over 300 years. A remarkable woman in many ways."

"She was a cruel, vicious monster!"

"Oh, yes, that too," said Nanny offhandedly. "And then, of course, the rest of the High Command perished when their Zeppelin blew up. That was a setback, but it did them little lasting damage. Others stepped forward to take their place. You can't destroy an organization by disposing of a few of its members, no matter how highly placed. The Sons of Destiny are like the hydra of Greek legend: if you cut off one head, two more grow in its place."

"All right." Nick had found his voice at last. "But why did they attack us? And why now?"

"That's hard to say, dear. Revenge was probably a strong motive. You did rather put a spanner in their works twelve months ago. They may also believe that if they manage to eliminate Master Luke, it would distract Sir Andrew from his latest project."

"I heard," said Luke, "that my father's latest top secret project has to do with atomic energy."

"Not as top secret as all that, evidently," observed Nanny with frigid disapproval. "Little pitchers have big ears."

"Well? Is it?"

"That's for me to know and you to find out."

Luke gave up. "So what do we do now?"

As if in answer, the study door was thrust open and

Sir Andrew Challenger was wheeled into the room by the poker-faced Bateman. He was followed by some half-dozen harassed-looking white-coated scientists, who were desperately attempting to make notes of his bellowed instructions and losing half the untidy bundles of papers they were carrying in the process.

"We need more power to the cyclotron!" roared Sir Andrew. "Double the power – treble the power! Even that's no good if we can't get the frequency higher, and are you sure that's the strongest dipole magnet you can find?" Catching sight of Luke and Nick, the irascible head of Challenger Industries broke off. "Oh, it's you two." He scowled even more deeply. "You'll forget everything you just heard if you know what's good for you." Turning his chair, he barked, "We'll finish this later!" and the relieved scientists fled, shedding more papers as they made a hurried exit.

Sir Andrew gave Luke and Nick his full baleful attention. "Hargreaves tells me my boat is a complete write-off," he rasped. "He says he'll have to start again from scratch."

"We're fine, Father," said Luke woodenly, "thanks for asking."

Sir Andrew's livid face turned an even more unhealthy colour. "Blast your impudence! You wreck my boat—"

"I'd've thought you'd be less worried about bullet holes in your boat than bullet holes in your son!"

"If you'd left my blasted boat alone, there'd have been no question of bullet holes in either of you!" Sir Andrew banged the desk with a clenched fist, causing Nanny's speaker to jump in the air. "The minute I let you out of my sight, you cause riot and wreckage over half of Westmorland – have you any idea how much that wretched Bassenthwaite woman is claiming in compensation? She's not only blaming you for ruining her idiotic picnic, mind! She says you've wrecked her daughter's marriage prospects for good!"

"What?" Luke and Nick exchanged startled glances. "I haven't even met her daughter..."

Luke's father wasn't listening. "Not to mention, the Air Ministry are trying to make out that I owe them the cost of replacing their blasted plane!"

"Perhaps it would be best if Nick and I cleared out for a while," suggested Luke without much hope. "Things might die down. I hear Greece is very nice this time of year..."

Sir Andrew wattled. "Are you mad? Let you go to Greece? On your own? How could I protect you with those Sons of Destiny madmen after your scalps?"

A plummy voice interrupted, "We can't be absolutely certain—"

"Shut up, Nanny!" Sir Andrew gave the loudspeaker a momentary glare. "Anyway, I shudder to think what you two would get up to in Greece – you'd probably start a war!" Sir Andrew seemed to run out of steam. He waved listlessly at a chair. "Oh, sit down." He nodded at Nick. "You, too. I was on the verge of pulling the funding on our world record scheme anyway," he went on in his usual growl. "I can't justify pumping resources into prestige projects when there's more urgent work requiring my attention."

"Like bombarding uranium with slow neutrons to achieve nuclear fission?" said Luke.

His father stared at him, aghast. "How the devil did you know about that?"

"You should warn your boffins not to talk about their experiments in front of the tea-lady. Anyway, I read the latest scientific papers, and what else would you be doing with a cyclotron?"

"We are so sharp," Nanny's voice intoned frostily, "one of these days, we might just end up cutting ourselves. *Then* we'd be sorry." Luke and Nick exchanged surreptitious grins.

Sir Andrew glared at them both. "Very clever," he said heavily. "So you have some inkling what I'm up to. And what you do now is, you ask no more questions and forget everything you've heard so far."

"That's not fair!" protested Luke. "Nick and I can't help picking things up when we're stuck around here all day every day, and who would we tell anyway? You've just told us we're not going anywhere..."

"And whose fault is that?" demanded Sir Andrew in a dangerous voice.

"We're sorry about the boat, Sir Andrew," put in Nick, "but Luke's right, isn't he? If we're not to set foot outside Kingshome Abbey, where's the harm in us knowing what's going on?"

"Particularly," added Luke, "as you're always saying you want me to succeed you as head of the firm and it's about time I showed some responsibility."

"Aren't some people getting too big for their boots?" asked Nanny vaguely.

Sir Andrew gazed at his son and nephew in silence. Then he gave a wolfish grin. "All right," he said. "You want to know what's going on? Then you can put this is your pipes, and see how you like it.

"Ever since the theory of neutrons was proved, there's been a race to discover the secret of nuclear fission. Everyone's at it – Rutherford in Manchester, Joliot-Curie in France, Fermi in Italy, Meitner in Germany..."

"And us," said Luke.

"And, as you say, us. There's a war coming – your friends, the Sons of Destiny, are hell-bent on getting it going as soon as possible. Whether they succeed or not, sooner or later, it will come.

"The power locked in the atom is incalculable. An atomic bomb would be so destructive, it would make all the explosives used in the Great War look like a Chinese firecracker in comparison. That's why this work is so important: whoever discovers the secret of nuclear fission first will rule the world. And if it's Adolf Hitler, God help us all."

Luke squared his shoulders. "Then we have to discover the secret first. I agree. So what are we waiting for? Nick and I are ready to help. What do you want us to do?"

Sir Andrew's grin widened. "Oh, you want to help? You want some *responsibility*? Don't worry – I've thought of a really *responsible* job for the two of you..."

4 LETTER

"**H**ere's another one," said Nick.

Luke glanced up, trying to force his bleary eyes to focus. "Another scheme for distilling petrol from potatoes? That's six so far."

"No, this one's for distilling it from rutabagas." Nick blinked. "What are rutabagas?"

"Swedes, I think." Luke let his head fall forward onto his folded arms and groaned aloud.

They were in a basement room with high, narrow windows, whose meagre light was reinforced by two naked hundred-watt bulbs dangling precariously from frayed wires. The walls and ceiling were the unhealthy cream colour of spoiled milk. The room had been a scullery when Kingshome Abbey was the country seat of a Victorian magnate. Now it was full of paper. Box files and lever arch binders jostled for space on dusty shelves with curling document wallets and dog-eared manila folders. Teetering piles of correspondence covered every flat surface and most of the floor.

In the centre of the room was a rickety table flanked by two cane-bottomed chairs. Nick sat in one and Luke in the other. In front of Luke stood an ancient Underwood typewriter. By his right hand was a wire basket. In this lay a dozen letters that Luke had so far typed with one-fingered deliberation. The basket was labelled OUT.

The IN basket was everything else in the room.

"My correspondence," Sir Andrew had told them with callous glee when showing them round. "Every crank and nutcase in creation sends me drivelling letters about the loony devices they've invented, which they imagine will be of interest to Challenger Industries. I haven't time to deal with their ravings, so I file them here."

"Fascinating," Luke had said, gazing at the mouldering letters, notes and diagrams with distaste. "So why are you showing it to us?"

"You wanted responsibility, didn't you?" Sir Andrew had boomed. "Well, responsibility you shall have. I'm appointing both of you as my confidential secretaries and I want you to reply to these letters." Bristling beard jutting out and blue-grey eyes sparkling with unholy glee, he concluded: "Every last one!"

So for the past three days, Luke and Nick had been wading their way through a mountain of correspondence, ranging from the mildly eccentric to the seriously deranged. There were designs for heavier-than-air balloons, cars with small front wheels and large back wheels that would stay level when going up hills ("for going down hills, simply turn the vehicle round and reverse!") and submersible aircraft carriers. These scintillating inventions jostled for space with schemes for producing gold from seawater, storing sunlight in jars (*condensed* sunlight, obviously) and stopping enemy tanks in their tracks with a "shield of impenetrable mental energy".

Every single one of Luke's replies began: *Dear Sir, thank you for your interesting and thoughtful letter and please accept my apologies for the lateness of this response. I am afraid that at the moment, our resources at Challenger Industries are fully engaged in a variety of projects and, regrettably, we cannot therefore fulfil your request for...* At this point the letters diverged, variously *reading five million pounds, three dozen trained seals,* or *an advanced chemical laboratory on the site of Buckingham Palace.*

Nick put the letter proposing a rutabaga petroleum refinery down and picked up another. He read for a moment and gave a bitter chuckle. "This one is even crazier. The bloke who wrote this reckons he's found a way of getting bits of silicon to remember stuff."

Luke gawped at him. "Silicon as in rock? How can rock remember stuff?"

"Oh, it gets better. He says we'll eventually be able to do all sorts of things with it – make calculations, record music and movies…he reckons by the end of the century, machines with silicon memories will practically replace adding machines, record players, typewriters, telephones – and by linking them up we'll have a worldwide communication network with instant access to all human knowledge." Nick gave a pitying sigh. "Completely barking, poor feller." He put the letter down and looked around in despair. "It'll take us the whole holiday to reply to this lot!"

"I'm sure that's the idea." Luke stood up and stretched. "We could be working on something really important, like nuclear fission. My dad's right about that – if we don't get it before Hitler does, we're sunk. And what are we doing instead? Dealing with nutcases who think they can distil petrol from root vegetables." He sighed. "Oh, well, let's get on with it. The most recent stuff first, remember. There might be something worthwhile in here, but anything over three years old that hasn't been invented yet is definitely rubbish. Your turn to type." He reached for a letter from the nearest pile.

Nick shuffled between paper stacks, sat down at the typewriter, and fed a blank piece of paper between the rollers. "Ready." When no reply came, he raised his head. "What's up?"

"I'm not sure." Luke was staring intently at the letter he was holding. "Listen to this." He began to read. "*Dear Professor Challenger, I hope you will not think it forward of me to write to a total stranger, but I have discovered something I reckon you'll find interesting...*"

Nick gestured at the mounds of paper surrounding him. "Haven't they all?"

"Sssh!" Luke motioned him to silence. "Listen... *My name is Jessica Land and I am the great granddaughter of Ned Land. You may have heard of Great-Grandpa Land: he was a harpooner, Canadian by birth, and seventy years ago, give or take, the United States government hired him to track down and kill some kind of sea monster that had been spotted all over the world's oceans, and had recently taken to colliding with ships and giving their captains the heebie-jeebies.*

"Great-Grandpa signed aboard the US Navy frigate SS *Abraham Lincoln, under Commander Farragut. Also on board was some Professor from the Museum of Paris, France. Their job was to find the monster causing all the trouble. If it turned out to be a submarine, they were to sink it. If it was some kind of sea creature, Great-Grandpa Land was supposed to kill it."

"Hang on," said Nick, "this is starting to sound familiar."

"You bet it is ... The* Abraham Lincoln *finally spotted the monster 200 miles off the coast of Japan and gave chase. They got left behind, but the following night, lookouts spotted the beast resting on the surface. Commander Farragut called Great-Grandpa to harpoon the monster – which he did, and, he says, scored a hit that would have killed any genuine whale stone dead – but the harpoon just bounced off the critter's hide with a ringing noise, as if it was made of metal. The next news was, the monster blew out two huge jets of water that swept over the ship's decks and washed the French Professor, his servant and Great-Grandpa Land into the sea.*

"After splashing about for a spell, they all found themselves clinging to the 'monster', and when they reckoned it was fixing to dive beneath the sea, they up and hammered on its metal hide until the crew of the submarine – they'd now figured out that that's what it was – let them in, and they came face-to-face with Captain Nemo…"

"The *Nautilus*!" Nick clicked his fingers. "The sub was called the *Nautilus*. I knew it sounded familiar! It's all in the book by that French feller – what's his name?"

"Jules Verne."

"That's the boy! What's it called? *20,000 Leagues Under The Sea*!" Nick paused. "I always wondered about that. A league is about three miles, isn't it? So how can you go 20,000 of them under the sea? The deepest part of the ocean is only 36,000 feet or so."

"Verne was talking about distance, not depth," Luke told him. He grabbed a letter proposing a method of growing square apples (for easier storage) and scribbled on the back with a stub of pencil. "So, assuming Verne is talking about *nautical* leagues, 20,000 leagues in UK nautical miles would be 59,961.67."

"What's 38.33 nautical miles between friends? Call it 60,000." Nick did a hurried calculation. "Phew! That's over two and a half times round the world." Then he threw the pencil down with an air of disgust. "What are we doing? The whole thing is nonsense anyway."

"Is it?"

"Of course it is! It's just a story."

"People thought the Lost World was just a story," Luke pointed out, "until we went there last year."

Nick gave him a pitying look. "I've read *20,000 Leagues Under The Sea* – they made us do it at school – and it's scientific nonsense!"

"I'm pretty sure there's a copy in the library," said Luke, pocketing the letter. "Why don't we go and take a look? I fancy a change of scenery anyway."

"I won't argue with you there."

They left the musty piles of correspondence and made their way to the library. Their route took them across the kitchen yard, where a pilot dressed in regulation flying leathers and goggles waited apprehensively as a team of scientists made last-minute adjustments to an engine strapped to his back and the stumpy helicopter rotors above his head. Satisfied, they started the engine and stepped back. The rotors began to turn. So did the pilot, in the opposite direction; faster and faster, like a figure skater going into a spin, until he was no more than a blur. Nick and Luke watched open-mouthed as the unfortunate man took off and sailed above their heads in a beautiful parabolic curve, which terminated when he crashed through the roof of the next-door stables in an explosion of tiles, dust and hay. Two waiting medical orderlies gathered up splints and a stretcher with a *here we go again* air and made their way unhurriedly towards the scene of the crash.

Luke pushed his way through the gaggle of agitated scientists and re-entered the house. The corridor he and Nick took was lined with laboratories and workshops where Challenger Industries inventions were being developed and tested. In one room, a man in a white mess jacket mixed coloured drinks from a number of bottles in a silver cocktail shaker. He screwed on the lid, shook the mixture, threw the shaker into a blast chamber and ducked behind a wall of sandbags. Moments later, the shaker exploded violently. A scientist, watching dispassionately from behind a window of bulletproof glass, made notes on a clipboard.

"I see my father's still experimenting with secret weapons," said Luke disapprovingly as they passed a heavy steel door with a large red and white notice fixed to the wall beside it: *SHOOTING GALLERY – NO ENTRY WHEN RED LIGHT IS ON*. He turned a corner. "I wish he wouldn't—" He broke off as the wall to his right exploded in a shower of plaster, which cleared to reveal a wicked-looking metal spike. It had been driven through the wall from the other side and come to rest six inches from his nose. Luke ran a finger carefully over the sharp point. "I see the compressed-air crossbow is coming along well." He gave Nick a wry smile. "Imagine what Colonel Mochizuki might have done with one of those." Nick shuddered.

They reached the library. A few moments' search produced a well-used copy of *20,000 Leagues Under The Sea*, which Luke spread out on the leather top of a desk. He fixed Nick with a serious look. "Let's assume for a moment that Jules Verne's book isn't a work of fiction – that Ned Land and this Professor what's-his-name..." He checked the book. "Yes, here it is, Professor Aronnax. Let's suppose they really did go on an undersea journey in a revolutionary submarine designed and built by a scientific genius, and told Jules Verne about it, and he wrote up their adventures as a novel."

Nick shrugged. "If it makes you happy."

Luke flipped pages until he found the passage he wanted, and began to read. "This is the bit where Captain Nemo is explaining how the *Nautilus* works. He says it's powered by electricity, and when Professor Aronnax says electricity isn't powerful enough, he says the electricity he uses isn't electricity as the rest of the world knows it."

"That's convenient," said Nick sarcastically. "I'm convinced!"

"He says he extracts sodium from seawater and mixes it with mercury to make batteries: the heat needed for this process is produced by burning coal..."

"You see?" scoffed Nick. "Tommyrot! A coal-powered submarine! And Verne claims it could do fifty knots – rubbish! Just wait until you read how his diving suits work – I fell about when I read that bit. It was enough to make a cat laugh. It makes some of those letters we've been reading sound like cold common sense."

Luke was still reading. "You're right – but there is one form of power that could move a submarine at fifty knots and enable it to cruise 60,000 miles without refuelling."

Nick stared at him. "What sort of power would that be?"

"Nuclear power."

Nick regarded him seriously. "Now I know you're crazy. Just because we've been talking about atomic energy, you come across a letter from some American lunatic and make an Olympic record-breaking jump to a conclusion that doesn't begin to make sense! This is the 1930s, the greatest age of scientific discovery in history, and even we can't create atomic energy – and you reckon this Nemo character could do it seventy years ago? Pure applesauce!" He wagged a finger at Luke. "Even supposing he could do it, why didn't Nemo tell Aronnax that's how the *Nautilus*'s engines worked? Why give him all that guff about coal?"

"I can think of several possibilities," said Luke

gravely. "Maybe Nemo wanted to throw the Professor off the scent – he was a marine biologist, remember, not an engineer. Or maybe Aronnax did know how the engines worked but decided not to tell Verne. Or maybe he did tell Verne, but Verne suppressed the truth because he thought his readers wouldn't understand it, or because it was too dangerous a secret to be revealed."

"Or maybe the whole thing is complete and utter codswallop!" Nick made an impatient gesture. "In any case, it doesn't make any difference whether the *Nautilus* existed or not, or how the engines were powered if it did." He flipped the pages of the book until he'd nearly reached the end, scanned a page, and tapped a passage in the text. "Read that! According to the book, the *Nautilus* went down in the maelstrom – the famous whirlpool off the coast of Norway."

"That's what the book says, yes." Luke held out Jessica Land's letter. "This tells a different story." He continued to read...

"I'm not sure who first told stretchers—"

"Stretchers?" interrupted Nick.

"Lies, I suppose. You know – as in 'stretching the truth'? Here..." Luke held out the letter. "Read it for yourself."

Aloud, Nick read, "*...I'm not sure who first told stretchers about what happened to the* Nautilus. *The*

Professor might have promised Captain Nemo that if he let them go, he would pretend the submarine had sunk so no one would go looking for it. Or maybe it was Monsieur Verne made up the story, or even Great-Grandpa himself – my momma always told me he loved to tell stories, the taller the better.

"All I know for sure is this: after he retired from the sea, Great-Grandpa got a letter from the Professor. The old man was dying, and seeing that he had no kin himself, he wanted to leave Great-Grandpa a memento of their trip with Captain Nemo.

"The Professor said that some years after they escaped from the Nautilus, he was sent a package by the Governor General of Madagascar. In the package was a waterproof cylinder, addressed to Professor Aronnax, and a note saying that it had been washed up on a beach and found by one of the local fishermen, who had taken it to the authorities.

"When the Professor opened the cylinder, inside it he found Captain Nemo's journal, which gave every detail of the Nautilus's voyages. Along with the journal was a letter to the Professor, telling him that, when he knew he was going to die, Captain Nemo had disbanded his crew and planned to scuttle the Nautilus. Just before he went down for the last time, he would throw the journal into the sea to drift wherever the tides and currents took it, and he hoped whoever found it would send it on to the Professor, who would be the best judge of what to do with it. It seems the journal ended up floating ashore on Madagascar.

"The Professor never told anybody he had the journal. But he didn't destroy it because of the knowledge it contained, and in his letter he said he was planning to leave it to Great-Grandpa Land in his will and pass on the responsibility for it that way.

"Well, from what I know of Great-Grandpa – he died before I was born, but my mom told me all about him – that may not have been a real wise move: but as it turned out, when the old Professor died there was a legal wrangle over his will that went on for years, and Great-Grandpa never did get to see Captain Nemo's journal. He hired fancy lawyers from Boston, but even they couldn't get their hooks on it, and Great-Grandpa died a disappointed man.

"But a month ago, the lawsuits were finally settled. As Great-Grandpa's last surviving relative, the Professor's lawyers sent the journal on to me. Anyway, the long and the short of it is that Captain Nemo's journal is in my possession, and the last entry gives the exact location of where he was when he sank the Nautilus. I won't tell you that location at present – all I'll say is, it's somewhere in the Indian Ocean. But I believe the Nautilus holds secrets *that could be very dangerous in the wrong hands. With the state of the world as it is, I'd rather we Americans had those secrets, but I tried the US Navy and they said no dice. So I thought I'd try the Brits.*

"I'm not in this for the money, but I can't go looking for a sunken submarine in a great big ocean all on my lonesome. It would need a proper survey vessel and some sort of deep-diving submersible to get to the Nautilus *(I forgot to mention that my dad was a professional diver, and he taught me, so I know what it would take). If Challenger Industries is interested in my story, please send a representative to meet with me. He'll find me at the* Who Dat? *bar in New Orleans, Louisiana. Just ask for Jess – everyone knows me there."*

Nick looked up from the letter. His expression was serious. "The whole thing is still barking mad, but whoever wrote this letter…I dunno – she doesn't *sound* crazy."

Luke took the letter. "Let's see what my dad thinks."

5 PROPOSAL

"I think you must have taken leave of your senses!"

Sir Andrew stared at Luke as if he'd suddenly grown another head.

"I thought you'd look at it that way," said Luke heavily.

His father spluttered. "What other way is there to look at it? I gave you that job to keep you out of mischief, not so that you could make my life a torment with every piece of half-witted nonsense that any rattle-brained crackpot has seen fit to send me!"

Nanny's disembodied voice floated from the loudspeaker on his study desk. "Your father has a point, Luke dear. To a casual listener, Miss Land's story might sound a little far-fetched."

Luke's gaze remained on Sir Andrew. "But you will admit that if the *Nautilus* really did exist, the only way it could do everything claimed for it would be if it ran on atomic power?"

"Or if it ran on moonshine and fairy dust! The whole thing is preposterous!"

Luke held up the letter. "If you read this properly, you'll see that the story Ned Land passed on to his family agrees exactly with what happens in Jules Verne's book…"

"Of course it does!" snapped Sir Andrew. "Because whoever wrote that ridiculous letter read the footling book and took good care that it should!"

Nick ventured to ask, "But why should anybody go to so much trouble…?"

"I'll tell you why! To convince credulous nincompoops like you two that they have something of value to sell."

"But she says she doesn't want money," Nick pointed out quickly.

"Oh, no. She just wants a fully equipped research vessel with a team of expert divers and the facilities to launch and recover a deep-sea exploration vehicle, that's all."

"Well, you've got one tied up in Honolulu with the crew sitting around twiddling their thumbs," said Luke blandly. "Wouldn't that do?"

Sir Andrew became very still. In a low, dangerous voice, he said, "How did you know about that?"

"It doesn't matter how I know. The ship is called the *Challenger II*, it's just fitting out now and it'll shortly be ready for sea trials. If it's got to be tested out anyway, why not test it by searching for the *Nautilus*?"

"Because the so-called *Nautilus* doesn't exist!"

Nanny's voice said calmly, "I don't think we can be altogether sure of that, Sir Andrew."

Luke's father gave a weary sigh. "*Et tu*, Nanny?" He rallied. "I thought you said this whole tarradiddle was far-fetched!"

"Actually, I said it might sound a little far-fetched to a casual listener. But I am not a casual listener," the voice continued serenely. "Since that business on Lake Windermere, I have been looking into what the Sons of Destiny are up to – and a little bird tells me that for several months now, they've been making enquiries about a journal, formerly in the possession of a certain Professor Aaron Xavier Perrier from the Museum of Paris, for which they are prepared to pay a great deal of money."

"What of it?" demanded Sir Andrew.

"Aaron X. Perrier – Pierre Aronnax. If you reverse the names – put them back-to-front, as it were – there's a certain similarity to the sound, don't you think? It's the sort of thing that might appeal to a novelist who's trying to disguise someone's real name. Writers are such simple souls. That made me think of Jules Verne's book, of course."

"Of course," said Sir Andrew sarcastically. "How are you on crosswords?"

"Actually, I find them rather childish. That is beside the point. I discovered that Professor Perrier disappeared from the Museum between June 1867 and August 1868 – precisely the period in which 'Professor Aronnax' set sail, first in the *Abraham Lincoln* and then in the *Nautilus*."

"Poppycock!"

"That made me wonder whether Monsieur Verne's story was quite such a work of fiction as it seemed, so I made some more enquiries. I discovered that there really was a famous harpooner called Ned Land, who appears on the US Navy List in 1867. His grandson, Jacob, was a professional diver, based in New Orleans, and according to the US census department, Jacob Land has a daughter called Jessica."

Luke waved Jessica Land's letter under his father's nose. "You see?"

"Balderdash!"

"The British Government certainly wouldn't have described the activities of the *Nautilus* as 'balderdash'," said Nanny severely. "They commissioned a report on a number of unexplained sinkings, including that of an unidentified warship that went down in the chops of the channel just where Jules Verne says Captain Nemo destroyed a hostile vessel belonging to an unnamed foreign power. The report was evidently so disturbing that it's been locked away in the deepest vault of the secret service ever since."

"And you've seen it, I suppose?"

"Yes. But I can't tell you what it says, I'm afraid. Your security clearance isn't high enough."

"Nonsense!" Sir Andrew exploded. "My security clearance is higher than that of anyone except the Prime Minister!"

"And me. Quite so," said Nanny smugly. "That's how secret it is."

For a while, Sir Andrew said nothing. His eyes held a sullen glint and his beard moved and bristled as though he was chewing a wasp. Then he rallied. "It's balderdash still! If those maniacs want to waste time chasing after a mythical journal that tells them how to find a non-existent ship, why should I care? Let them waste their time and their money on a wild goose chase!"

"But what if it isn't a wild goose chase?" Luke was determined to press home his advantage. "All right, I'll admit the whole thing's unlikely. It's unlikely the journal exists; even if it does, it's unlikely that the *Nautilus* is where the journal says it is; and if it is there, it's unlikely that anyone will find it or that, after all this time, there'd be anything on board worth finding if they did. *But it's not impossible!* And if the *Nautilus* does exist and its engines are intact, and the Sons of Destiny find them, then the secrets of atomic power could shortly be in the hands of our enemies. Then they really would be able to rule the world!" Luke leaned over the desk and looked his father straight in the eye. "Are you prepared to take that chance?"

Father and son held the pose for several seconds. Sir Andrew broke contact first. He lifted the telephone handset from his desk and barked, "Send for Spotiswoode!"

Banging the receiver down, he said, "Nanny, I want you to send a couple of your best men out to New Orleans to see this Land girl. They can take a look at this journal and if they think there's anything in it—"

"I'm not sure that's wise, Sir Andrew," Nanny interrupted thoughtfully.

"What? But you've just spent the last ten minutes persuading me to take this whole thing seriously!"

"Quite. It's just that if we send out some high-up from Challenger Security, the Sons of Destiny may well find out about it and take action before our people reach New Orleans. Softly, softly, catchee monkey, you know. In any case, how would a security expert assess whether the journal held any useful information or not? Ocean exploration isn't generally part of their training. Perhaps we should consider other means..."

Nanny's musings were interrupted by a hesitant knock at the door. In response to Sir Andrew's bellowed, "Come in!" it opened and Hilary Spotiswoode appeared.

Challenger Industries' Chief Marine Engineer was a slim man of medium height. He wore round spectacles with thick lenses, which magnified his eyes, giving him the appearance of a startled haddock. His high forehead and untidy dark hair standing permanently on end added to his air of confusion. He was wearing a checked shirt, a revolting bow tie and a patterned cardigan. The breast pocket of his rumpled suit bristled with a formidable array of pens. He blinked at his employer. "Ah – Sir Andrew?" He flourished the hat and mackintosh he was holding. "I was just about to leave for the station..."

"Sit down!"

"Um...excuse me, but my...ah...my train won't wait..."

"If I tell it to, it damn well will!"

Spotiswoode sat down abruptly in the chair that Nick had just vacated for him and fiddled with his hat.

"I'm going to tell you what we've been discussing," said Sir Andrew in menacing tones, "and if you laugh, you will be very sorry." He gave a succinct account of Jessica Land's letter and the reasons advanced for taking it seriously. "So," he concluded, "theoretically speaking, and if, against all reason, it turned out that the *Nautilus* really did exist – could your team on the *Challenger II* locate and raise it?" He gave the engineer a narrow-eyed look. "You're not laughing, are you?"

Spotiswoode quickly covered his mouth with his hand and shook his head. "Cough," he explained. "Ahem, ahem."

Sir Andrew glowered. "Well?"

"Um...well, the *Challenger II* hasn't been tested yet, of course, and it would depend on the depth at which the...ah...*Nautilus* was lying. But if that was not more that, say, 500 fathoms, that's to say...ah...3,000 feet, I think, all being well, the chances would be...ah...pretty good. Yes. Um. Of course..." He shot a quick glance at Sir Andrew. "Of course, raising wrecked submarines is not what our deep-diving apparatus is designed to do..."

"No," said Luke brightly. "It's designed to look for uranium deposits on the ocean floor."

Spotiswoode turned to Sir Andrew with an expression of complete panic. "I didn't tell him!" he cried. "I didn't breathe a word! Honestly!"

"He was guessing, but you've told him now, haven't you, you unspeakable donkey!" Sir Andrew looked daggers at his son. "Very clever. That confirms your suspicions, does it?"

"Well, I couldn't think of any other reason why you'd spend hundreds of thousands of pounds on a deep-diving submersible. You need uranium for your nuclear fission experiments and at some stage, if they succeed, you'll need more. There's no uranium to speak of in Britain, so if there's a war and the sea lanes are closed, you'll need some other way of getting a supply."

Sir Andrew glared at Luke, breathing heavily. Then he turned his attention to Spotiswoode. "All right. But you're ready to go?"

"Well...um...yes. I was just on my way to catch the boat train when you called me in. The *Challenger II* is due to sail in a couple of weeks and I'll be...ah... supervising her sea trials, and those of *Little Em'ly* of course..." Catching Sir Andrew's look, Spotiswoode broke off and looked sheepish.

"*Little Em'ly?*"

"Yes. Um...that's what we decided to call the submersible. '*Challenger Self-Propelling Bathysphere*' was a bit of a mouthful you see, so we decided to call her *Little Em'ly*, after a character...ah...in a book...ah... by Charles Dickens..."

Sir Andrew raised his eyes to heaven.

Luke took the plunge. "Sir, why don't Nick and I go with Mr. Spotiswoode?" Ignoring the rumblings that indicated the imminent eruption of Mount Sir Andrew, he continued, "Then we could all nip over to New Orleans and meet this Jessica Land, and if this journal of hers looks promising, we could go on to—"

Luke's father finally exploded. "*You* are not going anywhere!"

"You know, Sir Andrew," said Nanny in her most soothing voice, "what Master Luke is suggesting makes a certain amount of sense." Ignoring Sir Andrew's splutterings, the voice continued, "Supposing the Sons of Destiny know about the *Challenger II* – it is, after all, hard to keep a thing like building a ship entirely secret. They'll be expecting Mr. Spotiswoode to go straight to Hawaii for the sea trials, and if he goes haring off to New Orleans instead, they might start asking themselves why. But if, on his way to Hawaii, he merely conducted your son and his friend to New York, accompanying them in the role of 'responsible adult', you see..."

Sir Andrew stared at Spotiswoode in disbelief. "*Responsible?*"

"Just so. Assuming our enemies do take an interest in what your Chief Marine Engineer is up to, if he proceeded straight from New York to Hawaii, as expected, and Luke and Nick set off for the Southern states on a sightseeing trip, I don't see why the Sons of Destiny should take any further interest in the boys."

"But we know they're after Luke and Nick..."

"In this country, yes. Currently, we have no evidence that the Sons of Destiny are active in the United States. I know of no reason why Luke and Nick would be more at risk from them in America than they are here – if anything, the reverse is true."

Sir Andrew wasn't exactly breathing fire, but he was clearly coming close. "If you think, for one minute—"

"That's an awfully good idea!" Spotiswoode was oblivious to the danger signs. "And then once they've had a look at this journal-thingy, they can come on to Honolulu – it would be really helpful to have them on hand when we're testing out *Little Em'ly*."

"Would it!" snarled his employer.

"Oh, yes. They helped design it, after all."

Luke and Nick exchanged glances. Nick closed his eyes and said, "Oops."

Spotiswoode's perpetual air of surprise deepened. "Didn't they tell you? They said they had."

Sir Andrew looked sandbagged. "*They* helped you design...?"

"Oh, yes – Luke worked on the flotation tank, and the ballast system was mostly his idea..."

"Oh, lor'," muttered Luke.

"...And Nick did wonders with the propulsion units. What's more, they both actually piloted the prototype when we held initial sea trials a few months ago..." Spotiswoode finally cottoned on to the atmosphere in the room. "Ah..."

"Are you seriously telling me," grated Sir Andrew, "that you allowed these irresponsible numbskulls within a mile of your designs for my incredibly expensive and extremely delicate deep-diving equipment?"

"Well...ah...yes."

"Fine!" Sir Andrew's roar left all his previous efforts standing. He wheeled his chair away from the desk and headed for the door as he continued, "Take them to Honolulu, Hull, Hell or Halifax if you like! They can go with you on your blasted sea trials – they can damn well *conduct* the sea trials as far as I'm concerned, and if you all end up at the bottom of the ocean, it'll save me a lot of grey hairs and a fortune in blood-pressure medication!" He paused at the door, clearly searching for a parting shot; unable to find one, he gave a final, inarticulate grunt of fury – "G'ah!" – and went out, slamming the door and leaving a ringing silence behind him.

"Well, Master Luke, Master Nick, you'd better start packing," said Nanny matter-of-factly. "I'll have the car waiting in half an hour. Mr. Spotiswoode is ready now, I take it, so you can all go together. Won't that be nice?"

For once, Luke was slow on the uptake. "Pack – where are we going?"

"To America, of course, dear. Your father just gave you a direct instruction to go to America with Mr. Spotiswoode. Didn't you hear him?"

Nick gave a whoop of joy. Luke felt an incredulous grin spread across his face.

"Hold on a minute...um...Nanny." Spotiswoode's voice was agitated. "I'm not sure Sir Andrew meant all that *literally*..."

"People should always mean what they say," observed Nanny, "or what's the world coming to? I don't know what you're fussing about. You're going to have a lovely holiday in a warm climate, and if you manage to wrong-foot the Sons of Destiny as well, so much the better."

"But..."

"Hush, dear." Spotiswoode barely caught Nanny's last words as Luke and Nick took an arm each and hustled him from the room. "Nanny knows best..."

6 FOG

Grand Banks of Newfoundland
July 1934

Four days out from Southampton, the RMS *Majestic* hit fog.

It lay over the Grand Banks in smothering curtains. On falling into its insubstantial clutches, the liner's speed dropped from its usual twenty-four knots to twelve, then to ten. As night fell, the huge vessel was ghosting through the long, sighing North Atlantic rollers at little more than eight knots, with its foghorn sounding continuously.

Luke stood on the aft promenade deck, leaning on

the ship's rail and listening to the answering horns, bells and whistles of the fishing boats through which the *Majestic* was picking its way like a duchess at a toddlers' picnic. The ship's wake stretched away beneath him, bubbling and frothing as it left the stern until it settled down in a broad band of white phosphorescence, straight as a ruler, marking their passage. Even as he watched, a denser curtain of vapour closed in and the luminous trail vanished into grey obscurity.

He straightened up as footsteps heralded the approach of his cabin-steward. The man whipped a hand behind his back on seeing Luke, who immediately suspected that he had nipped outside for a crafty smoke. "Good evening, sir."

Luke returned the greeting. "Will we be in New York tomorrow, d'you think?"

"Well, we should be through this by dawn." The steward rubbed a drop of moisture from the end of his bulbous nose; his chins wobbled as he spoke. "It might lift earlier, with a bit o' Friar." The steward was a cockney – he seemed to delight in trying to baffle his passengers with snippets of rhyming slang. He was wasting his time with Luke, who knew that "Friar Tuck" meant "luck". "Then again," he went on, "it might not lift at all. My guess is we'll get in late tomorrow evening or first thing next morning. Depending."

"Thanks." Luke watched as the man shuffled away and was quickly swallowed by the fog. It was definitely getting thicker.

He left the promenade deck and strolled aimlessly through the immense first class dining saloon, where a few late diners were lingering over coffee or port and nuts. He found a vacant desk in the reading and writing room and tried to compose a letter to his mother, but he never found it easy to know what to say to her. *I'm in the middle of the ocean and there isn't a single fossil to be found* didn't seem a very good beginning, but he couldn't think of anything better. After a while he gave it up, put his chin on his hands, and stared gloomily at nothing.

The departure from Southampton, with bunting flying and the ship surrounded by bustling tugs and pleasure steamers packed with waving trippers, had been lively; and for the first three days of the crossing the weather had been good. But the fourth day had seen scudding grey clouds, a sullen sea and squalls of rain that had driven everyone off the decks and into the liner's great public rooms, crowding them with fretful passengers who all seemed to be as bored and listless as Luke felt. He'd gone for a swim in the liner's luxurious indoor swimming bath, but after ten minutes of being splashed and jostled, had given up trying to get any exercise. Now that dinner was over, a long evening stretched ahead with nothing to do.

He went back to the stateroom he shared with Nick, and found his cousin stretched out on his bed, poring over a technical manual of the ship. He glanced up as Luke entered. "Oh, there you are." He held up the book for Luke's inspection. "I borrowed this off the Second Engineer. It's fascinating. Listen: *The* Majestic *is powered by Parsons direct acting oil-fired steam turbine engines, driving quadruple four-bladed propellers, each of which has a width of sixteen and a half feet...*"

"Fascinating," said Luke. "Don't you ever read just for enjoyment?"

Nick was perplexed. "I *am* enjoying myself."

"I mean, why don't you try reading – I don't know – a novel or something?"

"A novel?" Nick couldn't have looked more disgusted if Luke had suggested he take a swim in raw sewage. "I don't have enough time to read books about real things. Why should I waste my time reading stuff that some half-witted author has made up?"

"Forget I mentioned it." Luke stretched. "I'm going to bed."

"Don't let me stop you." Nick carried on reading.

Luke changed into his pyjamas and slipped between the crisp, laundered sheets. He lay with his eyes closed and tried to relax. After a while, Nick's reading light flicked off. Soon afterwards, his steady, regular breathing indicated that he had fallen asleep more or less instantly.

But Luke couldn't sleep. He opened his eyes and stared at the ceiling.

There was a faint rattle from the door. Luke jerked his head towards the sound, and watched as the handle slowly turned. The door opened, admitting a strip of light from the corridor beyond. The door opened wider and a figure slipped through.

Luke's hand shot out and flicked a light switch.

Their cabin-steward stood, blinking in the sudden glare. His sallow face, lit from below by Luke's bedside lamp, looked ghastly. He was holding a steaming mug. After a moment's hesitation, he held it up. "Cocoa, sir?"

Nick raised his head and said, "Wassamarrarup?"

Luke stared at the man. "I didn't order any cocoa."

The steward looked flustered. "Didn't you, sir? What about the other young gentleman...?"

"Neither of us," said Luke sharply.

"Ah – my mistake. Must have been another cabin. Sorry to have disturbed you." The steward backed out, and closed the door.

Luke was instantly on his feet and reaching for his dressing gown. Nick peered owlishly at him. "What are you doing?"

"I'm going to follow him. Something's up."

"Rubbish," said Nick sleepily. "He just brought the cocoa to the wrong cabin, that's all."

"Then why didn't he knock? He always knocks. And I locked that door when I came in. He must have used his pass key to open it." Luke stood with his ear to the door, listening. He opened it a crack, and checked that the corridor was clear.

Nick groaned and turned his back. "Don't make a noise when you come in."

"Goodnight, Sleeping Beauty." Luke slipped out.

He hurried down the corridor to its junction with the longer passageway running fore and aft, and was just in time to see the steward go through the door leading to the outside decks. Sprinting noiselessly on slippered feet, Luke followed.

As soon as he emerged onto the open deck, he realized that the fog was thicker still. Droplets of mist immediately began to settle on the flannel of his dressing gown. He hesitated, unsure of where his quarry had gone – the steward could be anywhere on the promenade. Then, in the fitful glow of the ship's lights, he spotted a trail of footprints, dark against the silver, moisture-soaked planking. These led to a companionway. Luke descended it cautiously and, hearing muffled voices, inched forward.

The steward was standing in the shadow of a lifeboat and speaking in low, urgent tones. "...I tell you, they're in there."

Another figure – someone so wrapped and muffled against the fog that Luke couldn't distinguish a single feature – stirred and said something inaudible.

The steward's voice became petulant. "Yes, they woke up when I went in; but it's all right, I said I was bringing cocoa. I took some with me so they wouldn't be suspicious." The muffled figure said something else, and the steward's face became ugly. "Don't come the old acid with me, treacle. I done what you said, I made sure they was in their cabin, and I want my money..."

The muffled figure moved its arm. There was a sharp pop. The steward's eyes went wide and he clutched at his stomach. Then he sagged forward and slid bonelessly to the deck.

Luke didn't wait to see any more. He hared back to the cabin, woke Nick and flung his dressing gown at him. "Put this on. We're getting out."

"Womarra?" Nick groaned. "Oh, it's you." He rubbed at his eyes. "Did you find old Cockney Rhyming Slang?"

"Sort of," said Luke tersely. "He's brown bread."

Nick sat bolt upright. "Dead?"

"I think so. I didn't hang around to take his pulse."

"How?"

"He told someone we were in here." Luke flung back his sheets and began to arrange pillows and bolsters into the form of a sleeping body. "Then he shot him."

Nick stared at him stupidly. "Who shot who?"

"Whoever the steward was talking to, shot him." Luke flung the sheets back over the fake sleeper in his berth and, as Nick struggled into his dressing gown, began work on the second bed.

Nick's voice was more alert. "Wasn't there a lot of noise?"

"He used a silencer. Will you get a move on?" Luke put the finishing touches to Nick's bed. Then he switched off the cabin light and led the way out into the corridor, closing the door behind him. He and Nick tiptoed past cabin doors until they reached a recess. A mirror on the opposite wall gave a partial view down the corridor. Luke and Nick flattened themselves against the wall, and waited.

A few moments later, a muffled figure appeared at the end of the corridor and, moving with catlike tread, crept along it to the door of the cabin they had so recently vacated. Hardly breathing, Luke craned his neck to keep the figure in view as it raised a hand holding a key. Sweat pricked his brow – the assassin must have taken the key from the steward's body. There was a soft click, the door opened, and the figure slipped inside. Barely a second later, Luke and Nick heard half a dozen barely audible *pop*s. After a short silence, thumps and muffled curses indicated that the gunman had discovered that he had just ruthlessly murdered a collection of feather pillows.

Luke and Nick shrank back in their refuge as the cabin door opened again and the gunman emerged, peering to left and right. Making a decision, he turned in their direction and began to inch down the corridor, making inexorably for the recess where they were hiding.

The assassin had almost reached them when a man in evening clothes, with bow tie undone and shirt-tails awry, came into view, walking unsteadily and using alternate walls of the corridor for support. The gunman instantly turned on his heel and made off the way he had come. Luke and Nick sagged with relief as their would-be murderer disappeared from sight. The intoxicated passenger fitted his key into a cabin door lock at the third attempt, and stumbled inside.

Luke grabbed Nick by the shoulder. "Get Spotiswoode – and whoever is in charge of security on this ship. The officer of the watch, I suppose."

"What are you going to do?"

"Follow him."

"Follow the man who just tried to kill us? Are you mad?"

"There are over 2,000 passengers on this ship – the murderer has only got to take his overcoat off and he could be practically any one of them! Do you want to spend the rest of the trip dodging bullets? Go on!" Luke gave Nick a shove, and set off in pursuit of the assassin.

The door to the outside deck was swinging closed as Luke slipped down the passageway. He opened it a fraction and listened. There was no sound but the ghostly booming of the ship's foghorn and the answering noises of anxious fishing boats. Luke slipped through the door.

He examined the deck carefully, but could see no footprints. With no clue as to where his quarry had gone, he crept down the companionway he had taken earlier. There was no one in the shadow of the lifeboat where the steward had met his murderer, and no sign of the steward's body. Presumably, the assassin had got rid of it – heaved it over the rail, perhaps. Luke glanced towards the stern. There was no one there. On impulse, he crossed to the rail and examined it closely; there – was that a bloodstain? Perhaps the murderer had left it when he pushed the steward's body over…

A memory that had been tugging at Luke's

consciousness suddenly surfaced. He had assumed that the murderer was a man, but the steward had addressed his killer as "treacle". That was cockney rhyming slang: "treacle tart" meant "sweetheart" – so the murderer was a woman. And the only reason he had thought she was out on deck had been the swinging door – but what if the murderer had pushed the door open, and stayed hidden inside the ship while he went past? That would mean she was now *behind* him...

The thought had hardly registered when Luke caught a sudden movement out of the corner of his eye. Reflex alone saved him – he dived to the deck as the silenced gun spat, and a splinter of wood flew off the rail above his head. He converted the dive into a roll and kicked out. More by luck than judgement, his foot caught the assassin's hand – the gun went spinning away.

Luke leaped to his feet. His assailant was wearing a hat with a low brim and a heavy overcoat. In between, a scarf was wrapped tightly round the head, leaving a mere slit for eyes. He had barely registered these details before the assassin sprang to the attack. Luke felt himself being hurled back, with inexorable force, against the ship's rail.

Gloved hands tightened on his throat and thrust at his jaw, forcing him back further and further over the stern, with nothing beneath him but a sheer drop into the cold, grey sea. He was choking. His back felt as if it was about to break. Twisting his head sideways, he stared down into the churning water of the ship's wake; "four propellers", Nick had said, "each sixteen and a half foot across" – they'd make mincemeat of him.

With the last of his strength, Luke fought back. In the struggle, his attacker's hat flew off, letting loose a waterfall of dark hair. Luke snatched at the scarf and yanked hard, revealing his attacker's face for the first time. His eyes bulged – he gaped and cried out in shock. With an animal snarl, his assailant took advantage of his distraction, forcing him even further back over the rail, to the point of no return...

"Luke!" He heard Nick's yell, and the death-grip was suddenly released. A clattering of feet on the deck heralded the arrival of the rescue party. Luke's would-be murderer released her grip with a curse, took two steps back – and vaulted far out over the rail to disappear into the darkness.

Luke doubled over the rail, coughing, massaging his throat and staring into the thundering waters. His attacker had disappeared without trace. Maybe she had suffered the fate to which she had so nearly sent him, but somehow he doubted it. She hadn't seemed suicidal, and the force of her leap might well have carried her clear of the ship's propellers. In any case, Luke thought wildly, an assassin who had already returned from the dead once could probably be counted on to do so again...

As he struggled to make sense of what he had just seen, he found himself surrounded – by Nick, holding him by the shoulders and repeatedly asking whether he was all right; by Spotiswoode, spectacles askew and hair ruffled, bleating questions; by ship's officers shouting orders at men who scurried to obey...

"Luke!" Nick's voice was urgent. "Who was it? Did you get a look at him?"

Luke lifted a stricken face. "Her. It was a woman."

"A woman?"

"But it couldn't be," gabbled Luke. "She's dead. Dead as mutton. I saw her die a year ago, with my own eyes..."

"Luke, talk sense. Who was she?"

Staring Nick directly in the eye, Luke said, clearly and with deliberation, "Colonel Mochizuki."

7 JESSICA

Pennsylvania Station,
New York, NY

Luke and Nick were still arguing as they boarded the Crescent train for New Orleans thirty-six hours later.

"It can't have been Colonel Mochizuki," Nick said for the umpteenth time as they hurried across the vast, echoing station concourse. "I mean, all right, we know she was persistent – she chased us halfway round the world, after all – but there are limits! We both saw the allosaurus get her. Roar roar, chomp chomp – remember? People don't survive being eaten by a dinosaur."

Luke cast his eyes up to the soaring glass roof. "I

know that. I also know that she was on the *Majestic*, the night before last."

"That's not possible! Look, the woman who attacked you was Japanese, that I can believe, but you only saw her face for a second. How can you be sure it's the same person?"

"Because she was trying to kill me!" Luke hurried his pace as they reached the platform and threaded their way between bustling passengers and piles of luggage. "It's amazing how it concentrates the mind."

"But—"

Luke rounded on Nick. "I know it's not possible! But I also know what I saw." He stopped and checked the number of his ticket against the one painted on the side of the Pullman car. "This is ours." He handed the ticket to the conductor, a grey-haired man who took it without haste and examined it carefully through wire-framed glasses.

"Well, we'll probably never know who she was," said Nick. "After she jumped ship, if the propellers didn't get her, she must have drowned."

"Unless she was picked up. Don't forget, the shipping company insists there were no Japanese names on the passenger list, and none of the crew could remember seeing a Japanese woman before the attack."

"Then how...?" Nick's eyes widened as he caught on.

"You mean, she might have got aboard in the fog from one of those fishing boats, and been picked up the same way after she jumped?"

"A fishing boat?" Luke shrugged. "Maybe."

"Well, I suppose..." Nick broke off and gazed over Luke's shoulder with a puzzled expression. "Hello, here's Spotiswoode. We said goodbye to him at the hotel – I didn't know he was coming to see us off."

Luke swung around as the engineer, hair, spectacles and bow tie awry, came panting along the platform, suitcase in hand. He put it down and thrust a rumpled ticket towards the conductor, who did not deign to take it but merely gave it the indifferent glance of a man who refused to be hurried.

Luke stared at Spotiswoode. "What are you doing here? You're supposed to be going straight on to Hawaii."

Spotiswoode looked flustered. "Yes, well, that was before you nearly got yourself chucked off the *Majestic*. I've had quite an eventful morning, let me tell you. The police dropped by to tell me that the steward – or what was left of him after he'd been through the ship's propellers – was hauled out of the Atlantic by a fishing boat last night, but they couldn't find any trace of the woman who attacked you. So I got on the phone to your father, and he ordered me to go with you to New

Orleans." He ran a hand through his hair, making it even more disordered. "He wanted me to hire half a dozen bodyguards from the Pinkerton detective agency," he continued as the conductor returned Luke's ticket and accepted Nick's, "but Nanny said she had new information that the Pinkertons may have been infiltrated by...er..." He glanced at the conductor and lowered his voice. "...the you-know-who..."

"Oh, for pity's sake!" Luke was exasperated. "If you're talking about the Sons of Destiny, say so!"

Spotiswoode made frantic "shushing" motions and pointed at the conductor, who looked up and caught him in the act – the engineer made an unconvincing attempt to convert the gesture into a wave to a non-existent friend.

Luke sighed. "Stop jumping at shadows! I'm sure this gentleman isn't a member of the Sons of Destiny."

The conductor sniffed. "No, sir. African Methodist Episcopal Church, always have been."

"There you are, you see." Luke retrieved Nick's ticket from the conductor, and passed him Spotiswoode's. The man examined it with pursed lips, as though determined to spot some irregularity.

Spotiswoode glared at Luke. "You can laugh! It's dashed inconvenient, that's all. This diversion is going to cost me days. I have better things to do than nursemaiding you two!" Spotiswoode took his ticket from the conductor, drew himself up haughtily, took a step towards the door of the railway car, and tripped over his own suitcase.

The glimmer of a smile flitted over the conductor's careworn face as he raised a whistle to his lips. "All aboaaaard!"

New Orleans, Louisiana

Night was falling as Spotiswoode paid off the taxi that had brought him, Luke and Nick from their hotel to the *Who Dat?* bar.

The bar was just too far outside the fashionable French Quarter to be popular with well-heeled customers, and it showed. The *Who Dat?* had a veranda, swing screen doors, and a peeling sign lit by a dozen electric bulbs, several of which were missing. Crates of empty beer bottles stood to one side of the door. A mangy dog sat in the dusty road outside, scratching itself.

Spotiswoode had grumbled all through the forty-hour, 1400-mile journey from New York about the time he was wasting on what would probably turn out to be a fool's errand, and his mood was not lifted by his first sight of their destination. He eyed the *Who Dat?* bar with distaste. "What a dump! Honestly. And why give it such a ridiculous name?"

"It comes from the Minstrel shows," Nick informed him breezily. "One feller says, 'Who dat?' and another feller says, 'Who dat saying who dat?', and then the first feller says, 'Who dat up there sayin' who dat down here?' and the second feller—"

"I get the picture," said Spotiswoode glumly. "Very droll."

"Come on." Luke led the way inside.

The bar was almost empty. A few customers sat in booths, but there was no one seated at the counter. Behind the bar, bottles sat in front of fly-specked mirrors advertising drink brands. Most of these had gone out of fashion even before the US government had banned the sale of alcohol completely during the Prohibition years of the 1920s and early 1930s.

Spotiswoode gazed around at the scuffed furniture and stained walls. "Do you know," he said in disparaging tones, "I believe I like the inside of this place even less than I liked the outside." Luke elbowed him in the ribs.

The bartender looked as though he had been carved out of basalt. Evidently having heard Spotiswoode's disparaging remark, he put down the glass he was wiping and gave the newcomers a look from which welcome was entirely absent. "Can I do somethin' for you folks?"

"Beer, please," said Spotiswoode.

The bartender gave him a look of contempt. "I ain't servin' you no beer."

Spotiswoode looked surprised. "I thought Prohibition had finished."

"Just for you, I brung it back."

Luke decided this had gone on long enough. "We're looking for Jessica Land."

The bartender's face was inscrutable. "Yeah? Who's askin'?"

"My name is Challenger."

"Hmmmpn." The bartender put down his towel and slipped through a curtained doorway at the back of the bar. From behind the curtain came a muffled conversation. Luke glanced around the bar, meeting the gaze of several customers who were eyeing the proceedings with wary curiosity.

Then the door alongside the bar was flung open, and a girl strode into the room.

She was slim and of medium height, with green eyes and a freckled face. She wore a checked open-necked shirt with rolled-up sleeves and denims. But by far her most striking feature was the mass of red curls that flowed around her head, shimmering in the fitful lights of the bar. Luke's mother had red hair, but hers was a muted shade, soft and wavy. This girl's hair was like wire, and its bright and vibrant tint gave her the appearance of a flaming torch.

She planted her feet and folded her arms. "Which of you is Challenger?"

"I am," said Luke.

The girl snorted. "The hell you are. Andrew Challenger is a big guy in a wheelchair. I seen pictures."

"I'm his son, Luke."

The girl rounded on the barman. "You jackass, Lou. You told me Challenger was out here."

Luke's temper flared. "I *am* here. My father sent me to find out whether you had anything worth his while."

The girl gave him a scornful look. "Well, isn't that just peachy. I write the Big Cheese, and I get the office boy."

"I'm guessing you'd be Jessica Land," said Nick in his most charming voice as Luke struggled to bite back a furious retort. "My hot-tempered friend really is Sir Andrew's son. I'm Nick Malone."

The girl glared at Luke and Nick. "So that's how seriously Sir Andrew takes my offer – sending a couple of kids and..." She gave Spotiswoode a particularly vitriolic glance. "...Groucho Marx."

Spotiswoode was stung. "Oh, I say!"

"You look about the same age we are!" snapped Luke.

"If it's any of your business, I'm sixteen. Anyhow, I've been looking after myself for quite a spell."

"Ah, be still," soothed Nick, "all of you." He gave the girl a winning smile. "Be reasonable now – Sir Andrew doesn't travel himself, but he sent the three of us all the way across the Atlantic to see you." He put a companionable arm on Spotiswoode's shoulder and drew him forward to be presented. "And Exhibit A here is Sir Andrew's Chief of Marine Engineering."

The girl stared at the Chief of Marine Engineering with frank disbelief. "What? *Him?*"

Spotiswoode bridled. "Now look here—"

"Don't let his rugged good looks fool you," said Nick hurriedly. "The man's a demon with a slide-rule. He's designed a submersible that will find what you're looking for – if we can all reach an agreement."

The girl considered this. "Oh. Well, I guess that's different." She leaned back against the bar with her elbows on the counter. "Oh-kay. I'm Jessica Land. What's your offer?"

Luke had himself under control. "What are you selling?" he shot back.

"Oh, gee, I'm sorry. Didn't my letter make it clear to your tiny mind?"

"We know what you claim to have. We're here to find out whether you're telling the truth or whether you're just another snake-oil merchant – or a nut."

Jessica's eyes flashed. "You know something? You are commencing to seriously tick me off."

"Well, I'm glad it's mutual. Show us the merchandise and we'll talk business. Otherwise, stop wasting our time."

The giant bartender rumbled, "Young man, I find your attitude disrespectful. Hey, Jess, you want I should beat up on 'em a little?" Spotiswoode looked alarmed. Nick gave Jessica his most winning smile.

"Pipe down, Lou." Jessica hesitated. Then she said, "Okay, cards on the table. I'm not crazy about the way Sir Andrew chooses to do business, but what the hell. So here's the deal. Ned Land was my great-granddaddy, and he did get shanghaied by this Nemo character, and he did leave me the Captain's journal, like I said. The journal says where he sunk that submarine of his. I'd go after it myself – I got my daddy's diving suit and I know how to use it – only, like I said in the letter, I calculate it's too deep for a normal dive, and anyhow, I'd need a support vessel to get me there."

"So you're selling the information about where the *Nautilus* is?" said Luke.

"No. I told you, I'm not selling anything. I need a ship,

and diving equipment, and I know that don't come cheap. I want to find that sub, and prove that my granddaddy's story was true. And I don't want the Germans, or the Italians or the Japanese or the Ruskies to get what's in there; I want us to have it, the States or the Brits, I'm not particular – I reckon it'll come to the same thing in the end."

Luke regarded her steadily. "And what do you want for yourself?"

"To go find the *Nautilus* with your team. My board and keep, which I'll work for. Ten per cent of the salvage."

Luke was startled. "Only ten per cent?"

Jessica smiled for the first time. "Careful, Mr. Challenger, or you'll talk yourself into givin' me more. I told you, I'm not in this for the money. But Lou and his folks have been good to me since my daddy died, and I'd like him to be able to set up in a better joint than this. And I want my own boat and gear – I figure on setting up a diving business when all this is over, and I need capital for that. I reckon ten per cent should cover it, even if the sub ain't all granddaddy cracked it up to be.

"So, what do you say? Deal?" Jessica spat in the palm of her hand, and held it out.

Luke glanced quickly at Nick, who was grinning like a Halloween lantern, and Spotiswoode, who looked as if the conversation had got away from him. He said carefully, "Providing we judge the journal is authentic – deal." He spat in his palm, and he and Jessica shook hands.

The red-headed girl absently wiped her hand on her denims, crossed to the bar and said, "Lou."

"Hmmmpn." The bartender reached down behind the counter, and brought out a battered cigar case, which he placed on the counter top.

Luke, Nick and Spotiswoode crowded round Jessica as she opened the box to reveal a small, leather-covered notebook. "There it is," she said quietly. "Captain Nemo's journal."

Luke examined the notebook. Was it really Nemo's diary, or a clever forgery? Yellowed by time and stained by water, it had an air of authenticity. Luke felt a sudden conviction that Jessica Land was telling the truth. He reached out to take it from the box...

A voice behind them said, "Keep your hands on the bar, and don't turn around."

8 SWAMP

Luke cursed himself for his lack of caution. Caught off guard by Jessica Land's abrasive greeting, he had forgotten all about keeping an eye on the other customers in the bar. A swift sideways glance confirmed his suspicions: the two men drinking in the booth furthest from the bar had left their seats. One was at the door, keeping watch. Luke glanced at the bar mirrors and was rewarded with a distorted view of the other man standing right behind them. Something cold and hard poked Luke in the ribs: the muzzle of a handgun.

A slow, deep voice in his ear said, "We ain't fixin' to have no trouble, so without you do somethin' real dumb, everybody gonna get out of here alive. Jus' keep your hands where I can see 'em." An arm slid between Luke and Nick and reached for the cigar case. As it did so, the man's shirtsleeve pulled up to reveal a tattoo – that of a striking snake coiled around a spear. Luke and Nick exchanged a glance; a silent message passed between them, instantly understood by both.

In a split second, Nick slammed a fist down on the reaching hand while Luke spun round and chopped at the hand holding the gun. The gunman gave a roar of surprise; the gun went off, shattering a bottle of tequila behind the bar, and clattered to the floor. The man at the door gave a shrill whistle. The one at the bar set about Luke and Nick with his fists until Jessica snatched a tin tray from the bar and whanged it against the side of his head. Spotiswoode stood gawping until Nick shoved him to the floor.

Then came a sudden rush of feet outside and the shockingly strident clatter of a machine gun. The bar's windows imploded; dust and plaster showered from the walls and ceiling. Luke and Nick dived to the floor, while the drinkers ducked down in their booths. Jessica hauled Spotiswoode under a table.

Then Lou turned out the lights.

The next few seconds were a nightmare of muzzle-flashes from guns, oaths and screams, thundering footsteps and hurtling bodies colliding with tables, chairs and each other. It was impossible to tell friend from foe, which didn't stop Luke laying about him for all he was worth. He had the satisfaction of feeling his fist connect with soft tissue, and hearing the grunt of his victim, but his next punch hit nothing but empty air and threw him off balance, to land with a crash on top of a struggling figure that he instantly seized in a vicelike grip. He held on as the firing ceased and the floorboards shook to the hurried tread of departing footsteps.

The figure he was holding struggled wildly. Luke tightened his grip and snapped, "Stay still or I'll slug you one."

"Luke, you ape! It's me, Nick."

The lights came on again. Luke cursed and rolled away from Nick who rubbed at his neck. "You half-throttled me," he complained.

Ignoring him, Luke darted towards the bar. The cigar box was empty – Captain Nemo's journal was gone.

Lou erupted from behind the bar carrying a Winchester 12 pump-action shotgun. Closely followed by Luke and Nick, he strode out of the doorway, and stood four-square on the veranda, roaring defiance and blazing away at the retreating thieves.

Under a street lamp across the road from the bar stood an Asiatic woman wearing a long leather coat and dark glasses. Luke recognized her instantly – Colonel Mochizuki, who had seemingly returned from the grave to seek his death; first on the *Majestic*, now here.

Mochizuki had a Challenger Mark III sub-machine gun in her left hand, and Captain Nemo's journal in her right. She held up the little leather book, waving it in mockery. Then, with lightning speed, she thrust the book into a coat pocket and raised her weapon into a firing position. For an instant, Luke was rooted to the spot; then he and Nick simultaneously threw themselves at Lou, bearing him to the ground as the machine gun roared and flashed. Bullets peppered the air above their heads and sent splinters leaping from the clapboard wall behind them.

Luke glanced up as the woman stepped forward to finish her work – but at that moment, the wail of a police siren rent the night. As the woman hesitated, a powerful car, a pearl-grey DeSoto 8, swept from a side alley and came to rest, rocking on its springs, between her and her target. She yelled something inaudible, and her hirelings in the car screamed back, obviously insisting that she get in so they could make a getaway. Lou decided the matter by clambering to his knees and firing his Winchester one-handed. The round shattered one of the DeSotos's headlights; the Japanese woman, still cursing, jumped on the running board, and the vehicle sped off.

Jessica appeared in the lighted doorway. "Everyone okay out there?"

Luke cast an inquiring glance at Lou, who was clutching his left arm. Blood was seeping through his fingers. "Walking wounded!" he yelled. "How about in there?"

"Okay, give or take a bottle of hooch. You sayin' they hit Lou?" Jessica's voice was harsh with concern.

"In the arm – take care of him."

"Luke Challenger, you come back here!" Luke ignored Jessica's call. Hauling Nick to his feet, he sprinted off in pursuit of the car. Jessica's voice pursued them down the street. "I said come back. *Dammit!*"

Halfway down the block, a Harley-Davidson Model D motorcycle combination was parked at the kerb, while its owner, a slick-looking man wearing more hair cream than was socially acceptable, tried to charm one of a group of giggling young women into its sidecar. Ruining his plans for the rest of the evening, Nick tumbled into the sidecar while Luke vaulted into the saddle and stood on the kick-start. The engine roared; Luke twisted the throttle, released the clutch, and he and Nick took off with a squeal of tyres, leaving the would-be Lothario in a cloud of dust.

"That woman...that was..." Nick was lost for words. Luke, steering with grim concentration, said nothing. Nick took a deep breath. "All right. I take it back. If that woman wasn't Colonel Mochizuki, I'm a monkey's uncle!" He shook his head. "But how? People don't come back from the dead!"

"I don't know," said Luke, "and right now, it doesn't matter. We have to get that book."

"Right, good plan," said Nick, "but that car we're following is full of desperate criminals with guns and we're unarmed – what are you going to do if we catch up with them?"

Luke twisted the throttle as hard as it would go. "Improvise!"

The chase took them through the narrow streets and alleys of the French Quarter. Partygoers on their way to jazz joints and dance halls, honky-tonk bars and night clubs, scattered in panic. The rear window of the DeSoto was smashed from within; the wicked-looking muzzle of a machine gun poked out and spat fire. Nick ducked down in the sidecar and Luke flattened himself against the fuel tank to present as small a target as possible.

The DeSoto took a right turn on two wheels, tyres screaming, and roared down a narrow street. Ahead of it, a large delivery truck was swinging across the road to reverse into an alley. Nick whooped and punched the air.

"They'll have to stop!" he yelled. "They'll have to… woah!" He broke off as the car, engine roaring, powered straight for the narrowing gap between the truck's tailboard and the walls of the buildings. The DeSoto mounted the kerb, demolishing a fire hydrant that erupted like the fountains of Versailles, and, with a screech of tortured metal and a shower of sparks, shot through the gap and away.

The startled truck driver hit his accelerator and the truck kangarooed backwards, closing the gap. *"We'll have to stop,"* yelled Nick, "we'll have to…oooh!"

Luke swung the handlebars and the bike skidded to a halt inches from the truck. He kicked down through the gears and opened the throttle again. The bike roared back the way it had come, and plunged down a dark alley.

For the next block, the ride was very exciting. The Harley plunged through rutted lanes, demolished link fences and tore through the yards of sleeping houses, smashing cane furniture and collecting washing from neglected lines. A dog, maddened by the snarling monster's invasion of its territory, followed them, nipping at their wheels. Nick fought his way clear of a pair of oversize bloomers as they completed their backyard tour and surged out onto the street at the end of the alley. Luke swerved into the centre of the road and stood on the brakes, bringing them to a halt.

They found themselves at a road near the river. Halfway down the street, an empty cart, pulled by two blinkered horses, stood outside a corn chandler's; otherwise the street was deserted apart from the lights that swung round a corner and raced towards Luke and Nick – the lights of a car with only one headlight.

"That's them, for a pound! We must have taken a short cut." As the roaring vehicle bore down on them, Nick's jubilation quickly waned. "That thing weighs over two tons – they'll smash us to pulp!"

At precisely that moment, a metal pole, used for propping up the washing line in the yard behind them, clattered to the ground alongside the Harley. Luke eyed it for a moment with deliberation – then he picked it up and handed it to Nick. "Time for a spot of jousting."

Nick struggled to rise from his seat and get his legs underneath him so that he was kneeling in the sidecar. He tucked the improvised lance under his right arm. "Just call me Sir Lancelot." Luke grinned savagely, revved the engine and let out the clutch with a jerk.

The car and motorcycle thundered towards each other along the deserted street at a combined speed well in excess of a hundred miles an hour. Luke ignored the pistol bullets that whined around his head like wasps – he guessed that a speeding car on an uneven road made a lousy gun platform, and that the chances of the gunmen hitting a moving target, except by accident, were slim.

At the last possible moment, Luke twitched the handlebars to pass down the right-hand side of the onrushing car. At the same moment, Nick swept up his arm and hurled the clothes pole. The missile smashed through the car's windscreen. The DeSoto swerved, rocking to the left, the right, left again – and crashed onto its side, sliding down the street in a fountain of sparks.

Luke pulled a skid-turn and headed back to the car. He pulled up, dismounted, zigzagged across to the wreck and peered through the windows. His caution proved to be unnecessary. Just two men remained in the DeSoto, groaning from their injuries. They clearly had no interest in continuing the shooting match.

"Luke! The cart!"

Luke glanced up, and swore. The Japanese woman and the three remaining raiders had commandeered the horse and cart from outside the chandler's. One of the gang took the reins; a volley of shots around the horses' ears sent the terrified animals stampeding away down the street. Luke raced back to the bike and set off in pursuit.

It was an unequal chase, and Luke soon realized that he and Nick were rapidly gaining on their enemies. But as he closed the gap, the Japanese woman stood up in the back of the cart, balancing like a circus acrobat, brought up her machine gun, and fired.

Most of the slugs went wide, but a lucky shot hit the bike's front tyre, instantly shredding it. Luke tried to control the bucking, swerving machine, but he was flung from the saddle. He skidded and rolled in the dust of the road while the bike and sidecar slammed through a pair of corrugated-iron gates into a riverside boatyard. Nick ducked into a foetal crouch as the machine ripped through the yard, hurling stored sailboats, skiffs and canoes aside like skittles, before burying itself in the wooden walls of a boathouse.

It was some time before Nick dragged himself out of the wreckage of the sidecar, groaning. He felt for broken bones and shook his head to clear it. He turned to see Luke, limping a little but otherwise unscathed, coming through the wrecked gates.

"Are you okay?" Luke demanded. Nick nodded. "Listen," Luke went on urgently, "they're ditching the cart a few hundred yards up ahead. They've got a boat waiting on the river. They must always have planned to switch from the car here. We can still catch them."

Nick rubbed his bruised elbow. "I don't see how," he complained. "I couldn't run ten yards, let alone a couple of hundred..." He broke off as a powerful boat engine started up nearby. "And anyway, they've reached the water – we can't follow them there."

At this point, Nick realized that he had lost his audience. Luke was staring avidly at a strange-looking machine sitting alone in a cleared space at the top of the yard's slipway. "Oh," he said softly, "I wouldn't be too sure about that..."

Out on the river, the raiders were heading into midstream at a leisurely pace. The atmosphere in the boat was relaxed. The Japanese woman, who was at the wheel, was grimly satisfied by her acquisition of the long-sought journal, and the members of her gang were beginning to feel that they'd successfully accomplished their getaway – with fewer of them left to divide the fee they had been promised for their co-operation, meaning each would get a bigger share...

These pleasant reflections were interrupted by a shattering roar as an outlandish machine leaped from the darkness like some screeching metallic demon and, veering crazily from side to side, hurled itself upon them. The men in the boat gave hoarse cries of alarm; one flung himself overboard. The woman let rip a frantic curse and gunned the engine, speeding away from the new danger in blind panic.

The airboat Luke and Nick had commandeered was basically a flat-bottomed punt with an oversized aero-engine on the back driving a propeller protected by a steel cage, from which hung two vertical rudders that Luke was attempting to control with the stick to the left of his raised pilot's seat.

Nick twisted in his front seat, and, straining to make himself heard above the bellow of the engine, yelled, "Remember – forward for left, back for right. Squeeze the lever for more power."

"Do you want to drive this thing?" demanded Luke.

Nick shook his head. "I just know how it works, I've never driven one!"

"Me neither – but don't worry, I'm getting the hang of it." Luke squeezed as instructed. The engine note rose to a howl as the ungainly machine hurtled in pursuit of the raiders.

Luke grinned. The airboat was fast! There was no way the Japanese woman could escape him now!

The occupants of the boat evidently realized this. The vessel suddenly turned, heading straight for the bank. Luke stared in disbelief. Were their enemies trying to commit suicide? Then he noticed a dip in the bank – the boat was heading for a bayou, a backwater leading into the swamplands lying to the south-east of the city. Banking crazily, Luke followed.

Grasses and reeds appeared before the low, straight bow of the airboat and disappeared under the speeding hull with a swishing noise that was all but drowned out by the scream of the engine. The occupants of the motorboat were shooting again. Their aim was improving – as they fled down a channel of clear water, one of their bullets ricocheted from the cage around the airboat's propeller, and another ripped through the seat beside Nick, who turned to stare at Luke. With a grimace, Luke cut the throttle, allowing the airboat to drop back.

The motorboat surged ahead of it. Once the airboat was out of sight, it too throttled back. The Japanese woman sat with her hands on the wheel, listening intently. For several moments, there was no sound but the burbling of the boat's motor as it ran on tickover.

Then, with a howl like all the fiends of hell, the airboat burst from the reeds to the right of the channel, hit a sandbar, and rode right over the motorboat, whose crew was flung, screaming, into the dark water.

Luke made a U-turn and steered back cautiously, but it was immediately clear that there would be no more resistance. The remaining gunmen were floundering in the water, while their damaged boat settled heavily below the surface some distance away. As they watched, there was a sudden flurry of water around the first gunman, who disappeared with a scream. Seconds later, the second man went the same way.

"Alligators." Nick's voice was shaky.

Luke headed for the disturbed water, but there was no sign of the men, no possibility of rescue. He cut the engine. In the sudden silence, he said, "Where's Mochizuki?"

He and Nick listened intently for some time. Then, some way off to their left, they heard the cough and roar of an aero-engine starting up.

"Another airboat?" said Nick.

Luke started the engine. "Let's go and see."

But as they headed towards the source of the sound, they realized that it was not an airboat. A floatplane was racing down a dead-straight channel between the whispering reeds. Luke swerved in pursuit, but it was hopeless. The plane was already moving faster than the airboat. They caught a single glimpse of the Japanese woman staring at them through the cockpit window, her lips pulled back in a savage grin of triumph. Then the plane lifted off the water and climbed into the night sky.

Luke gunned the engine to send the airboat up the slip into the boatyard and killed the motor. He and Nick climbed stiffly out of their seats, and headed for the gates. Luke was only mildly surprised to find Jessica outside the yard, leaning against the bonnet of a battered pickup truck. "Is Lou okay?" he asked.

Jessica made a face. "Flesh wound. He's had worse." Her voice was husky with affection. "Dam' old fool, blazing away like that..."

"And Spotiswoode?"

"Oh, him. He got cut by flying glass. I dabbed some iodine on – he screamed like a baby with the colic. He's lying down in the back room."

"How did you find us?"

"Just followed the trail of damage. Are you all through playing boy scouts now?"

Luke sat on the kerb, head lowered in defeat. "It looks like it. The Japanese woman has the book and she got clean away."

Jessica gave a short bark of laughter. "Your Asiatic friend has jack."

Nick stared at her. "How's that again?"

"I said, she has nothing. What kind of a fool do you take me for? You think I'd just bring out that kind of information in a bar full of strangers?"

Nick began, "But you showed us the book..."

"If you'd listened to me instead of haring off like blame fools, I could have stopped you wasting your time. Yes, I showed you the book: Captain Nemo's journal – Volume One."

Luke said, "Volume...?"

"One. I was going to show it to you to prove it's authentic, but it just deals with the time my granddaddy was on the *Nautilus*. There's nothing important in it that wasn't in Jules Verne's book anyhow. Those gangsters, whoever they might be, were welcome to it. The stuff you need to find the *Nautilus* is in Volume Two."

Nick said, "And where is Volume Two?"

Jessica looked smug. "I burned it."

Luke gawped. "You burned it?"

"Sure. I didn't want it falling into the wrong hands, did I?"

Luke held himself in check with a commendable effort. "But if you burned it..."

"Of course, I read it first. Every word. Did I mention that I have a photographic memory?" Jessica tapped her head. "It's all in here. So, you see, you have to take me with you, whether you like it or not. Oh, and by the way, my fee just went up. It's now twenty per cent. That should just about pay for the repairs to Lou's bar, and all the vehicles you just wrecked!"

9 KIDNAP

Pearl Harbour, Oahu Island, Hawaii

The journey across the southern USA on the Sunset Limited train had taken three days. For the following two days, the Challenger party had kicked its heels in San Francisco waiting for the SS *Lurline* to sail for Honolulu. On the eleventh day after they had left New Orleans, Luke, Nick and Jessica were lounging in the Challenger Marine office overlooking Pearl Harbour. Jessica was reading a magazine, while Nick stared hungrily at every detail of the *Challenger II* tied up against the wharf below. Luke was rereading the veritable snowstorm of telegrams that they had sent and received on their journey.

The first one read:

TO: Sir Andrew Challenger, Kingshome Abbey,
Wiltshire, United Kingdom
FROM: Hilary Spotiswoode, Bourbon Orleans
Hotel, New Orleans, LA, USA
CONVINCED MERCHANDISE GENUINE FROM
JL STORY AND OPPOSITION ATTEMPT TO
SNATCH IT STOP RECOMMEND COMMENCE
SEARCH AS DISCUSSED

Sir Andrew's reply had been:

TO: Hilary Spotiswoode, Bourbon Orleans
Hotel, New Orleans, LA, USA
FROM: Sir Andrew Challenger, Kingshome
Abbey, Wiltshire, United Kingdom
WHAT DO YOU MEAN OPPOSITION ATTEMPT TO
SNATCH MERCHANDISE QUERY EXPLAIN
CIRCUMSTANCES BLAST YOU

The resulting flurry of telegrams had begun with Spotiswoode's explanations of the raid on the *Who Dat?* bar. It had continued with his justification for believing

Jessica's story, and the reasons he had decided that Luke and Nick would be safer going on to Hawaii with him rather than returning to England alone, or under the supervision of hired protectors who might turn out to be in the pay of their enemies. Spotiswoode's communications had been liberally punctuated by Sir Andrew's demands for more details. Eventually Spotiswoode's temper had snapped and he had fired off the following terse message:

TO: Sir Andrew Challenger, Kingshome Abbey, Wiltshire, United Kingdom
FROM: Hilary Spotiswoode, Fairmont Hotel, San Francisco, CA, USA
WE SAIL TOMORROW STOP DO WE HAVE YOUR PERMISSION TO SEARCH OR NOT QUERY WITH RESPECT CANNOT PROCEED IF YOU INSIST ON SHILLY SHALLYING

The reply had been equally forthright.

TO: Hilary Spotiswoode, Fairmont Hotel, San Francisco, CA, USA
FROM: Sir Andrew Challenger, Kingshome Abbey, Wiltshire, United Kingdom
DON'T TAKE THAT TONE WITH ME DAMN YOUR

EYES STOP VERY WELL PERMISSION GRANTED BUT
ITS MOONSHINE STILL

Another telegram had arrived ten minutes later,
apparently as an afterthought:

TO: Hilary Spotiswoode, Fairmont Hotel,
San Francisco, CA, USA
FROM: Sir Andrew Challenger, Kingshome
Abbey, Wiltshire, United Kingdom
JUST RECEIVED BILL FOR DAMAGES FROM NEW
ORLEANS AND IF YOU VALUE YOUR HIDE DO NOT
REPEAT NOT LET MY HAM-FISTED SON OR HIS
CACK-HANDED COUSIN ANYWHERE NEAR MY
PRECIOUS EQUIPMENT OR ELSE

This had been followed by one final, mysterious
communication:

TO: Luke Challenger, Challenger Marine
Office, Pearl Harbour, Oahu Is, Hawaii,
USA
FROM: Office Of Sir Andrew Challenger,
Kingshome Abbey, Wiltshire, United Kingdom
YOU WILL BE CAREFUL WONT YOU LUKE DEAR
QUERY OUR ENEMIES WILL STOP AT NOTHING

STOP SIR ANDREW ISN'T KEEN BUT I MANAGED
TO PERSUADE HIM STOP REMEMBER NANNY KNOWS
BEST

Luke put the pile of telegram forms back on the desk. "Nanny thinks we haven't seen the last of the Sons of Destiny."

Jessica looked up from her magazine. "You boys have a nanny?" Luke and Nick exchanged a glance but said nothing. "I guess you need someone to wipe your noses and change your diapers. Anyway," Jessica continued, "what's the deal with this Sons of Destiny outfit? You said they were behind the attack on Lou's bar, but who are they?"

Luke gathered his thoughts. "Well, they're a kind of secret society. They believe in some kind of mumbo-jumbo about the Spear of Destiny – they're convinced it's the spear that pierced Christ's side at the crucifixion, and whoever holds it will rule the world…"

"Just the sort of guys you two would get mixed up with. They sound like a bunch of nuts."

"But highly dangerous nuts. They have the same roots as Hitler's Nazi party, and they have members in Germany, Italy, England, Japan, Russia, you-name-it – and, as we now know, the United States. They've had a couple of pops at me and Nick already. They'll know they've got the wrong diary by now, and I can't see them giving up just like that. The question is, what will they try next?" Luke broke off as Spotiswoode came into the office. "How's it going?"

The engineer mopped his brow. "We're still having trouble with the propulsion units."

Nick bounded up eagerly. "Would you like me to take a look...?"

"No!" Spotiswoode held up both hands as though trying to fend off a large and boisterous dog. "No," he repeated more quietly. "In any case, it's just a leaking seal – but I can't get a replacement until tomorrow."

Luke stood up. "Well, in that case, I'm going to the beach." He turned to Nick and Jessica. "Coming?"

Waikiki beach was busy in the July sunshine. The sky was dotted with puffy clouds, scudding along at a fair rate of knots. The wind was kicking up a decent surf, blowing sand into picnic lunches and causing chaos among a group of boys nearby who were wrestling with an oversized kite that weaved across the sky as though alive and threatened at any moment to lift them off their feet.

Nick had declined Luke's invitation on the grounds that he didn't feel like swimming, though Luke strongly suspected the real reason was that he hadn't given up hope that Spotiswoode would relent and let him help prepare *Little Em'ly* for sea. Luke thought this a forlorn hope, and Nick would have done better to enjoy a day's surfing than mope around a stuffy office.

Jessica, wearing a red bathing-suit and slip-on sandals, was selecting a surfboard from the hire rail with the same care that some girls would use in choosing a pair of shoes. Luke wondered what he thought of her. He admired her toughness and self-reliance, but couldn't help feeling that her habit of speaking her mind could be altogether too much of a good thing. Jessica had certainly mellowed during the journey to Honolulu, but she still had the annoying tendency to treat him and Nick as if they were about eight years old. Luke was uncomfortably aware that he had limited experience with girls; all the surroundings in which he had spent most of his time – Kingshome Abbey, his mother's fossil-hunting digs and his despised public school – had been pretty much male preserves. Maybe all girls were as forthright and prickly as Jessica. It was an alarming thought.

Jessica chose her board and joined Luke at the owner's shack. A man with a drooping moustache and an eye-popping Hawaiian shirt grunted as Luke paid him a deposit. "You folks been surfin' before?"

Luke nodded. Jessica said, "Sure."

"Well, watch yourselves out there today. There's an offshore wind, so you should get some good surf, but if the waves get too high, come back in. You don't want to be trying to surf a pipeline unless you're experts. And watch out for rips."

"We will." Luke deposited a bag with their belongings with the man for safe keeping, tucked the board under his arm and followed Jessica down towards the sea.

They pushed their boards into the water and began to paddle out. The waves were rolling in nicely; Luke and Jessica took them side by side, duck-diving through incoming waves until they had reached the edge of the surf zone. They lay face down on the boards, paddling in a leisurely way to keep control, rising and falling on the swell and watching out for promising waves.

"Where did you learn to surf?" asked Luke.

"California. You?"

"Australia, a couple of years ago." Luke gave Jessica a wry grin. "My mother was digging up fossils as usual – I preferred the beach." He gazed out to sea. "I like the look of this one."

Jessica studied the oncoming wave. "Nah – I reckon it'll crumble. I'll wait."

"Suit yourself." Luke turned his board towards the shore and paddled faster. As he felt the energy of the wave lift the board, he angled it carefully, and then shifted, first to his knees, then to his feet.

To begin with, the board slid smoothly down the slope of the wave, just below the crest. But Luke soon realized that Jessica was right. The wave, instead of powering smoothly towards the shore, was beginning to break up and lose definition. Even so, he was quite close to the shore before the wave washed out completely. Luke slipped off the board, surfaced, shook water from his eyes, and looked for Jessica.

He was just in time to see her being hauled off her board by three men and bundled into a motorboat.

As the boat's engine roared and it sped away, Luke saw instantly that there was no way he could catch it. Instead, he grabbed his board and waded for the shore as quickly as the clutching waves would allow. He had no plan in doing so, apart from getting to a telephone and alerting the coastguard. But as he ran, his eye was drawn to the group of struggling boys and their huge, unwieldy kite...

The surf-shack owner came pounding down the beach, waving his fists, as Luke, perfectly balanced on the board and holding onto the kite strings for dear life, swept out to sea through the surf zone. "Hey!" the man yelled. "Where you going with my board?" Then his eyes widened. "Hmmm," he mused, watching as Luke rode up a wave, leaped from the crest and continued on his hell-for-leather race in pursuit of the boat. "Kite... surfboard...I think I just had me a great idea!"

His thoughts were interrupted by the arrival of half a dozen island boys who surrounded him, bouncing with excitement and all talking at once. "Hey, Mister! That guy took our kite. He said he left his money with you, and you give us twenty dollar for it."

The man scowled at them. "Scat! I just thought of a brand-new way of surfin' and you're distractin' me from my inventin'."

"Twenty dollar! Twenty dollar!"

Out in the bay, Luke felt as if he had a tiger by the tail. The board bucked and slapped beneath his feet and the kite strings felt as though they were about to tear his arms from their sockets. But this combination of kite and surfboard was fast, there was no doubt about it – he was probably doing at least thirty knots and he was catching up with the motorboat. He could see Jessica struggling in the grip of two men wearing what looked like sailors' uniforms. As he drew closer, he realized that her captors were Japanese and was instantly sure that the Mochizuki woman was behind Jessica's abduction.

The boat raced parallel to the shore, going west, with Luke tearing along in pursuit and gaining hand over fist. By now, the kidnappers were definitely aware of his presence. They were urging the driver to go faster and snatching handguns from their belts to shoot at their pursuer. Luke heard the crack of small arms fire and smiled grimly. Let them shoot – they hadn't a snowball in hell's chance of hitting him at this distance. When he got close enough to attempt a rescue, of course, that would be a different matter.

Luke's arms were numb by the time the boat began turning in to shore, and he realized they were heading towards Pearl Harbour. An aircraft carrier flying the Stars and Stripes was riding at anchor, just off the harbour mouth. Luke glanced at it as he passed, and saw that a launch full of sailors in immaculate white ducks was just pulling away from its side, presumably heading for shore leave. With a gasp of relief, he hauled on the left-hand string and steered straight for it.

The sailors stared open-mouthed as he swept alongside. A petty officer gestured furiously. "What in the nation are you playing at, buddy? Sheer off!"

Luke's hands were full of kite string, but he nodded vigorously in the direction of the fleeing boat. "American girl," he yelled at the top of his lungs, "kidnapped!"

"What's that you say? Kidnapped?" The officer held a hurried consultation with a colleague, then waved an arm. "Come aboard!"

Gratefully, Luke let go of the kite strings and

coasted to the launch's side. Grinning ratings hauled him aboard.

The petty officer scowled at him. "Now – what's all this about?"

Luke pointed. "The men in that boat – I think they're Japanese – they kidnapped an American girl from Waikiki Beach. Her name's Jessica Land…"

"That's enough for me!" chirped up one of the ratings. "Come on, Chief, let's go. I ain't had me a real good dust-up since Fat Charlie's in Singapore."

"Shut your yap, Kowalski." The petty officer gave Luke a narrow-eyed stare. He pointed at the kite, which had settled on the water some distance away. "You followed this girl all the way over here from Waikiki with that contraption?" Breathless, Luke could only nod. "I always knew Brits were crazy – but this better be on the level."

One of the ratings had a telescope clamped to his eye, following the progress of the kidnappers' boat. "Chief, they're signalling! They – holy cow!" Every sailor in the boat turned and gaped as, barely a mile away, a submarine conning-tower broke the surface.

The petty officer swore luridly. "That's a Japanese sub or I've never seen one. All right! Helm, lay a course for that boat! Full speed ahead! Jump to it, you men! Action stations!"

The helmsman opened up the engines and the launch surged in pursuit of the kidnappers' boat, its sides lined with sailors grinning at the prospect of action. The submarine rose further from the water, so that its long deck was just awash. A figure appeared on the conning tower – even from that distance, Luke was sure that it was Colonel Mochizuki – and beckoned frantically to the men holding Jessica.

But the launch's powerful engines ate up the distance, and it was soon apparent that it would be upon the kidnappers' boat before they could reach the sub. Luke glanced at the conning tower as they made their final approach, and saw two figures apparently locked in furious argument. Then they disappeared, and moments later, waves began to break over the deck of the submarine.

The kidnappers had raised their guns to fire, but on seeing their only hope of salvation preparing for departure, they cut their engine, threw their guns overboard, folded their hands on top of their heads and waited glumly to be captured.

The launch pulled alongside the drifting boat and Luke reached out to lend Jessica a hand. She gave him a look he found difficult to read and said, in a rather strained voice, "Thanks, boy scout."

Luke said, "You're welcome."

The submarine, now moving swiftly through the water, continued its dive. The conning tower, with the number I-40 painted on its side, slipped beneath the waves.

The petty officer shook his fist at it. "Yah! Git! This is Pearl Harbour, buddy, property of the US Navy and you ain't been invited! You just haul your sorry ass out of here and *don't come back*!"

10 DEPARTURE

Forty-eight hours later

Captain Fulton, the commander of the *Challenger II*, was a blue-eyed, bull-necked veteran with close-cropped white hair and a neat beard. He wore an immaculate white uniform with gold braid at the shoulder. He seldom raised his voice, and the word on the lower decks was that no one had ever seen him smile. He greeted any remark – even "Good morning" – with great seriousness, and took his time over replying; as if mentally checking the time to see that it really was morning, and then reviewing his current situation to decide whether the morning might on balance be considered "Good".

The Captain was in the ship's chart room when Luke and Nick found him. "Sir," said Luke without preamble, "what's this about you not wanting us to come with you?"

The message had been delivered by the *Challenger II*'s second officer. Luke had been furious when he had received it, and Nick was watching him nervously, as though he were a large dog of uncertain temperament, who might at any minute begin to growl, bite or start chewing the carpet. Nick had never actually seen Luke chew the carpet, but in his current mood, he wouldn't rule it out.

The Captain looked up from his charts and regarded Luke steadily for a full fifteen seconds before replying. "Mister Challenger, your father is the owner of this vessel. He decides where it goes and what it does. It is my job to follow his directions, whatever I might think of them. If he wants me to go hunting non-existent submarines, I'm ready to do so until kingdom come. But he has sent me no instructions concerning you or Mister Malone. I am master of this ship under God, and no power on earth can compel me to take anyone into my crew against my wishes. There is no room on this ship for passengers."

Luke gritted his teeth. "We wouldn't be passengers. It was Nick and I who persuaded my father to look for the *Nautilus* in the first place..."

This time, the Captain's reply was uncharacteristically prompt. "I am aware that I have you to thank for engaging my ship and crew in a pointless search. You are not helping your case, Mister Challenger."

Nick stepped in while Luke fought down his rage. "Captain, we could be very useful. Luke and I both helped design *Little Em'ly*..." He broke off as Spotiswoode appeared in the doorway, clutching a book of tide tables. "Ask Mr. Spotiswoode, he'll tell you." He addressed himself to the engineer. "You think we should be along on this voyage, don't you?"

Spotiswoode looked uncomfortable. "Well, obviously, I greatly value your contribution to the design... But I am quite capable of looking after the *Challenger II* and *Little Em'ly* myself, you know. And I have to agree with the Captain that a survey vessel is no place for two fifteen-year-olds..."

Luke gave Spotiswoode a furious glare. "You're wasting your time, Nick. He's been nobbled by my father. Haven't you?" he demanded.

Spotiswoode blushed. "Ah...Sir Andrew has made it clear to me that he is opposed to your further involvement..."

Nick regarded him with contempt. "Thanks for nothing. Traitor."

Captain Fulton returned the chart he had been studying to its drawer and reached for his peaked cap. "We will cast off in one hour. Mister Challenger, Mister Malone, I'd be obliged if you would leave the vessel as soon as possible." He stepped out of the room. Luke and Nick exchanged determined glances, gave the uncomfortable Spotiswoode a scornful parting glare, and followed.

They caught up with the Captain outside the mess hall. He was engaged in earnest conversation with a nervous-looking wire-haired scientist with a thin face – Luke knew he had joined the expedition from Berkeley University, but couldn't remember his name. The scientist was talking nineteen to the dozen and waving sheets of calculations under the Captain's nose. Fulton listened with weary patience before promising to give whatever was disturbing the young man his urgent consideration. As the man from Berkeley scurried off, he turned his attention to Luke. "Still here, Mister Challenger?"

Luke made a determined attempt to be diplomatic. "Sir, Nick and I are more than capable of taking care of ourselves."

"I know that – it's the manner in which you choose to do it that disturbs me. Quite apart from the trail of damage you've left in England and New Orleans, there is the matter of your intervention in the attempted kidnapping of Miss Land..."

"They were carrying her off!" Luke retorted furiously. "Ask her if you don't believe me!"

"I'm sure Miss Land would confirm your story. In fact, I believe she is doing so to the Hawaiian justice department as we speak."

"There you are, then! What was I supposed to do?"

"Report the matter to the authorities and let them deal with it."

"By the time I'd done that, it would have been too late to get Jessica back. Her kidnappers don't know she's burned Nemo's journal. They tried to kidnap her to make her tell them where it is, or to force us to swap her for the journal if we had it. If they'd found she'd memorized it, and they couldn't find the *Nautilus* without her, they'd never have let her go."

"Nevertheless, the official view is that your intervention was damaging. You enlisted the aid of the United States Navy in committing what the Japanese Ambassador in Washington is describing as an act of aggression against a Japanese submarine engaged in peaceful pursuits in US waters." Luke was speechless. "The Pacific Fleet is stirred up like a hornet's nest, there are questions being asked in the White House, and the Governor of Hawaii is threatening to impound my vessel. You've created an international incident, young man."

"I didn't create anything," said Luke hotly. "The Japanese tried to kidnap—"

"I don't pretend to understand the ins and outs of international relations – all I know is, your actions have heaped coals of fire upon our heads." Captain Fulton finally noticed that Spotiswoode was frantically signalling him from the bridge deck. "Yes?" he called brusquely. "What is it?"

"Radio signal, sir." Spotiswoode looked worried, even by his own perpetually anxious standards. "I really think you'd better hear this."

The Captain said, "Very good," in a tone that made it clear that it was anything but, and set off up the accommodation ladder.

Nick shook his head. "It's no good arguing. We won't change his mind."

"We're not finished yet," said Luke savagely. "We'll stow away if we have to – we're not being left behind..." He felt a tap on his shoulder. "Now what? Oh, hello, Saul."

Saul Baird, *Little Em'ly*'s laconic Texan pilot, grinned at Luke. "Whoa, my friend. You look like you're fit to be tied. What's got your panties in a knot?" Luke told him. Saul wiped imaginary sweat from his brow. "Phew.

Lucky day for me," he said seriously. "From what I hear, you handle submersibles better than I do."

"What's Nick been telling you?" Luke glared at his cousin, who looked abashed. "A load of tommyrot, I expect. I'd never even seen *Little Em'ly* before we got here. It's true that Spotiswoode mocked up a three-quarter sized prototype and did some trials in Portland Harbour last Easter, and Nick and I managed to bullyrag him into letting us have a go, but that's all."

"Put in some hours?"

"A few – we had a surface air supply so we could stay down pretty much as long as we liked. But it wasn't like piloting the real thing – the prototype couldn't dive below thirty feet, for a start..."

Saul held up his hands. "Don't bother me none – me and Del got us a contract. Anyhow, good to know we got backup if we need it."

"I don't suppose you...?"

"You want me to put a word in?" Saul shook his head. "I can try, but it won't do any good. I been with the Old Man long enough to know once his mind's made up, you'd need dynamite to shift him. Hey, Del!" He beckoned over his co-pilot. Saul was tall and rangy with long hair and a moustache that ran halfway down his throat. Delaware Silvers, in contrast, was a whippet of a man – small, wiry, all nervous energy. "Looks like the Cap is fixin' to throw our friends here off the boat," Saul told him.

"That's too bad." Del looked downcast for a fleeting moment. Then he said, "In that case, there's a couple of things you can help us with before you go."

Saul gave him a wry look. "Always the diplomat."

Luke grinned despite himself. "Sure. How can we help?"

Del addressed himself to Nick. "It's the batteries. They're not giving us as much power as they should. Peak rate is fine but they're discharging faster than spec."

Nick was instantly the eagle-eyed mechanic. "Must be a high resistance somewhere. Let's take a look." He and Del headed for the afterdeck.

Saul rubbed his chin. "I got me a problem of my own. See, I'm used to midget subs – they don't go deep but you can steer 'em wherever you want. *Em'ly*'s different. When we were doing preliminary trials, flying her round down there, below about six hunn'erd feet I couldn't steer her as far as I wanted. It's the weight of the cable. You start moving away from directly below your support vessel and the cable kinda pulls you back like an elastic band. You waste a lot of battery power gettin' nowhere. You feel like a real small dog on a heavy ol' chain."

"But if you see something you want to investigate, you can release the cable and take a look, can't you?"

"Sure, but you can't reattach the cable if whatever you went to look at turns out not to be as interesting as you thought. You have to drop ballast, and surface, and the cable has to be winched up, and you have to recharge the batteries and it all takes time and costs money. We need a way of going over to take a closer look-see at stuff without dropping off the cable."

Luke thought for a moment. Then he said, "Why not move the ship?"

Saul stared at him. "The ship?"

"Why not? I know when a support vessel has a surface-supplied diver down it's usually at anchor, because if it starts to move the diver gets dragged around by his air-hose. But where the *Challenger II* is operating, it'll usually be too deep to anchor, and *Em'ly* will be above the ocean floor, not on it. If the ship moves, she'll just fly across the seabed underneath. All you need to do is work out a system of instructions with the steersmen so you can tell them to go right or left, double back and so on, and with the winchmen to take you up or down. That way you can get a good look at anything on the seabed before you decide to release the cable."

A big grin spread slowly over the Texan's face. "Yeah – I reckon that would do it." He looked past Luke's shoulder. "Like I told you, Capt'n. Boy's got a head on his shoulders."

Luke glanced around. Captain Fulton was standing just behind him, his face expressionless. "Don't try your soft soap with me, Baird. I accept Mister Challenger might have his uses on this trip, but that is not my only consideration." He scowled for a moment towards the aft deck where Nick and Del were deep in discussion about the electric motor, whose watertight casing they had just removed. Then he turned his attention back to Luke. "Radio room, five minutes. Bring your friend."

By the time Luke had succeeded in dragging Nick away from an intense discussion about brushes and commutators, the Captain and Spotiswoode were already present. The shortwave radio was hissing and crackling as its operator struggled to hold on to the signal.

"This is being relayed via New York and Los Angeles." Fulton nodded towards the radio. "There's a slight time delay and the signal breaks up now and then, but *Nanny*" – he made a face as if he'd bitten into a bad oyster – "thinks you should all hear this." He took the microphone from the radio operator, pressed the transmit button and said, "Hello, Challenger Headquarters. This is *Challenger II, Challenger II*. Come in please. Over."

Nanny's voice, tinny and faint with distance, issued from a loudspeaker above the radio set. "*Hello,* Challenger II. *This is Nanny. Are you all sitting comfortably?*"

Captain Fulton pressed transmit again. "Affirmative."

"*Then I'll begin. I have news, and I'm afraid it isn't very encouraging. Luke, dear, some American senators are very cross with you and Nick. They may be in the pay of our enemies; then again, they may simply have business interests in Japan. At any rate, they are lobbying hard to arrange warrants for your arrest. You'll need to get away from United States territory as quickly as possible.*"

Luke glanced at Captain Fulton. "All the more reason to take us with you."

"Or put you on a ship to Shanghai or Singapore."

"*There's more, I'm afraid,*" said Nanny. "*Intelligence confirms that Japanese Navy Experimental Submarine I-40 is known to be operating in Hawaiian waters...*"

"We could have told her that," muttered Nick. "In fact, I'm pretty sure we did..."

"*...and that aboard her, acting as political officer – that means, making sure the submarine commander does what the Japanese government wants him to – is one Kaigun Daisa – that's 'Captain' to you and me – Mochizuki.*"

Nick shook his head. "I still don't understand how she's come back from the dead."

Luke snorted. "If the Japanese think she's taking orders from their government, they don't know much about her. She's working for the Sons of Destiny..." He paused. "Hang on a minute." He gave Captain Fulton an enquiring look and Fulton passed him the microphone. "Nanny, did I hear that right? *Captain* Mochizuki?"

"Yes, dear. I thought that would interest you. And just to put the icing on the cake, as it were," Nanny continued, *"a little bird tells me that there's also a German submarine on the loose in the Pacific, and believed to be in your vicinity: Unterseeboot U-X1. It's the German Navy's latest experimental model, designed to go deeper than the submarines currently in service, and its commanding officer is Korvettenkapitän Wolfgang Roth."*

Fulton almost snatched the microphone from Luke. "The Sea Wolf?"

"Quite so, Captain. One of the most distinguished U-boat commanders of the Great War. He sank over a hundred allied ships. A formidable adversary – always supposing that he is a member of the Sons of Destiny, or acting under the orders of those who are—" Nanny's voice was interrupted by a blast of static. The radio operator turned down the loudspeaker and fiddled with dials, listening intently to his headphones. At length he gave up and turned to Captain Fulton with an apologetic shrug.

Fulton turned to Luke and Nick. "This changes nothing. I know about the Sons of Destiny – I know that they are a secret organization and therefore not bound by the rules of international diplomacy. We can't be sure what Kapitän Roth may be up to, but from what Spotiswoode tells me, this Mochizuki woman is hell-bent on revenge, and this is not a fighting vessel. If there's trouble, we have no way to protect you."

"Captain..." Spotiswoode's reluctance to speak was obvious, but he steeled himself and carried on, "I'm afraid it changes everything. Luke and Nick can't stay in the United States without falling foul of the authorities, and I don't think we can just stick them on a ship to some Asiatic port that, for all we know, could be crawling with their enemies. That's assuming they ever got there – this Mochizuki woman seems to be able to board and leave ships in mid-ocean more or less as she pleases – and at least the boys are among friends here."

Jessica appeared in the doorway, so furious that her face was almost as red as her hair. "The flatfoots in the police department here are as bad as the New Orleans kind. And as soon as I get back, I hear about these guys being bum-rushed off of this tub! What's the big idea?"

Captain Fulton gave her a quelling look. "This doesn't concern you, Miss Land. You're here on sufferance for the information you possess, no other reason."

"No?" Jessica's eyes glinted. "Well, now, Captain, I

don't like the way you seem to assume that anyone who still has all their own teeth is a complete waste of space. I reckon we're all three of us good enough to earn a place with your crew on merit, if you weren't too stick-in-the-mud to see it. But that don't signify, I guess. The clincher is that you need me, and I'm not going anywhere unless these guys come too." She folded her arms and scowled.

Captain Fulton said nothing for several seconds. Then he gave a single, brief nod. "It seems I have no choice. Very well." He checked his watch, giving Luke and Nick time to hide their grins of delight. "I'll see that you're allocated a cabin. Now, clear the bridge, please. I'm about to give the order to cast off."

Luke and Nick followed Jessica down to the crew's quarters. Luke touched her lightly on the arm. "Thanks."

Jessica gave him a half-smile. "I guess that makes us even. I pay my debts, Luke Challenger. That's all. You read me?"

"Oh – yes, right."

"Well, good."

"Yes."

"Okay. Fine. And my fee is still twenty per cent."

"Right."

"Right." Jessica stalked off.

Luke turned on Nick. "What are you smirking at?"

"Oh, nothing." Nick's grin widened. "Nothing at all."

As the *Challenger II* steamed out of Pearl Harbour, heading for the open sea, a steel tube rose from the surface of the ocean and swivelled until the lens at its end was directed at the departing vessel. A few seconds later, a quarter of a mile away, a second periscope surfaced, also turning to focus on the Challenger vessel.

For several seconds, the periscopes continued their watch. Then they began to move as the submarines whose eyes they were set off in pursuit. Moments later, the periscopes sank, soundlessly and unobserved, beneath the waves.

11 COMPANY

Central Pacific Ocean: 7°34' N, 171°09' E,
near Marshall Islands

Luke was standing at the rail, gazing across the flat afterdeck of the *Challenger II*. His position overlooked two gigantic drums – one wound with several thousand fathoms of steel cable, the other holding the umbilicus that would carry *Little Em'ly*'s electricity supply and communications. Beyond these, right at the stern of the ship, stood the crane that would raise and lower the submersible, and *Little Em'ly* herself, securely fastened to the deck.

The submersible was basically a cigar-shaped tank,

filled with gasoline. It had a spherical observation gondola set into its belly, which made it look like a pregnant guppy, though this was invisible for the moment as it sat in a semicircular housing set into the deck. There was a single rudder at the stern and diving planes like stubby wings protruded from each side of the hull; behind these were the pods housing the electric motors that would propel the craft. A small slatted deck on top of the submersible's back contained the connection points for the lifting cable and the umbilicus and a hatchway from which a tunnel led down through the hull to the gondola.

At the moment, Luke had no interest in *Em'ly* or anything else on the *Challenger II*. His eyes glued to a pair of high-powered binoculars, he was staring back over the stern of the ship to where its wake tumbled across the surface of the peaceful ocean, a ruler-straight line of white foam gleaming with phosphorescence in the light of the half-moon.

Jessica appeared beside him, for once not wearing one of her seemingly inexhaustible supply of check shirts, but a cream-coloured blouse with a soft collar and leg-o'-mutton sleeves. She leaned on the rail beside Luke and said, "Hi, there."

"Oh – hello." Luke continued to stare through the binoculars.

Jessica waited for him to put them down and take a little more notice of her presence. When this failed to happen, she said, "Kinda beautiful, isn't it?"

Luke's eyes remained glued to the binoculars. "Hmmmm?"

Jessica gave him an annoyed glance and said, in something more like her normal abrasive tone, "Our wake. The way it just stretches off to the horizon." Her voice softened. "You can't see anything else on a night like this; just dark sea, dark sky, the stars, the moon – and the wake. It's like this ship is the only thing left in the whole world, and we're sailing away into the unknown and leaving the past behind. It's a strange feeling. I wonder what causes it."

"Cavitation," said Luke promptly. "The bubbles come from the shock wave made by the ship's propellers. Of course, there's also some splashing from the hull, and some of the foam comes from pollution in the water..."

"You sure know how to sweet-talk a girl," Jessica observed sourly. "I meant what causes the feeling, not the wake."

"Oh, sorry," said Luke, without relaxing his vigil. "I don't know. In any case, I'm not watching the wake."

"Then what are you watching?"

"I'm watching for conning towers."

"Excuse me?"

"Conning towers." Luke lowered the binoculars and rubbed his eyes. "There are two subs out there, and they're following us, I know it. They can run submerged all day using their batteries, but they have to surface at night so they can renew their air and run their diesel engines." Luke lifted the binoculars to his eyes again. "In fact, I don't expect actually to see the conning towers..."

"Gee, what a disappointment that must be for you."

"...they're only the size of a small boat; but on a night like this, I may be able to see the bow wave they produce."

"Well, your life is clearly just throbbing with excitement," Jessica told him sourly. "I'd hate to interrupt such a fascinating activity. So long, you fun lovin' fool."

The clatter of her steps as she left, rather than her words, penetrated Luke's concentration. "Hmmm?" he said. "Oh, yes...'night."

After a while, it occurred to Luke that he may have been less than polite. He'd practically ignored Jessica, who had been making some effort to be nice to him since they had put to sea. So when he heard the sound of returning footsteps, though he didn't take his eyes from the binoculars, he said, "Look, I'm sorry about earlier. I didn't mean to be rude. I'd be happy to talk about the wake if that's what you'd like."

"Why would I want to do that?" asked Nick.

Luke lowered the binoculars and stared at him. "I thought you were... Never mind," he went on as Nick's grin began to reappear, and resumed his search.

"Still looking for phantom submarines, Mister Challenger?"

Luke turned to find that Captain Fulton and Spotiswoode had joined them. "Yes, sir. You said Nick and I were to stand watch, like the regular crew."

"So I did. I didn't order you to chase shadows, however."

"Those subs are out there," said Luke stubbornly. "I'm sure of it. The Sons of Destiny are an international organization. When we met their High Command last year, it had members from Germany and Japan. I can't prove it, but I'm sure Kapitän Roth and Captain Mochizuki are co-operating. When they failed to kidnap Jessica, they lost their last chance to discover the whereabouts of the *Nautilus* – unless they follow us. They *must* be out there."

Fulton said nothing, and Nick said, "I still don't get how that Mochizuki woman is still alive. It's a complete mystery."

"But not as big a mystery," said Luke, "as why a colonel in the Japanese Army suddenly becomes a captain in the Imperial Japanese Navy."

"Because they don't have female captains in the Japanese Navy?"

"Well, not in command of ships. Mochizuki's a political officer, though; I suppose the rules are different."

"Well, then, what's the problem?" asked Nick. "Maybe she fancied a career change. Army colonel and navy captain are equivalent ranks, after all."

Luke said nothing.

Captain Fulton considered. "Even if you're right, and we are being shadowed, giving yourself eye strain isn't going to get us any further. I don't know about the Japanese commander, but Roth is far too canny to allow himself to be spotted. They don't call him the Sea Wolf for nothing."

"If they're following us," said Nick, "couldn't we just turn around and catch them by surprise?"

"We're a lot bigger than a sub's conning tower," said Fulton. "Any move we make, they'd see at once and either crash-dive, or make a turn themselves. We wouldn't catch Roth napping that way."

"Wait a minute," said Luke slowly. "If we can't spot them on the surface, maybe we can find them under it – Nick, couldn't we pick up the subs on the ship's echo sounder?"

Nick shook his head. "Wouldn't work."

"I'm afraid he's right," said Spotiswoode. "The echo sounder sends out a signal and then counts how long it takes to bounce back from an object to work out how far away it is. Normally, it bounces off the seabed – to get it to detect smaller targets, we'd need to increase the power and the sensitivity, but it still couldn't tell you what the echo was bouncing back *from*. It could be a sub, but it could be a rock or a reef, or even a shoal of fish."

"To find a sub," Nick put in, "you'd need proper anti-submarine detection equipment – ASDIC."

Luke wasn't to be put off. "So, could you convert the ship's echo sounder into an ASDIC set?"

Captain Fulton stared at him. "Now just a minute..."

Nick fired up immediately. "Should be able to. We can make it more directional, so we can use it to find out where the target actually is. And we're carrying hydrophones for underwater sound detection. If we rejig the echo sounder and use it and the hydrophones together, we can pick up an underwater target *and* listen for engines. Echo plus engines equals submarine."

"As you were!" snapped Captain Fulton. "If you think for one minute I'm going to allow you to monkey around with the *Challenger II*'s echo sounder, especially while we're passing though an island chain – where, I might add, I'm not confident that all the reefs are properly charted – and leave us navigating blind while we chase something we don't even know is out there, you can think again."

"But you've got a spare echo sounder, haven't you, sir?" said Nick.

Spotiswoode nodded vigorously. "We can recalibrate that one while we're still using the regular echo sounder, then swap them."

"That's right," said Nick. "In any case, the set-up might come in useful later. If we lose contact with *Little Em'ly* while she's diving, it could help us find her...oh." He broke off suddenly. "No," he said, giving Luke an apologetic look. "Even using the hydrophones to find the subs won't work if they're behind us."

"Oh Lor', yes." Spotiswoode looked as if he'd been sandbagged. "If we were trying to listen out for something behind us, all we'd pick up is the sound of our own engines."

"True," said Luke. "*If* they're behind us – but they won't *be* behind us if we turn round. In daylight, even if they see us doing it, they'll just lower their periscopes and go deeper. They'll think they're safe." He turned to the commander of the *Challenger II*. "Captain?"

* * *

The conversion of the spare echo sounder took the rest of the night and most of the following day. Nick, Spotiswoode and the *Challenger II*'s radio operator worked for fourteen hours at a stretch, rewiring, soldering, testing. Luke had tried to help, but electronic engineering was not his long suit. Finding himself more of a hindrance than otherwise, he had wandered off to find Jessica – but she, apparently engrossed in a movie magazine, had made it clear that she was not in the mood for conversation. In fact, she'd given Luke the distinct impression that if he were lying dead in a ditch, that would be fine by her.

So Luke had spent the rest of the day playing chess with the young scientist from Berkeley (whose name he still could not remember). The Berkeley man was some sort of expert on atomic energy. His job would not really begin until the *Challenger II* had succeeded in locating the *Nautilus*, and he was feeling both bored and seasick. Luke wasn't fond of chess, but their games seemed to help the Berkeley man feel less nauseous, so Luke good-naturedly continued to play and tried not to feel resentful when he lost.

By late afternoon, Nick and Spotiswoode had declared themselves satisfied with the result of their labours; Luke and Jessica had joined them on the bridge along with Captain Fulton and his senior officers. All eyes were on the improvised equipment's dials, and the machine's sound output had been switched to the bridge loudspeakers.

"Ready?" asked Captain Fulton. On Spotiswoode's nod, he said, "Helm – starboard one-eighty. Bring her about. Engines ahead full."

The quartermaster on duty spun the wheel. "One eighty, engines ahead full. Aye, sir."

The ship turned, listing slightly to the right as she did so. A minute later, the *Challenger II*'s bows were cleaving through the foam of her own wake, heading back the way she had come.

The radio operator switched on the hastily assembled ASDIC set. A series of high-pitched *PING!*s sounded in the bridge speakers. For a while, nothing else could be heard. Then, the *PING!*s began to lengthen to a sound like *PING-ER!* At the same time, a faint whirring of engines became audible. On the dials of the ASDIC set, needles began to twitch.

"There they are, by God!" Captain Fulton sounded grimly satisfied. He watched as the operator scanned for the strongest echo. "Bearing zero-three-zero, range 3,000 yards and closing..."

The whirring sound in the speakers was growing louder, and was now joined by vibrations of a slightly different frequency.

"Another one!" Spotiswoode was beside himself with excitement. "Bearing zero-four-three, range 3,500..."

"They're turning." Luke pointed at the dials. "The bearings are changing. They can hear us coming. They're heading away from us..."

They continued to watch and listen as the engine noise of the shadowing submarines built to a climax, then began to fade away.

"Orders, sir?" Fulton's Chief Officer cast an anxious glance at the dials. "Do you want to follow them?"

"Follow them, Mister Marsden? Which one should we follow? And for what reason?" asked Fulton. "So we can ask them to keep the noise down? No. We know for certain they're there, and they know we know. We've given them something to think about – that'll do for now." When the last engine sound had died away and the last needle on the dials quivered to rest, he straightened up. "Resume original course."

As the helmsman spun the wheel, the Captain caught sight of the ship's barometer. "Is this thing broken?" he asked.

The helmsman stared at the instrument open-mouthed. "No, sir. Checked it myself, yesterday."

"Well, that reading can't be right. I've never seen a glass fall so steeply." Captain Fulton tapped the glass.

This made no difference – the barometer needle continued to hang sullenly at the bottom of the scale.

Jessica looked over Fulton's shoulder and whistled. "That's the lowest pressure reading I've ever seen."

The Captain checked the log for the readings over the last few hours. "Nothing unusual earlier," he said in measured tones, "but it's dropped like a stone in the last hour."

Luke, who didn't count meteorology among his areas of expertise, was bewildered. "So what does it mean?"

Jessica pointed to the windows of the bridge. Beyond them, from horizon to horizon, gigantic black clouds were piling in upon the *Challenger II*, racing across the sky, bloated with rain and shot with lightning. The ship's easy motion began to be interrupted by drunken lurches as the seas built with extraordinary rapidity, going from smooth rollers to a short, vicious chop. Spray crashed over the deck, and a sudden wind howled around the bridge.

"It means," said Jessica grimly, "that we are in for one mother of a storm."

12 KNOCKDOWN

Central Pacific Ocean: position unknown

The violence of the storm was appalling.

Thunder roared and hammered at Luke's ears. Lightning flashed continuously – spears, bolts and sheets of electric fire that burned their images on his retinas even through closed eyelids. Rain drummed on the roof of the bridge and streamed down the windows.

The *Challenger II* was lifted as though by a giant hand, as a mountainous wave rolled beneath it. The stern rose up and up, until the deck was sloping at the angle of a pitched roof – then, as the wave passed under the ship, the stern fell into the trough behind and it was the bow's turn to rise and point at the roiling clouds.

"Secure all hatches!" Even on the bridge, Captain Fulton had to bellow to make himself heard above the rolls of thunder, the howling wind and lashing rain. "Helm, keep her stern to the waves whatever you do."

Nick, clinging to one of the stanchions that supported the bridge roof, yelled, "What happens if he doesn't keep the stern to the waves?"

Jessica answered him. "We broach. If a wave catches us sideways on, we roll over and sink!"

Nick gave Spotiswoode a disgusted look. "You said you designed this ship to be safe!"

Spotiswoode was wide-eyed with apprehension. "It *is* designed to be safe – at least, as safe as any ship can be in a storm like this! What it isn't designed to do is float upside down! Don't worry – as long as we have the engines we can steer, and as long as we can steer we'll be..." He gulped as the *Challenger II* gave a sudden lurch. "...fine," he concluded, turning green around the gills.

Nick tightened his hold on the stanchion as the vessel lurched again. "I thought this was the Pacific," he complained to the world in general, "the 'peaceful' ocean."

"Normally it is," Jessica told him, "but from what I

hear, when it does raise up a storm, it's generally a humdinger!"

Luke peered through the blurred glass of the windows facing the stern of the ship. On the afterdeck, the scurrying figures of the crew struggled to secure the hatch covers that had been left open to allow cool air below. The suddenness of the storm had caught them by surprise, and it was all they could do to keep their footing on the pitching deck as they were continually washed by waves and showered with spray. The work was going slowly.

Then, something else caught his eye. He looked up, and his mouth was suddenly dry with horror.

Far astern, but rushing upon the ship with the speed of an express train, was a wave that dwarfed the others – a monstrous, rearing, foaming mountain of a wave; a watery juggernaut that towered above the *Challenger II* like the wrath of Neptune.

Luke grabbed a loudhailer from its bracket and hauled open the bridge door. The wind slammed it against the rail. Instantly drenched and blinded by rain and spray, he raised the instrument to his lips. "Big wave!" he yelled at the top of his lungs. "Coming in astern! Brace, brace!"

One or two of the nearer crew heard him and looked up. Their eyes followed his pointing finger. After a split second's hesitation, they hurried to warn the others.

There was pandemonium. Some crew scuttled for the safety of the enclosed decks, others grabbed on to rails, stanchions or cables. A few continued to try to wrestle the obstinate hatches closed. There was a moment's lull in the rain, as though the ocean were holding its breath.

Then the wave was upon them.

It rolled over the stern of the *Challenger II*, breaking over *Little Em'ly* and her crane. It surged forward, dashing itself against the vessel's superstructure. As it roared past, Luke flung himself back into the shelter of the bridge, slamming the door behind him – a pointless act, as the force of the wave simultaneously smashed the windows through which Luke had first seen it, filling the wheelhouse with water and flying glass. The wave rolled on, swamping the bows, before finally disappearing into the gathering darkness.

The ship wallowed beneath tons of water, like a sleeper beneath heavy blankets, reluctant to rise. After what seemed an age, the *Challenger II* haltingly shouldered the seas aside and rose at last to the surface.

At exactly the same moment, the regular beat of the engines faltered, then stopped dead. All the lights went out.

The Captain and Chief Officer exchanged appalled glances. The officer rang *Ahead Full* on the engine telegraph. Nothing happened.

"Losing steerage way, sir," the helmsman reported.

Jessica wiped dripping hair from her eyes. "This is not good."

"Get down there, Mister Marsden," snapped the Captain. "Find out what the problem is."

The Chief Officer made for the door, but before he could open it, one of the ship's engineers hauled it open and stuck his head inside. "Engine room flooded, sir," he bawled.

The Captain's face betrayed no emotion. "Pumps?"

"We're using the auxiliary generators, sir." The lights flickered and came back on. "One for electrics, one for the pumps."

"When can you restart the engines?"

"Have to get the water level down first, sir. It's going to take time."

The Captain clenched his fists, the knuckles white. "We don't *have* time." He nodded to the engineer. "All right. I understand. Do your best."

As the engineer hurried back to his duties, Nick turned an anxious face to Luke and Jessica. "What happens now?"

Luke said, "Without the engines, we can't steer the

ship. We just have to sit here and take a battering from the waves. And if the ship swings round so we're taking the waves from the side…"

"We roll over and sink, yes, thanks, I remember that bit. So what do we do?"

"That depends," said Captain Fulton. "Are you a religious man, Mister Malone?"

"Not really…"

"Then I suggest you become one very quickly. Prayers may help us, I can't think of anything else that will."

Luke felt a familiar burning sensation in his chest – the Challenger inheritance that gave him his temper, his spirit, his refusal to admit defeat. "There must be something we can do. Some way of keeping her bows or stern on to the sea."

The Captain shook his head. "Without the engines, our rudders are useless." He turned to his Chief Officer; the two men conferred with their heads close together.

Luke racked his brains. He'd done a fair amount of sailing, and read thrilling accounts of survival at sea. An idea came to him. "What about a sea anchor?"

The Captain looked up and gave him an angry glare. "A brilliant idea, Mister Challenger, but for one minor drawback – we're not carrying a sea anchor. Suggestions, Mister Spotiswoode?" he concluded, drawing the unhappy engineer into the discussion.

"What's a sea anchor?" demanded Nick.

"You use it to hold a ship in position, or steer it if the rudder fails. It's usually a sort of underwater sail, a big funnel of canvas or tarpaulin, but it could be anything really as long as it floats and drags on the ship's stern..." Luke broke off as the ship gave a sudden lurch. Everyone on the bridge grabbed for any support they could find as another wave struck the *Challenger II* on the beam. The ship began to roll, further and further, to an incredible angle. Decks and ceilings became walls, walls became floors. The bridge wing on the ship's starboard side dipped into the roaring sea, which sucked and gurgled hungrily.

Spotiswoode gave a yell as he lost his grip and began to slide towards the hissing water. Jessica let rip a hair-raising New Orleans curse and grabbed him by the belt, straining to hold on as the bridge shuddered.

For several agonizing moments it seemed inevitable that the *Challenger II* should continue to roll until she was upside down. Luke's heart hammered as the vessel hung at the point of no return; then, slowly, hesitantly, she began to roll back.

Captain Fulton staggered across the heeling deck to peer out of the shattered windows. "One more like that will finish us."

But the reprieve from death had inspired Luke. He

weaved his way towards the Captain. "Sir, we could use *Little Em'ly*..."

Captain Fulton had had enough. "Mister Challenger! I am trying to deal with an emergency! I have had enough of your idiotic suggestions. Clear the bridge!"

Luke gave him a furious look, then turned to Nick. "Come on!"

Battered by the wind, which tried to tear them from the heaving accommodation ladder, they staggered downwards, clinging to the rail. As they reached the deck, soaked to the skin and wiping moisture from their eyes, Jessica joined them. "Where are you two going?"

"Aft," said Luke shortly. "I'm sure my idea will work. We haven't time to argue with the Captain, so we'll try it without his approval."

"And what is this big idea?"

"We can use *Little Em'ly* as a sea anchor. If we put her in the water and veer out a couple of hundred yards of cable, her weight on the end of it will bring the bows round to face the sea. The *Challenger II* can ride the storm out while the crew get the engines restarted."

"But *Em'ly*'s rigged to dive," protested Jessica. "A sea anchor needs to be near the surface."

"Yes," said Luke. "That's why I'll be on board *Em'ly*, dropping ballast and using the engines and diving planes to stay in position and at the right depth."

"You'll be on board *Little Em'ly*?" Nick was horrified. "That will be incredibly dangerous!"

Luke gestured at the wild sea and tearing sky. "Compared to what?"

"Right," said Jessica, "count me in."

Luke stared at her. "You want to come with us?"

"No, I'd rather go cry in my cabin, waiting to drown. Of course I want to come with you!"

Despite the peril of their situation, Luke grinned. "Let's go, then."

They fought their way to the vessel's stern. Darkness had fallen, but the storm had not abated – lightning forks continued their march across the sky and the sea washed over the heaving afterdeck. Wherever there was shelter they took advantage of it, but several times they had no choice but to watch the swell, and then sprint across an open, unprotected stretch in the short interval between waves.

The deck was deserted. *Little Em'ly*, still firmly clamped in place, dipped in and out of the waves like an adventurous toddler on her first day at the seaside.

A platform ran along the inboard side of the submersible. Luke and Jessica cast off the restraining straps that held *Em'ly* to the deck. Then they climbed onto the platform and clung to the rail while the wind buffeted them and the rain hammered down like a waterfall.

Nick, meanwhile, had climbed into the tiny cabin that housed the controls for the crane. He gave Luke and Jessica a "thumbs up" signal, and began pulling levers. The crane swung from its "at rest" position until the jib was hovering over *Little Em'ly*. Nick operated more controls and the drums behind the crane began slowly to rotate. Two cables began to descend from the end of the jib. One of these was the lifting cable – a strong wire rope, which in normal use would raise and lower *Little Em'ly*, but which, in the current emergency, Luke hoped to use as a towline to drag the *Challenger II* around to face the deadly seas bows-on. The other cable was the rubber-coated umbilicus that carried electric power to the submersible's motors, and the telephone line that, once *Em'ly* was launched, would be Luke's only means of communicating with the ship.

Luke cupped his hands around his mouth and yelled into Jessica's ear, "I'll attach the cables and go through the hatch. As soon as it closes, go around and unlock the clamps. There are four, two on each side. Watch out, *Em'ly* will probably swing when she gets loose. Stay low." Jessica nodded. Luke began to climb the fixed ladder that gave access to *Em'ly*'s hatch.

The storm chose that moment to strike the *Challenger II* with another big wave. Once again, the ship rolled, even further this time, it seemed to Luke, as his feet slipped from the rungs and he clung onto the ladder for dear life, kicking against empty air. After what seemed an age, the ship began to recover. Captain Fulton had said the next wave would finish them – luckily he had been wrong; but Luke knew they had only been granted a brief reprieve. As the *Challenger II* came upright again, Luke was relieved to see that Jessica had managed to hold onto the rail. He gave her the briefest of signals – "Okay" – and resumed his climb.

There were handholds welded to the plate on *Em'ly*'s back. Luke clung to them as he reached for the dancing cables. After several misses, he managed to snatch the lifting cable out of the sky. Despite the warmth of the tropical night, his hands were shaking with cold and tension, but eventually he succeeded in securing the shackle at the end of the cable to the ring set in *Em'ly*'s spine. He had half a mind to leave the umbilical power cable, but he knew that, without the external power source, the submersible's batteries would quickly run down – he had no idea how long it would take to ride out the storm, or to restart the *Challenger II*'s engines. He lunged for the umbilicus...missed...lunged again, caught it, and secured it to the attachment point behind the lifting cable. He held on as another wave swept over him. Then, already exhausted, he wrestled with the hatch. For a moment it resisted – then the wheel that locked it in place began to turn, and, after an agonizing interval, he hauled it open and dropped into the tunnel beyond.

Here, he was at least out of the wind and rain, but as he struggled to close the hatch, Luke realized that the motion inside the tunnel was no less than that outside. Fortunately the tunnel was narrow, and he was able to jam himself inside it to prevent himself being thrown about, but he began to feel a rising tide of nausea. Forcing it down, he spun the locking wheel until it would turn no more. At the same moment, a muffled clang signalled that Jessica was at work releasing the clamps that were holding *Em'ly* to the deck. Luke hurried down the tunnel – which was no more than eight feet in length – and dropped into the gondola, immediately hauling its hatch closed behind him.

As he secured this, he heard the second and third clamps being released. *Em'ly* began to twitch as though straining to be off.

He dropped into the pilot's seat and strapped himself in as the fourth and final clamp was released. Luke felt the submersible rise as Nick operated the crane – and then *Em'ly* was dancing crazily in mid-air. Through the gondola's tiny forward observation window, he caught sight of Jessica stretched out full-length upon the deck and hoped she was following instructions and lying low, rather than having been knocked down. Then the jib swung the tiny vessel over the ship's stern. Luke was shaken like a rat in a terrier's jaws and the lights of the afterdeck blinked crazily through the gondola's three circular observation windows – port, forward, starboard, and back again. He felt a lurch as the crane began to let out the cable...there was a noise of pounding water, a rush of bubbles past the windows, and the frantic motion eased. *Little Em'ly* was at sea.

As Nick let more cable out, Luke gathered his wits sufficiently to check the depth gauge and realized that the submersible was sinking fast. He reached for the controls, and began to dump ballast until *Em'ly*'s plunge was checked. Loose cables snaked past the central window. Luke set the submersible's electric motors to full astern and the cables rose and disappeared overhead as *Em'ly*, at a depth of thirty feet, slipped back from her mother ship. The cable began to jerk as it tightened, and the motion of the waves tried to tug the *Challenger II* and her offspring apart.

Luke snatched the telephone handset from its bracket. "Nick, Nick, can you hear me?"

"*Luke.*" Nick's voice was faint and distorted. "*You're pulling the cable straight back. The ship's still lying side-on to the waves – we need to swing her to bring the bows into the waves. Give* Em'ly *full left rudder.*"

Luke complied. After a pause, he heard Jessica's voice through Nick's microphone: "*Another wave!*"

"*Luke.*" Nick's distant voice was hoarse with appeal. "*Pull hard, my old mate. Pull really, really hard.*" Another pause. "*If this doesn't work, release the cable. If we sink, no sense in your being dragged down with us. Good luck.*"

"You, too." What more was there to say? The motors were screaming. *Little Em'ly* bucked and strained at the end of her cable. Luke could do no more.

On the bridge of the *Challenger II*, Captain Fulton's voice was resigned. "Another big one. This time, there'll be no way back." His eyes widened as his view of the onrushing wave changed. The ship was swinging round, slowly, infinitely slowly, its bows turning to meet the wave. The Captain turned to his Chief Officer, thunderstruck. "How...?" He staggered to the windows overlooking the ship's stern, and saw the empty deck where *Little Em'ly* should be, the jerking crane, the straining cable. He breathed, "Challenger..."

The wave struck.

But the ship had turned just enough. She rolled again, heavily, but the wave had met her on the starboard bow, not on the beam. She rolled, but she rose again. And now the bows were facing the charging waves.

Luke heard screams over his headphones – of

desperation or joy, he couldn't tell. Then, with a snap and a jerk, the umbilicus tore free. *Little Em'ly* was still attached to the *Challenger II* by the lifting cable, but Luke was cut off from the outside world. More seriously, he had lost external power to the propellers. The motors were running on batteries. Luke did not dare to throttle them back. He hung up the useless handset and switched off the gondola lights to save power. Then he waited.

For a long time, he hovered between sleep and waking, awareness and oblivion. An hour passed. Another half hour. The note of the motors changed as the batteries ran down. Eventually, they stopped altogether. Luke felt a dull despair steal over him. He had failed. The ship would drift side-on to the waves again, and this time he was powerless – literally – to prevent it. All his struggles had been in vain.

Suddenly, he noticed that *Little Em'ly* was moving. For a moment, his fuddled mind couldn't grasp what was happening. Then realization came. *Em'ly* was being winched back... And that could only mean...

Ten minutes later the submersible was dangling over a sea that, though still angry, was no longer the churning menace it had been. Lightning flickered in the distance.

Em'ly settled into her berth like a duckling returning to the nest. Willing hands secured the submersible as the hatch opened from within, and Luke's tousled head appeared, to be greeted by a ragged cheer from the crew and the welcome rumble of the *Challenger II*'s engines.

Luke half-fell down the ladder into the arms of Nick, who greeted him with a slap on the back, and Jessica, who threw her arms round his neck and gave him a resounding (if salty) kiss. Startled, Luke put his hand to his lips.

Captain Fulton appeared on the platform. "Mister Challenger." For a moment he seemed lost for words – he finally settled on, "Well done." He held out his hand. Luke shook it.

Fulton gave him the slightest perceptible nod. Then he turned on his grinning crew. "You men – back to work!" He swung down onto the afterdeck, throwing orders to left and right. "I need damage reports. Are the pumps still gaining? I want a position as soon as the sun rises..."

Nick grinned at his friend. "How about you, Luke? What do you want?"

With great conviction, Luke said, "Breakfast."

13 PIRATES

Unknown island,
Pacific Ocean:
15° 38' N, 145° 34' E

Under a cloudless blue sky, the *Challenger II* cautiously picked its way through a gap in a coral reef and crept into a sheltered lagoon on the eastern side of a small island. Captain Fulton shouted an order, and the anchor plunged from the bow of the ship and dropped into the crystal-clear water with a splash that put seabirds to raucous flight from their perches on the rocks. Chain rattled out behind it. The ship's engines rumbled as it went astern until the anchor bit and checked its progress. Then the propellers ceased to turn and the engines fell silent.

The *Challenger II* had not come through the storm unscathed. The most serious loss had been the two crew members washed overboard by the first, disastrous wave as they tried to secure hatches. Their fate had cast gloom over the whole crew.

The ship had also suffered material damage. Several hull plates had sprung, tearing out rivets and leaving gaping holes. Though, fortunately, none had been below the waterline, they still had to be repaired. The engines had been kept going only by the skills of the chief engineer, who had practically wept at their condition as he coaxed another few hours' use out of machinery that was coughing clouds of black smoke from the ship's funnel and was desperately in need of a thorough overhaul. Stores had broken free during the storm and shifted about, spilling their contents higgledy-piggledy across the holds, lockers and storerooms. Radio aerials had been damaged, rails bent, equipment broken – the list went on and on. Much of the damage could not be fixed while the *Challenger II* was at sea, so Captain Fulton had decided to put in at the tiny island where the crew could make repairs without attracting unwelcome attention.

Luke stepped quickly out of the way as crew members emerged from their cabins carrying sodden bedding, which they laid out on decks and draped over rails to dry. For the first time since the storm, there was laughter and joking among the men. A work party was swinging one of the remaining ship's boats (two had been lost in the storm) out on its davits, preparing to go ashore and forage for fresh fruit and vegetables and replenish the ship's water supplies.

Jessica joined Luke at the rail to stare at the low hills of the island, with their grassy slopes and intermittent scrubland. "Fruit and vegetables?" she said. "They'll be lucky."

"Does anyone live here?" asked Luke.

Jessica shrugged. "Not according to the chart. It doesn't even have a name. Other islands in the chain are inhabited, but they're pretty well scattered. According to the Captain, there have been reports of pirate activity around the larger islands further south – Saipan, Tinian, Guam."

Luke was startled. "Pirates? I thought they died out years ago."

"Not in these waters. I shouldn't think they'll be around here, though, and even if they are, they probably won't attack us – they're mostly after cargo ships with small crews and valuable loads. Don't worry."

Luke was stung. "I'm not worried."

"Good. I'll tell you something else that might interest

you. The Mariana Trench runs round to the east of these islands in a kind of sickle shape. It's the deepest trench in the Pacific. And about half a day's sailing that way" – Jessica pointed to the south-west – "is the deepest point of any ocean on earth. Know what it's called?"

Luke nodded. "The Challenger Deep."

Jessica was put out. "It's not named for you, though," she said crossly. "It's called after the British Royal Navy survey ship HMS *Challenger*. They were the first to discover it, around sixty years ago."

"I know. That's why this ship is called the *Challenger II* – in honour of HMS *Challenger*, not because she belongs to my father. Anyway, we won't be going there. It's far too deep for us to dive."

Jessica pouted. "Is there anything you don't know?"

"I don't know where Nick is. Have you seen him?"

Jessica gave him an angry look. "Down with *Little Em'ly*. Repairing something, I think."

"Good. Thanks." Luke set off for the afterdeck. Jessica watched him go. Then she leaned back across the rail and stared into the rippling blue water.

As Luke approached, Nick emerged from one of *Little Em'ly*'s electric motors and pulled out a blackened part. "Will you look at that? You overloaded it!"

Luke glared at him. "I'm so sorry."

"Ah, well, I suppose you were saving everyone's life

at the time. Luckily we have spares." Nick wiped his hands on a rag. "What about those subs that were following us? Do you think the storm hit them as badly as it did us?"

"I doubt it," said Luke. "Even in the worst storm, it's only the top fifty or sixty feet of the ocean that gets disturbed. All they'd have to do is dive to a safe depth and wait it out."

"Still," said Nick, "that means they wouldn't be able to track us, doesn't it? Maybe they lost us."

"Maybe." Luke was far from convinced. "Anyway, we're going to be here for a day or two. Do you fancy going ashore? I asked Captain Fulton, he said it would be okay."

"No thanks, I want to get this fixed." Nick reached for a screwdriver. "Why don't you ask Jessica?"

"Jessica? Why?"

Nick shrugged. "I've a feeling she'd want you to. Don't you like her?"

"Well, of course I *like* her," said Luke defensively. "I mean, who wouldn't? She's bright, she's resourceful, she's..."

"Prickly?" Nick gave him a grin.

"Good grief, yes. I never know where I stand with her. Sometimes I think she likes me..."

"Gosh," said Nick. "Really? Do you think so?"

"But other times, I seem to get her goat without meaning to, and suddenly she can't stand the sight of me."

"And how do you feel about her?"

"How do you mean?"

"For pity's sake, it's a simple enough question. Do you fancy her?" Luke was silent for so long that Nick looked up from his work. "Ah, I'll take that as a 'no'. Poor girl."

"What do you think I should do?"

"Don't ask me," said Nick quickly. "I work with engines. I like engines. When they're broken, they don't try to hide it, they just stop working. Then you can find the problem and fix it. People are complicated, engines are simple." He dived back into the motor casing. Luke watched him work for a moment...then he went in search of Jessica.

An hour later, Luke and Jessica stood on the top of a rolling hill – the only one on the island. They had been landed on a sandy beach by members of the crew sent ashore to look for water. The men had located a stream and were busy filling casks while Luke and Jessica set off to explore.

Luke shielded his eyes from the sun and looked down

into the lagoon where the ship rode at anchor. "It looks like a pretty sheltered spot. Even if we get a strong wind from the east, the reef should offer decent protection."

Jessica pointed. "There's the gap in the reef we took to come in. There's another one to the north according to the chart – there it is, look. You can see the blue of the deeper water."

"Pretty narrow, though. I'd hate to have to steer the *Challenger II* through that." Luke surveyed the island. "Not much to look at, is it? How big, do you think?"

"Just over seven miles long, just under a mile wide," said Jessica. "According to the chart, anyways. The original desert island." She gave Luke a sidelong glance. "We could be castaways."

"What? Oh – yes..." Luke unslung the binoculars from his shoulder and raised them to his eyes, staring out to sea.

Jessica gave him a cold stare. "Don't you ever put those things down?"

"There's a ship." Luke pointed. "A sailing ship. Over there. Coming from the north." He handed the binoculars to Jessica, who took them without enthusiasm.

"I see it." Jessica turned the focus ring. "Island trader. Junk rigged. Nothing to worry about."

"No? Why does a trading vessel need so many men?"

Jessica turned to stare at Luke, then refocused the binoculars. "You're right. The decks are swarming with them."

Luke took one more look through the binoculars. "I thought you said pirates wouldn't be around here."

"What am I, an oracle?" Jessica was already backing down the hill.

Luke slung the binoculars over his shoulder. "Come on."

As they ran, Jessica shouted, "How long do you think we've got?"

"An hour, maybe. Run faster!"

The men filling water casks looked up in astonishment as Luke and Jessica, panting from their run, arrived back at the ship's boat. Luke explained the reason for their early return.

One of the seamen spat noisily. "Pirates? What makes you think they're pirates?"

"Well, they weren't flying the Jolly Roger and we didn't hear them shouting 'Oo-arr!'," snapped Luke, "but there were at least a hundred men on that ship. I don't think they're planning to sell us souvenirs!"

"Right." The petty officer in charge of the shore party blew a whistle. "Everyone back in the boat."

"But we've only filled half the casks," protested the sceptic.

"And if it turns out to be a false alarm, we can come back and fill the rest. Shove off!" The crew put their shoulders against the prow of the boat and heaved – it slid over the silver sand and bobbed on the waves. The crew hauled themselves over the gunwales and reached for the oars. "All right, steer for the ship – and put your backs into it."

Fifteen minutes later, Luke was racing up the gangway lowered from the side of the ship. He was met at the entry port by Chief Officer Marsden, who listened to his story and Jessica's confirmation of it, and took them both straight to the bridge. They repeated their story to Captain Fulton, who listened with mounting concern.

"Mister Challenger, Miss Land," he said when they had finished, "I'm not sure we're in any condition to leave. We're short on drinking water, I have dismantled equipment all over the ship, the starboard engine is in bits—"

"Then at least power up the port engine, sir. Get us ready to leave if we have to. And we should be ready to defend the ship."

Captain Fulton frowned. "I give the orders here, Mister Challenger."

"But Luke was right before, sir." Jessica was as near to pleading as Luke had ever seen her. "And I'm sure he's right now."

"I'm perfectly well aware of how much we owe to Mister Challenger." Fulton thought a moment longer. Then he raised his voice. "Call the engine room. Port engine to standby. Haul in the boats. Anchor crew make ready to weigh. Both watches on deck. Chief – break out the small arms." He gave Luke a sombre glance. "I hope you're wrong about this, Mister Challenger, but if you're right – if they come – we'll be ready for them."

Within a few minutes, armed men were taking up positions along the rail, mostly on the seaward side of the ship. Nick looked up from his work on *Little Em'ly*'s engine as a couple of sailors carrying Challenger C64 rifles pounded past. He stared as Luke ran across to join him. "Now what have you done?"

"Me? I haven't done anything. But I'm pretty sure there are pirates on the way."

"Pirates, now!" complained Nick. "If it's not one thing, it's another..."

"Stop complaining. We're on first-aid detail." Luke handed over a medical kit.

Nick made a face. "Don't we get a gun?"

"No," snapped Jessica, joining them. "As if I couldn't shoot straighter than most of these feather merchants."

She jerked her head towards Luke's chess companion from Berkeley. "That guy doesn't look as if he knows which end of his gun to hold. Huh."

Luke gave Nick a hand up. They joined the fuming Jessica at the rail.

Saul, *Little Em'ly*'s pilot, edged between them. He was carrying an ancient Lee Enfield rifle, which he treated to a disgusted look. "I was in the heads," he complained. "By the time I got out, this was all they had left."

A tense silence descended over the ship. Luke checked his watch. "Just an hour since we first spotted the ship. They can't be far away now."

Ten minutes passed, then twenty. Muffled conversations broke out. Several members of the crew darted unfriendly or amused glances at Luke.

Nick sighed. "Well, I suppose even Luke Challenger can make a mistake once in a..." He broke off and gave a low whistle. "Holy mother of God."

Two long, rakish boats were coming round the headland at the north of the bay. They were packed with men who, on catching sight of their prey, raised a bloodcurdling yell and paddled furiously towards the *Challenger II*.

"Proas," said Jessica. "Like big canoes, but with outriggers to keep them steady – that ship must have launched them."

Captain Fulton's voice, amplified by the loudhailer, echoed across the bay. "Keep your distance, or I fire!" He was answered with jeers and catcalls; the proas came on.

Fulton turned his loudhailer towards the waiting men at the rail. "Fire!"

Rifle shots rang out all along the rail, except from the guns of those hands unused to firearms who had forgotten to work the bolt and put a bullet in the firing chamber. Splashes around the proas showed where the bullets struck. At least some shots went home, sending up splinters from the proas, or striking their crews – three of the attackers toppled overboard.

But now the pirates were returning fire. Luke tried not to duck as bullets struck the steel plates behind him and ricocheted with a whine.

Saul gave a grunt. He looked down, and in an amazed voice, said, "Will you look at that..." Then he dropped his rifle and crumpled to the deck.

Luke was instantly at his side. The Texan has been hit in the shoulder. Luke tore his shirt aside, pulled a dressing from his medical kit and clamped it over the wound. He saw Jessica sprint towards a sailor who had fallen, clasping his arm...then he and Nick were lifting Saul and carrying him, as best they could, to safety.

The *Challenger II*'s small sickbay was overflowing by

the time they reached it. They made Saul as comfortable as they could in an adjacent cabin, and returned to the fray.

The fighting was concentrated around the afterdeck, which, as the lowest part of the ship, was most vulnerable to boarding. Grapnels flew from the attacking proas and caught on the rails. Luke snatched a penknife from his pocket and sliced through the rope attached to one; a pirate who was about to board suddenly found himself hanging on to a rope that was no longer tied to anything – he gave a scream and fell back into the water. More pirates were clambering aboard. Luke reached into a nearby ship's boat, grabbed an oar, and struck out. He was gasping for breath by the time a counterattack from the ship's crew brought extra firepower, which swept the pirates back into the sea.

The deck was suddenly clear. In a daze, Luke realized that the rattling noise he could hear was the anchor chain being raised. The deck swayed beneath his feet – the ship was moving.

He raced towards the bridge just as Captain Fulton gave the order, "Hard a'port. Engine half ahead. Take us out to sea."

Luke felt a flood of relief. The *Challenger II* might only have one working engine, but even so, neither the proas nor the pirates' ship would be able to keep up with her once she'd cleared the bay. They could make for a safe port, and refit...

Then he raised his head, and gave a groan of dismay.

At the mouth of the bay, a conning tower broke the surface. Another one appeared, slightly further south. Two submarines rose out of the sea. Hatches opened and running figures hurried to man the guns mounted on each foredeck.

Luke knew that those guns were capable of sinking the *Challenger II* in minutes. Between them, the submarines' field of fire covered the entire mouth of the bay and the gap in the reef that was their only way through. There was not the least possibility of escape.

Captain Fulton's voice sounded weary as he ordered, "Stop engines."

Luke realized that Nick and Jessica had joined him on the bridge. He raised the binoculars to his eyes just as a small group of officers appeared on the conning tower of each submarine. Among them, on the German U-X1, stood a stern-faced officer wearing a peaked cap and a captain's jacket.

"Korvettenkapitän Wolfgang Roth," he said quietly. "The Sea Wolf." He switched his gaze to the I-40, and a familiar figure with long, dark hair, wearing a Japanese Navy uniform. "And Captain Mochizuki."

14 PARLEY

The meeting took place on the beach.

Captain Fulton was accompanied by Spotiswoode, Chief Officer Marsden, the boat crew that had rowed them ashore, and Luke and Nick. The Captain had balked at their inclusion in the party, but Luke had insisted.

"Mochizuki wants us," he had told Fulton, "me in particular. If we don't go to her, she'll come and get us."

The Captain had rubbed his chin. "The wild card in this situation is Roth. I have no idea what he'll do. However, he has a reputation for being tough but honest.

I agree, I can't protect you from this Mochizuki woman – maybe he can, if he chooses to. Perhaps it *is* best you meet him."

However, the Captain had flatly refused to allow Jessica to join the shore party. "You're our insurance," he told her bluntly. "They want the knowledge you carry in your head – as long as we have you, we have something to bargain with." So Jessica, breathing fire, was confined to her cabin, with two guards on the door to foil any possible attempt at a kidnap.

Facing the *Challenger II* deputation was a mixed party from both submarines, and a tough-looking islander wearing an odd collection of clothes, most bizarre of which was an embroidered waistcoat, seemingly looted from his victims: the pirate chief.

The German submarine commander, Kapitän Roth, was a hawk-faced man whose hair was turning grey at the temples. Despite the heat of the day, he was wearing a peaked cap and full, if rather crumpled, naval uniform. The Japanese commander was a small man; his uniform, in contrast to Roth's, was immaculate, as was his moustache. But Luke and Nick had eyes only for his political officer.

Kaigun Daisa Mochizuki was wearing a jacket with a high collar, and close-fitting trousers. Her long, dark hair was gathered into a ponytail and she was wearing her usual tinted glasses. She reached up and took these off, to reveal eyes whose irises were so dark as to be indistinguishable from the pupils. In a low, mocking tone, she said, "Luke Challenger."

"Captain Mochizuki." Luke nodded as though greeting an old acquaintance. "But you have the advantage of me. I'm afraid I don't know your first name – any more than I ever knew your sister's."

Nick stared at Luke open-mouthed. "Her sister?"

Captain Mochizuki's dark eyes glittered dangerously. "Clever, Mr. Challenger. I am Kasumi Mochizuki. Colonel Amaya Mochizuki was my twin sister. I was engaged in secret operations in the South China Sea when you killed her a year ago."

"I didn't kill her," said Luke evenly. "Her own carelessness betrayed her – the allosaurus did the rest."

"Intelligence reports say that she died fighting you." Mochizuki sneered at Luke's shocked reaction. "Why look so surprised? Surely you have realized by now that I am also a member of the Sons of Destiny. Our leaders told me exactly how my sister died."

"Really?" said Luke. "None of the Sons of Destiny escaped from the Lost World, so how can you be sure what happened there?"

"We have friends in British Intelligence." Mochizuki's voice was low and bitter. "Your account of what happened on the plateau was known to us almost as soon as you gave it. Deny what you will, Luke Challenger. You were responsible for my sister's death and you will pay. And I will let you into a little secret." She leaned forward and said, in a harsh whisper, "Of the two of us, *she was the nice one.*"

"Captain Mochizuki!" Roth spoke in English, his voice harsh with disapproval. "We have discussed this. Our mission takes priority. You will take no action that has not been agreed by myself and Commander Yoshida." Mochizuki said nothing, but replaced her dark glasses so that her eyes were hidden once more. The commanding officer of her submarine stared from her to Roth and back again, evidently not understanding the exchange.

"Kapitän Roth." Fulton's voice was angry but controlled. "You have no right to prevent my ship leaving this island. You are an officer of the German Navy. Your behaviour amounts to an act of war."

"Not at all, Captain." Roth's voice was calm and his accent hardly noticeable. "Only a sovereign government can declare war, and if my present actions were to become widely known, my government would deny any knowledge of them. It would be fully justified in doing so as it has, in fact, no idea of my current whereabouts."

"No," said Luke. "You're not acting for the German government. You're following orders from the Sons of

Destiny." Roth gave him a slight, ironic bow.

Fulton was not prepared to concede his point. "You fired on my men. Six of them are seriously wounded."

"An unfortunate occurrence; but in fact, neither my men nor Commander Yoshida's have fired on your crew or your ship." He indicated the pirate chief. "That regrettable attack was made by Raga here, and his followers."

"Acting under your orders."

"Not directly. We had lost contact with you in the storm; by a happy coincidence, we were engaging Raga and his followers to search the islands for you when our lookouts spotted your smoke – I take it your engines suffered some damage?" Fulton remained silent. "After that, I regret Commander Yoshida and I were unable to prevent our new friend from making an attempt on your ship. He is an impetuous fellow." Whether or not the pirate chief understood these words, he chose this moment to give Captain Fulton a savage grin and finger his sword.

Fulton glowered. "Are you seriously telling me that my only quarrel is with your pirate friend? That if I chose to leave this island, you and the Commander here would not prevent me?"

Roth smiled bleakly. "Come, Captain, let us be realistic. Nobody knows where you are, and I see from the damage to your ship that you have no radio communications. You are entirely at our mercy. However, we see no profit in unnecessary bloodshed. It has become clear that the person who holds the key to the location of the *Nautilus* is Miss Land. Does she still have Nemo's journal?" Fulton said nothing. "I think not. My guess is that you would not have allowed her to accompany your expedition if she did not possess information that she refused to disclose until you were near to your goal. Hand her over to us. I give you my word that she will be released safely once we have raised the *Nautilus* – in the meantime, we will allow your vessel to go on its way in peace."

"The vessel, yes." Captain Mochizuki's voice was hard and clear. "Luke Challenger, no. Twice he has slipped through my fingers. There will not be a third time. He is mine." Luke felt a cold hand clutch at his heart.

"That will do, Captain Mochizuki." Roth's voice was low and dangerous. "Commander Yoshida and I have already made it clear to you that your private desire for revenge cannot be allowed to compromise this operation." Mochizuki said nothing, but her hidden eyes remained firmly on Luke.

Captain Fulton said, "Perhaps you will allow me a few moments?" Kapitän Roth raised an eyebrow at Mochizuki, who said something in Japanese to the commander of the I-40. He said something in reply, and bowed formally to the captain of the *Challenger II*. Mochizuki gave Roth a brief nod, and the German inclined his head with grave courtesy. "Please. Take as long as you need."

Fulton walked a few steps down the beach, followed by his party. He stopped, and with his back to Roth and Mochizuki, and in a low voice, said, "Opinions?"

Luke was itching to speak, but he knew better than to butt in straight away. Nick was still shaking his head and muttering, "Her sister – Colonel Mochizuki's *sister*..." He gave Luke an accusing glare. "You might have told me. When did you work it out?"

"Well, I couldn't know for sure until I'd seen her up close, but I knew she couldn't have survived the allosaurus – an identical twin sister was the only sensible explanation." Luke gestured Nick to silence. "Listen."

Marsden was speaking. "If you ask me, sir, all that stuff about wanting to avoid unnecessary bloodshed was plain hooey. The Sea Wolf never cared how many lives were lost in his U-boat attacks. There's only one life he's interested in saving: Miss Land's. He needs what she knows, and if they attack and she gets killed, he's lost everything."

Fulton gave a brief nod. "Mister Spotiswoode?"

"Well, I mean to say," gabbled Spotiswoode, "I'm sure that's right, but we can't protect Miss Land, can we?

We might be able to fight off the pirates again, but if the submarine crews join in, especially if they use the deck-mounted guns, we haven't a hope." He caught sight of the disgusted glares Luke and Nick were giving him, and concluded, "I'm just saying..."

Fulton turned to Luke. "Mister Challenger?"

Luke gathered his thoughts. "Sir, even if we were to seriously consider handing Jessica over to them, I don't see that it would help us. "

"Roth might be prepared to let Luke go," added Nick, "but Mochizuki won't."

"Her commander is under orders to co-operate with Roth," protested Spotiswoode. "He'd keep her in line."

"I'm not sure how much her commander understands of what's going on," said Fulton. "He clearly doesn't speak English, for a start. Or German, I daresay. That Mochizuki woman could probably get him to swallow any kind of taradiddle if she put her mind to it."

"That's not what I meant," said Luke. "I was thinking about the ship. I don't know how deep that German sub can go, but I'm betting it's not nearly as deep as we can send *Em'ly*. Even if Jessica takes Roth straight to the *Nautilus*, she's hinted that it's not lying in shallow water – so how's he going to reach it? Even if he did, how could he lift it without the *Challenger II*'s salvage gear? Mr. Marsden's right, sir. His first demand is Jessica. If you give in to that, he'll use her as a hostage to force us to agree to others. He can't do without our ship, and he can't let any of us go. If word gets out about what he and his precious Japanese friends are up to, every navy in the world will be after them, including their own."

"What Mister Challenger says makes a lot of sense." Fulton suddenly looked old and weary. "What do you think they'll do? Kill us?"

"I don't reckon, so, sir," said Marsden slowly. "Roth may be ruthless, but I never heard of him doing away with prisoners or trying to stop our side rescuing men from the water, like some U-boat captains did. Maybe he'd just strand us on this island with enough stores to see us through until he's got what he wants."

"Yes, that's all very well," complained Spotiswoode, "but what about the Japanese?"

But Luke was no longer listening. He stood gazing out to sea – from the beach to the *Challenger II* and the submarines beyond. Suddenly his mind was teeming with possibilities – with perspective, vectors, angles; the phases of the moon...

He turned to Fulton. "Sir," he said, "can you stall them?"

Fulton gave him an appraising look. "Stall them?"

"Yes, sir. I have an idea, but it would take too long to explain now – it would look suspicious. And we'll need darkness, several hours of darkness, to make it work."

Fulton pondered for a moment. Then he turned on his heel, and returned to the deputation of his enemies.

In his most imperious manner, he said, "I have a great deal to consider. I wish to talk your proposal over with my crew. I must request a truce. I will give you my answer tomorrow morning at dawn."

Commander Yoshida looked blank. Captain Mochizuki's features stiffened with fury. The pirate chief maintained his air of scornful superiority so that it was impossible to tell whether he had understood or not.

Kapitän Roth seemed merely amused. "You English – how you love your little displays of democracy." He shrugged. "A truce. Very well, if it will help avoid deplorable scenes of violence. Dawn it is." He indicated the two watchful submarines with a negligent wave of the hand. "I do not think you will be going anywhere in the meantime."

He turned and strode away towards the folding boat that had brought him from his submarine. Captain Fulton led the way to the ship's boat that had brought his party ashore. But the Japanese members of the deputation remained unmoving, and as he made his way to the boat, Luke knew that Captain Mochizuki's eyes were on him – he could feel the woman's burning hatred, her insane desire for revenge. And even in the warm afternoon air, he shivered.

15 DECOY

Captain Fulton showed Luke and Nick into his cabin and closed the door behind him. "All right," he said, "I'm listening."

"First of all, sir," said Luke, "I need to know when the engines will be repaired."

"Tonight. By midnight if not before," said Fulton. "The Chief has worked wonders."

"Good. Now – have we any explosives on board?"

Fulton considered. "It depends what you mean – flares, of course, to signal for help in an emergency. Demolition charges for clearing underwater obstacles and generating shock waves for seismic measurements…"

Nick clicked his fingers. "I get it! Great idea – we use the explosives to make mines, divers take them out to the subs and attach them to the hulls, we light the blue touch paper and retire – kaboom!"

"Mister Malone," said Fulton crushingly, "our enemies may be pirates – we are not. The Japanese and German governments don't know what their submarines are up to; any attack on them by us could be enough to plunge our countries into war, and I absolutely forbid any such attempt."

Luke nodded. "I agree, sir. Look how Japan reacted when a bunch of US sailors helped us get Jessica back and just gave one of their subs a dirty look. But blowing them up wasn't what I had in mind." Nick looked disappointed. "What we want," Luke continued, "is to give them the slip."

Fulton looked dubious. "I approve of your aim, but I don't see how it can be achieved."

"Well, sir, it depends on a number of things. The first, as I said, is darkness, and tonight is the dark of the moon. The second is secrecy – not a breath of what we're planning must leak out."

"All right," said Fulton. "What will you need?"

"I'll need to talk to the diving team, sir. And your

chief engineer. Saul and Del, too, if they're up to it."

A shadow crossed Fulton's brow. He had lost both *Little Em'ly*'s pilots to injury in the brief but bloody pirate attack. "You can talk to them, but I don't think either will be back on active duty for several weeks at the very least."

"That's all right, sir. Now, the first thing we have to do is to get rid of one of those subs. What I have in mind won't work if both remain on station."

"And how do you propose to do that?"

Fulton's eyes narrowed in calculation as Luke told him.

The pirates had anchored their ship in the next bay to the north, and set up their camp on the headland between it and the lagoon where the *Challenger II* lay.

The pirates were well organized. Raga might have been an uneducated renegade deckhand who had worked his way up to his current position by unspeakable acts of savagery, betrayal and cold-blooded murder, but he had sufficient idea of the demands of leadership to impose some order on his crew, and, as night fell, to post pickets around the camp to guard against surprise attack. He did not trust the *mat salleh* – the foreigners – Germans or Japanese alike, and he knew they did not trust him; that was why they would not allow him to anchor in the same bay as the white devils' ship. They thought he would raid it during the night and carry off anything that was valuable. Normally, they would be right. But Raga feared their submarines that could follow him unseen beneath the sea and attack without warning. He was already regretting his agreement with Roth and the Japanese woman. He was not in a good mood.

So when one of his sentries appeared, dragging a dishevelled figure by the scruff of its neck and hurling it to the ground at his feet, his reaction was characteristically ungracious. "*Mannerless pig!*" he roared in Chamorro, the language of the islands. "*Why do you disturb me?*"

The sentry was used to his commander's outbursts. "*I found this foreign devil sneaking around the camp,*" he grunted. "*He jabbered at me in his barbaric tongue – I could not understand him so I brought him to you.*"

Raga glared at the grovelling figure. "Up, dog," he growled.

Spotiswoode raised his head. "Oh, thank God, you speak English!" Raga stared at him in silence. Spotiswoode shuffled forward on his knees. "Listen, Mr...Raga, isn't it? Listen...er...*Lord* Raga...I've come to you for protection."

Raga eyed him with deep mistrust. "Protection?"

"Yes, sir. The Germans and the Japanese mean to attack our ship, and kill everyone on board. I don't want to die. I tried to persuade the Captain to give them that rude Jessica girl, but he wouldn't. I thought if I came to you..."

"You want join my crew?"

"Well, not exactly – I thought you could hide me when the attack comes and then, when you leave the island, you could take me to the nearest port..." Raga scowled. "Or leave me here," Spotiswoode amended hurriedly, "with some food and water, you know; I'm sure another ship would come by eventually..."

"What you do for us?"

"Oh, well, yes," gabbled Spotiswoode, his eyes terrified behind his thick spectacles, "obviously it has to be a *quid pro quo* – ah, I don't suppose you understand Latin? I mean, you scratch my back, I scratch...what I mean is, I can spy for you. I can let you know what Captain Fulton is planning..."

Raga leaned forward with a cunning expression. "What *is* English captain planning?"

"I don't know, he won't tell me!" Raga sat back, looking bored. "But I'm sure I can find out!" Spotiswoode whimpered. "And if you want to raid the ship, I can show you where the valuables are. I mean, you want money and things, don't you? The Germans and the Japanese don't care about all that, they just want the ship."

Raga pondered for a moment. Then he snapped, "You go! Find out what English will tell other foreigners in morning! How many men on ship, how many guards? Where you keep money, food..." Raga's eyes glistened. "Rum!"

"Rum? Oh yes, we have rum," said Spotiswoode eagerly. "Lots of rum – in fact, I brought you a barrel as an earnest of good faith..." He caught Raga's blank stare. "That is, as a present. I swam ashore with it and left it hidden near the beach..."

"Good. Come back two hours before dawn. Now, go!" Raga turned to the sentry who had brought Spotiswoode in and said in Chamorro, *"Take this miserable wretch back to where you found him."*

"Can I not cut his heart out?" The sentry's voice was wistful.

"No! He may be useful. He has hidden rum. Make him show you where. Bring it back and share it among the men." Raga dismissed the sentry and Spotiswoode (still gabbling thanks as he was led away), and sat back, well pleased. The men had been grumbling since he formed his compact with the foreigners – eventually, one might be emboldened to challenge his leadership. The rum would keep them amused. And it might still be possible to turn a profit on this voyage.

Raga allowed himself a secret smile. The fish-eyed *orang putih* seemed to believe that his treachery would save him. The pirate chief chuckled. What fools foreigners were.

"Did he fall for it?" Luke asked as he helped the dripping Spotiswoode up the gangway on the landward side of the *Challenger II*.

"Hook, line and sinker." Spotiswoode shivered. "They've taken the rum. I say, do you think I could have a blanket or something? I'm most frightfully wet."

Luke clapped him on the back. "A dozen blankets if you want them. Terrific work, well done."

"You're a brave man." Captain Fulton held out his hand. Spotiswoode took it, flushing with pleasure.

As the hero of the hour was led away dripping, Luke listened carefully. Sounds of whooping, cheering and laughter were already rising from the pirates' camp. He grinned. One obstacle to his plan had been removed. Even if the pirates noticed anything untoward happening in the bay, the rum should keep them busy.

He ran silently down to the dark afterdeck. The only lights the *Challenger II* was showing were her anchor light and a couple of feeble lamps illuminating stairways. There was a slight risk that this might make their enemies suspicious; Luke hoped that they would assume that the lights were being run on batteries while the generators were being repaired.

An irregularly shaped structure loomed above him. Figures crawled all over it. Luke hissed, "Nick!" There was movement in the darkness as his friend joined him. "How's the raft coming on?"

"Nearly there," Nick told him. "I don't know how long it will hold together, though."

"It won't have to last long – a few hours. Lights in position?"

"In position and working." A shadowy figure slid across the deck and whispered something to Nick, who reported, "That's it. All set."

"Then let's get it in the water."

In many ways, this was the most difficult part of the operation. The raft had been lashed together since nightfall from old wooden barrels, boxes, planks, spare masts and booms from the remaining ship's boats and anything else that came to hand. It had to be lowered into the lagoon on the landward side of the ship, where prying lookouts on the submarines outside the reef could not see it, and this had to be done as silently as possible, and in almost complete darkness. Unseen figures strained on ropes and cursed in low voices. There were moans and screeches, instantly stilled, as the unwieldy construction brushed against obstacles. But at last it was done, with barely a splash. The raft rode alongside the ship, hardly bobbing in the calm water.

Jessica was already on the platform at the foot of the gangway, wearing diving gear. The *Challenger II* was carrying the latest breathing apparatus, and the new-fangled swimming fin that had been developed only the previous year. Jessica had insisted on being part of the diving team in the underwater survey of the narrow northern gap to the lagoon that had been conducted in utter secrecy that afternoon. Now she was ready to take to the water again, to help manoeuvre the clumsy raft into position.

Luke kneeled beside her. "Okay?"

"Sure." Jessica rinsed out her diving mask. "I told you, I'm a diver. The water is my element."

"Good luck." Luke stepped away as Jessica slipped into the water, joining two other divers. He gave Nick a hand to step onto the raft. "Remember your signal?"

"Once the raft is in position, I use my torch to signal to the ship. Three flashes," said Nick wearily. "If everything's ready, the Captain sends Cookie out of the galley. He chucks a bucket of slops over the side, then he goes back in; when he closes the door, that's the signal for the switchover. We've been through this a dozen times!"

"All right." Luke knew that Nick's bad temper was due to nervousness. So much of the plan depended on timing, so much could go wrong. "Good luck."

He caught the flash of Nick's teeth as he grinned. "You, too." Then the raft began to move away, propelled by the divers, over the inky waters of the lagoon.

Luke returned to the bridge. "Time to give the signal, sir."

Fulton gave him a brief nod. He took a torch, aimed it towards the top of the hill and pressed the switch to give three quick flashes. There was no reply – but if things were going to plan, a lookout on top of the hill would be passing on the captain's signal...

All hell broke loose.

From the other side of the island came a succession of explosions. Birds rose, screaming, into the air. Distress flares appeared, creating a red glow in the sky. These were followed by a pause. Luke raised his binoculars to study the submarines that were blocking their exit. Figures appeared on the conning towers of both.

Another half-dozen explosions erupted. More flares went off. There was evident consternation aboard the submarines. Aldis lamps flickered as they exchanged messages in Morse code. Then there was a noise of diesel engines, and white foam appeared at the stern of one of the vessels, which began to slip through the water.

"It's the I-40," breathed Luke. "Mochizuki's going." He had been certain that one of the submarines would be dispatched to investigate the disturbance; the only question had been, which one? But he had been correct in his guess that Roth would not leave Captain Mochizuki alone with the *Challenger II*, for fear that her lust for revenge would lead her to make a premature attack on the ship. Luke filed the fact of that distrust away in his mind for future use.

Out in the bay, just inside the reef, Nick watched the departing Japanese submarine; then, heart pounding, he signalled the divers to move the raft into position directly between the *Challenger II* and the U-X1. On the raft stood a careful reconstruction of the ship's lights and surrounding superstructure as they would be visible to the submarine, scaled down to match the reduced distance at which they would be seen. The trick would only work if the lights were seen from one position. From the second submarine, the dummy lights would have appeared in the wrong place – hence the diversion to get rid of one of the submarines. It seemed to have worked.

Although the island was only a mile across, it was

three and a half miles to its nearest end. From the I-40's starting position outside the reef to the site of the explosions was almost fifteen miles. Mochizuki would take over an hour to get there, more time to investigate, and another hour to return. There had been a chance that Roth would send a landing party to find the cause of the explosions; but Luke had correctly surmised that a submariner, faced with an unknown danger, would think first in terms of an attack by sea – and in any case, Roth had not sent anyone ashore all day long, probably because he did not trust his pirate friends.

Nick checked his position carefully. It was as good as he could make it. He signalled to the divers, who took weights made from worn-out engine parts from each corner of the raft, and lowered them to the seabed on lines, effectively anchoring the raft in position. Nick pointed his flashlight towards the ship and switched it on and off – once, twice, three times. Then he connected the battery and waited, his hand on the switch.

The cook came out of the galley. He dumped the slops. He went back in; the door clanged. Nick switched on the lights. Simultaneously, the lights on the *Challenger II* went out. Nick hoped that if the lookouts noticed any momentary shift or blink of the lights, they would put it down to their own eyes playing tricks. At any rate, his job was done.

He slipped into the water to join Jessica and the other divers for the long swim back to the ship.

On board the *Challenger II*, Luke had already taken his place at the controls of *Little Em'ly*.

With as little noise as possible, the crane operator lifted the submersible from its clamps and swung it over the stern. Then he lowered it into the sea, running the winch as slowly as it would go in order to make as little noise as possible. It was too much to hope that the whole operation could be carried out in complete silence, but as long as everything was done quietly there was a good chance that the noise of the pirates' celebrations would drown out any stray noises from the ship.

Some minutes passed before *Em'ly* reached the water and lay on its surface, her tiny deck just awash. A diver detached the lifting cable and replaced it with one of the ship's mooring ropes, which had been run from the bow. The man appeared in the forward observation window, and gave Luke the "thumbs up". Luke started the motors. Keeping the port side of the *Challenger II* visible in his starboard window, he moved slowly to the bows of the ship, and then kept going. The mooring rope and the umbilicus stretched out behind him until the rope tightened, checking his progress. Twenty minutes or so had passed since *Em'ly* had been lifted from the deck. Luke took a deep breath and increased power to the motors.

He picked up the telephone handset. "Commencing tow."

"Mister Challenger." The voice was Captain Fulton's. *"We have slipped our anchor."* This had obviously been accomplished very quietly – Luke hadn't even heard it. *"The demolition party has returned undetected. So has the raft party. All secure. It's up to you now. Take us to the gap. Starboard ten."*

"Aye, sir. Starboard ten." Luke would not be able to see the gap in the reef until he was much closer. He would have to rely on directions from the bridge. If the communications failed, they were finished! But then, so many things could still go wrong. The pirates, even in their rum-fuddled state, might notice something amiss. The lookouts might take their eyes off the raft and spot the slow-moving shadow of the *Challenger II* slipping from its mooring. But Lady Luck had smiled on them so far. Luke steered further to the right.

Time passed with agonizing slowness. The *Challenger II* had to be well out to sea before the I-40 returned; once that happened, it would not take long for Roth to realize he had been tricked. And they could not use the ship's engines until they were several miles offshore, or the sound would alert their enemies. But *Little Em'ly* towing her mother ship with her silent electric motors was (as Saul had said) like a small dog pulling an overweight owner – she could only go so fast.

Then he was at the gap in the reef, and there was no time for anything except following the course that the divers had laid down earlier in the day and drawn on a chartlet that Luke held balanced on his lap. It was approaching high water – a big, spring tide that should give sufficient depth for the attempt. After a long curve to port, Luke began a starboard turn through forty-five degrees; he groaned at the slowness of the ship's response to the change of direction, but eventually she came round – she must have missed the coral on that side by a coat of paint. Another turn, then another... At one point there was a long, low moan from behind him as the *Challenger II* scraped along the reef. Luke held his breath, pointlessly, hoping that the sound was less noticeable on the surface of the water than it was beneath it.

Captain Fulton's voice issued tinnily from the telephone. "*Steady as she goes, Mister Challenger.*"

"Aye, sir."

Another turn, another curve – and they were through. The seabed dropped away beneath *Em'ly* and the coral walls disappeared to either side. Now he only had to tow, once more straining *Little Em'ly*'s engines to the limit, to take the ship as far as possible from the island.

An hour later, he received the welcome message: *"Thank you, Mister Challenger. Come aboard."*

By the time Luke's feet touched the deck for an enthusiastic reunion with his friends, the ship, with both engines now working, was steaming away from the island at full speed. He reached the bridge as Captain Fulton ordered a course of one-eight-zero degrees.

"They'll be expecting us to return to our old course," said the Captain. "Let's see if we can surprise them." He checked his watch as the first hint of grey appeared in the east. "Nearly dawn. I said they'd have their answer then and, thanks to you, they have." He smiled with grim satisfaction. "I'll be damned if I let them catch me a second time."

16 DIVE

Indian Ocean: 009° 52' S, 108° 51' E,
off the coast of Java
August 1934

"**A**s far as I can figure it," said Jessica, poring over the chart, "the *Nautilus* should be just about...here."

"Stop engines," ordered Captain Fulton.

"Stop engines," repeated the officer of the watch. "Aye, sir." He signalled with the engine telegraph; seconds later, the engines that had propelled the *Challenger II* over thousands of miles of ocean were stilled.

The ship had left the Pacific Ocean as it threaded its way through the crowded islands of the Moluccas into the Banda Sea and then, by way of Bali, into the Indian Ocean. The sharpest eyes on board had kept a round-the-clock lookout for any trace of their pursuers, but neither the I-40 nor the U-X1 had been seen. Captain Fulton was convinced that the submarines had lost track of the *Challenger II*.

Luke was not so sure; though Fulton had been careful to pass through the narrowest straits at night, they had been travelling in some very crowded seas – there was at least a reasonable chance that one of the pursuing submarines would pick up news of their whereabouts from a fishing boat or an island trader. Moreover, the crewmen wounded in the pirate attack (including Saul and Del, *Little Em'ly*'s unfortunate pilots) had been put ashore to be treated at the Dutch mission hospital on Bali, where they would receive better care than was possible at sea. Captain Fulton had impressed the hospital with the need for secrecy, but there was no guarantee that news of the visit would not leak out.

Even so, on the basis that no news of their enemies was good news, the mood on board was buoyant; and now that a series of careful sightings, allied with detailed checks of the ship's chronographs, had brought them to their current position, this was bolstered by a real sense of anticipation. Two weeks ago, it had seemed impossible that the *Challenger II* should achieve its mission – now, spirits were high. The persistence of their enemies had convinced the crew, more than any argument Luke, Nick or Jessica could make, that the *Nautilus* was real and that the fabulous submarine of Jules Verne's book could be found and recovered. Nick, Spotiswoode and the ship's engineers laughed and joked as they carried out final checks on *Little Em'ly* before her first dive into the unknown.

Luke had been appointed *Little Em'ly*'s pilot for the diving programme. Captain Fulton had been reluctant to agree to this, but Luke's successful handling of the submersible on two previous occasions and lack of a viable alternative had brought him round.

Luke was taking an enforced rest on Captain Fulton's orders when Jessica came knocking on his cabin door. He politely swung his legs out of the way for her to sit on his bunk. Jessica was holding a framed photograph, which she held out for Luke's inspection.

The photograph – an early, hand-tinted type – showed an old man wearing a fisherman's sweater. He was mending a net, smoking a corncob pipe and grinning at the camera. Luke said, "Your great-grandfather? Ned Land?"

"That's him, the old rascal. The picture was taken around thirty years ago, not long before he died. But that wasn't what I wanted to show you." Jessica carefully removed the back of the frame, and from behind the photograph drew out the carefully folded page of a notebook.

"I told you I destroyed the second volume of Captain Nemo's diary," she said quietly. "That was almost true, but I really should have said I destroyed *most* of it." She unfolded the paper and passed it over. "I kept the last page."

Holding the fragile manuscript with reverence, and straining to decipher Nemo's tiny, meticulous writing, Luke read:

And now, I am come to the end of all my adventures. I feel the hand of death upon me, and the hopes I once had of an undersea kingdom where I could be at peace and free from the evils of humankind have long since dissolved, to be borne away on the tide, as my friend Perrier always tried to persuade me they would.

Of one thing I am sure: mankind is not yet ready for the secrets I have discovered, particularly that of how the Nautilus, my undersea home, is propelled. I shall be forever grateful to that excellent fellow Jules Verne for falsifying my doom, and that of the Nautilus, in his entertaining (if inaccurate) account of my voyages with Perrier and the impulsive Land;

and, in subsequent tales of my adventures (I mean in his book The Mysterious Island) of rendering my fate even more obscure by giving me a wholly false biography and locating the scene of my demise on a non-existent island in the South Pacific. Therefore I have little fear that the secrets of the Nautilus will ever be discovered by accident.

However, perhaps one day, humanity will learn wisdom and be able to derive benefits from my discoveries without using them to hasten its own self-destruction. I no longer feel able to judge: therefore I shall put this account into a waterproof container and leave it for the sea — which has been my home for so many years, and whose impulses and currents I trust as I would trust the judgement of no man — to deliver it to my friend Perrier, and to his heirs, to be kept safe and secret until it is their belief that the world is ready to learn what my legacy has to teach.

And now, the last remaining members of my crew have gone ashore (they will say nothing of my fate, dependable fellows), and I shall stay only to complete this account, before flooding the tanks and riding down into the ocean deep with Nautilus to what I hope and trust will be my last resting place and eternal home beneath the sea.

. . .this rough magic
I here abjure. I'll break my staff,
Bury it certain fathoms in the earth,
And deeper than did ever plummet sound
I'll drown my book.

"I don't get the last bit," said Jessica.

"It's lines from *The Tempest*," said Luke. "Shakespeare. They made us do it at school. I thought it was pretty dull at the time." He reread the closing lines of Nemo's farewell message. "I think, now, I have an idea what old Will was getting at."

"He didn't though, did he? Nemo. He didn't drown his book."

"Not literally, no. Maybe he just wrote that because he was tired of playing god. And the book...he left it to the sea to decide what would happen to it. Lucky for us the journal reached Professor Perrier in the end, or we wouldn't have a clue where to look." He passed the paper back to Jessica. "Thanks for showing me this."

"That's okay." She returned it to its hiding place. Her face serious, she said, "Kinda puts it in perspective, though, doesn't it? I mean, we're not just looking for a submarine. What we find – *if* we find it – won't be just nuts and bolts and secrets. It'll be a man's life. A man's vision."

Luke nodded. "A great man."

After a moment's silence, Nick popped his head through the door. He grinned at Jessica. "Oh, hello." He turned to Luke. "We're all set. Briefing in the mess hall, five minutes."

Captain Fulton rapped the table for attention. The buzz of conversation in the crowded mess hall died away to an expectant silence.

Fulton cleared his throat. "The first thing to say is, don't get your hopes up too high." He waited for the mutter of consternation to die down. "Let me explain. Our mission is to find and raise the *Nautilus*. Now, whether or not you believe in the submarine's existence – and I have to say, the enthusiasm with which our enemies have tried to engage the services of Miss Land" – several of the crew grinned at Jessica – "has brought me round to a more open-minded position on that question – whether or not you believe the *Nautilus* is down there, I'm sure you will all make your utmost endeavours to locate it. What happens then depends upon where it is lying."

He tapped a chart spread out on the table in front of him. Crew members leaned over to examine it. "I have marked our current position," said Fulton briskly. "As you can see, it is right on the edge of the Java Trench – also known as the Sunda Trench. Whatever you want to call it, it's deep – in places over 20,000 feet." The diving team exchanged uneasy looks. "The depth beneath us is currently 500 fathoms – 3,000 feet. This is way beyond the depth that *Little Em'ly* has so far been tested. However, Mister Spotiswoode assures me that the crush depth – that is, the depth at which the hull can be expected to collapse under the pressure of the surrounding water – is at least a thousand feet more than this; and in the Great War, submarines on both sides reported that their vessels had accidentally dived below their official crush depth, and survived. Therefore, as Mister Challenger has agreed to take the risk, I have allowed a search depth of a maximum of 3,000 feet.

"However, the search area will take *Little Em'ly* along what amounts to an undersea cliff top overlooking a drop-off into the depths of the Java Trench. If the *Nautilus* is lying on this cliff top, we have hopes of salvaging her. If not, the chances are we will never even find her – or if we do, that she will be beyond any reasonable hope of recovery by any means currently in existence. Is everyone clear on this?" There were reluctant nods around the table.

"Very well. We will commence diving operations at 1200 hours. The plan, as put forward by Mister

Challenger and approved by Saul Baird from his sickbed, is that the *Challenger II* will tow *Little Em'ly* in a search pattern. We have moved five miles to the south-east of the supposed site of the *Nautilus*'s sinking. We will proceed at a maximum speed of four knots, following the 3,000 foot depth contour marking the drop-off to the trench, to a point ten miles to the north-west of that position. If we are unsuccessful, as there is no point in searching the trench, we will repeat the exercise one cable to landward of the cliff top, then two cables and so on. Any questions?"

Nick muttered to Luke, "A cable – that's about 200 yards, isn't it?"

Fulton heard him. "A tenth of a nautical mile: two hundred and two and a half yards, to be exact."

"Oh." Nick looked embarrassed. "Right. Thank you."

"The final question to be decided," continued Fulton, "is, who will be Mister Challenger's co-pilot for the dive?"

Nick's hand shot up. "Luke will need an engineer, sir. I'd like to volunteer—"

"Now hold on a minute!" Jessica was on her feet, eyes blazing. "Who found Captain Nemo's diary? Who brought us here? If it weren't for me, you guys wouldn't have a clue where to look!"

Nick looked shocked by this unexpected attack. He

managed to say, "I helped design the propulsion system—"

"And if this famous propulsion system of yours goes wrong down there, what are you going to do? Get out and fix it?" Nick shook his head. This was a clear impossibility and Jessica knew it. *Little Em'ly* didn't have an airlock, so Nick couldn't leave the submersible; and if he did, at any substantial depth he would be instantly crushed to death.

"Besides," continued Jessica, "I'm a diver – I know what to look for down there. And I've read Captain Nemo's journal. I've seen his plans and drawings for the *Nautilus* – I know exactly what it looks like." She gazed around the room, as if defying anyone to argue. "And what's more," she added, "I have twenty per cent salvage rights on this dive – and I intend to earn it."

Captain Fulton regarded her with a mixture of irritation and amusement. "I believe Miss Land has made her point. Well, if no one has anything further to add...we commence diving in fifty minutes."

Though understandably disgruntled, Nick felt it his duty to make sure Jessica was properly briefed about *Little Em'ly*. "You'll be breathing bottled gas," he told her. "At the depth you're going, there's no chance of running an air supply from the surface – the hose would collapse under the pressure. That limits the dive time – even with scrubbers removing carbon dioxide and water vapour, your supply is good for six hours at the outside, so you need to keep an eye on the clock."

He leaned across her in the cramped control gondola. "If you drop the cable, Luke will start the motors – using *these* controls – and change direction with the diving planes and rudder. Of course, you're diving too deep for conventional manual linkages – cables and so forth – to work, so all those things are controlled by electrical relays..."

"Nick, I know." Now that Jessica had got her own way, she was determined to be nice to Nick, but at the moment he was trying her patience. "I haven't spent the whole voyage reading magazines, you know. Saul and Del showed me round *Little Em'ly*'s controls ages ago."

"Oh – did they?" Nick looked so downcast that Jessica took pity on him.

"Still, it never does any harm to run through things one more time. Thank you." Jessica gave Nick a pat on the arm. "Mind – we're counting on you to haul our butts out of the fire if anything goes wrong down there."

Nick suppressed the thought that at the moment he'd rather kick Jessica's butt than haul it out of trouble.

"Well, bon voyage." He reached up and began to climb into the tunnel, leaving the cabin clear for Luke.

When he had gone, Jessica took the picture of her great-grandfather and wedged it behind an electrical cable above the control board.

Luke dropped into the gondola, carrying a small white box with a dial and what looked like a microphone sticking out of the top. Jessica raised her eyebrows. "What's that?"

"Geiger counter," said Luke. "The scientist from Berkeley – what *is* his name? I can never remember it – he gave it to me. It measures radiation. He says, if Nemo's submarine really does have a nuclear engine, no matter how good the shielding is, after all this time the water around it will have a higher reading than background radiation, so it should help us to find the *Nautilus*." He switched the machine on – it chattered to itself like an outsized baby rattle for a few seconds, then settled down.

Jessica eyed it askance. "Is it going to make that noise all the time? It's like Chinese water torture, waiting for the next click."

"I daresay we'll get used to it." Luke secured the inner hatch. He unfolded the tip-up pilot's seat and strapped himself in. He gestured for Jessica to do the same in the co-pilot's seat, then he picked up the telephone handset.

"Em'ly to bridge – can you hear me?"

Captain Fulton's voice issued from the earpiece. *"Loud and clear, Mister Challenger."*

"Good. *Em'ly* to crane – Nick, can you hear me?"

"Every word."

"All right then. It's *Little Em'ly's* bathtime."

"Commencing lift." Four almost simultaneous clunks signalled the release of the clamps, and the submersible rose from the deck, rocking a little as the crane operator swung the jib and began to lower her into the sea. There was the now familiar splash and rush of bubbles; then the strange echoing silence of the underwater world as the submersible began her long plunge to the seabed.

"Well," said Luke, "we're off."

17 SIGHTING

For the first few feet of the dive, the shadow of the *Challenger II*'s hull loomed above them. Rays of sunlight speared through the water and danced playfully around *Little Em'ly* as their paths were bent by the waves above.

Luke and Jessica undid their safety harnesses as the motion caused by the *Challenger II*'s rocking in the waves died down. They folded their seats back and crouched on the rubber floor to peer out of the gondola's observation windows.

"I've not been down here in daylight before," said Luke. "It's beautiful."

Jessica slapped him on the arm, not altogether playfully. "Keep your mind on your work – we have a job to do."

Luke spread his palms to show that they were nowhere near *Little Em'ly*'s controls. "Look, no hands. We're being wound down on a cable – we won't have much to do until we reach the ocean floor except look."

"I guess not." Jessica craned her neck to see out of the port window. "And you're right – it is beautiful."

Luke pointed to a collection of long untidy strings and streamers dangling from the surface. "What are those?"

Jessica peered over his shoulder. "Portuguese man-o'-war." She shuddered. "It's a weird kind of jellyfish. I'm glad I'm in here, not out there. Those things can really sting... Oh, look!"

A pod of dolphins – perhaps the same one that had been racing the ship's bow wave in the last stage of its journey – had crowded round *Little Em'ly*. One of the inquisitive animals pressed his nose against the forward observation window, staring into the gondola. Jessica laughed. "Hey, they've got their very own humaniquarium. We should charge them. Fifty cents a peek."

In the upper layers of water, there was a good deal to see. As they slowly descended, a shoal of small, silver fish of the sardine type raced past the gondola, pursued by torpedo-shaped barracuda. A giant sunfish, whose flattened body and huge dorsal and anal fins made it look as if it had been built back-to-front, swam past, its mouth open in perpetual astonishment. Some time later, a green turtle sculled by with a purposeful air. Then, a dark shadow appeared at the edge of their vision: an enormous fish, sleek, graceful and slow-moving.

Luke was startled. "What's that?" he asked as the creature swam closer, revealing a pattern of white spots on its huge back. "A shark?"

Jessica nodded. "Whale shark. Biggest fish there is."

"It looks big enough to swallow *Em'ly* whole!" Luke bit his tongue; this was Jessica's world, not his, and she was being quite superior enough without his exclaiming like a half-witted schoolboy at everything they saw.

"Not quite that big," Jessica reassured him. "The glass makes things look bigger than they are. Anyway, it's a plankton feeder. Harmless."

As they went deeper, the dancing sunbeams faded and the light began to change. "The water filters out light," said Jessica, unable to resist the temptation to lecture Luke on the one subject about which she clearly knew more than he did. "Red, orange and yellow first. After 130 feet or so, you'll only see green, blue and violet. Deeper than about 600 feet, it's like a moonlit night down there, even when it's noon up above. I heard it's really dark after 1,000 feet, but I've never been that deep." She caught her breath nervously. "I guess we'll soon find out."

Their rate of descent was slow, about sixty feet per minute. It would take them a little under an hour to reach the seabed. Captain Fulton had wanted to give plenty of time for unforeseen problems to be spotted before they became a danger to *Little Em'ly* and her crew. Luke could appreciate the need for caution, but it meant that time passed slowly.

As the waters darkened, fish became increasingly harder to spot. Luke switched on *Little Em'ly*'s floodlights. They were dropping through a layer of plankton: small squid, prawns and other marine creepy-crawlies wriggled by outside the windows. Then Luke grabbed Jessica's arm. "Over there!"

Swimming just beyond the window was what looked like a giant inverted snail shell, white below and tiger-striped above. A spotted cowl protected a rudimentary eye and a forest of tentacles that protruded from the front of the shell. These waved dreamily until they encountered a shrimp – instantly, the tentacles darted to surround the struggling crustacean and draw it into the creature's shell.

"Is that what I think it is?" said Luke.

"A nautilus," breathed Jessica. "Fantastic. Those guys have been around for four hundred million years. I guess that's why Nemo named his submarine after them." She beamed at Luke. "Maybe it's a good omen."

"Let's hope so." Luke pointed at another shadow. "That's not a whale shark!"

"No." Jessica's fists clenched. "Great White. Those things are killing machines. Smart, too. Not a diver's favourite fish."

Her bleak expression prompted Luke to say, "Um – I never asked you how your father died. Was it...?"

"He was a diver." Jessica's voice was brittle. "One day he went down, and didn't come up. They never found him, so who knows? End of story."

Luke said, "I'm sorry."

"It happens."

"And I'm sorry I didn't ask before."

Jessica shrugged. For a while, there was silence between them as they descended into the depths.

Now they began to hear cracking and pinging noises as the pressure around the submersible increased, and the hull began to contract. Even though their flotation tank contained gasoline, which had been chosen because it was virtually incompressible, its seams were under strain. Despite Spotiswoode's reassurances, the creaking and groaning noises were disconcerting.

To take his mind off them, Luke gazed out of the starboard window – and gave a low whistle. "That is one ugly fish."

"Where?" Jessica leaned across Luke. A small fish, apparently attracted by the submersible's lights, was peering in at them with bulging eyes. Its body was so thin from side to side that it was difficult to see head-on. "Hatchetfish. I've only seen them in books. This species is called the lovely hatchetfish."

Luke stared at the misshapen, skeletal creature. "You're kidding."

"Probably named by someone with a warped sense of humour. You'll see uglier fish than that down here, though – uglier, and much, much weirder."

Jessica was right. A long, eel-like creature approached. It looked too slim to be a threat to the hatchetfish – until its lower jaw dropped to reveal a pouch many times as wide as its body. It swallowed the smaller fish whole before swimming away with a flick of its tail. Jessica caught Luke's startled expression and grinned. "Pelican fish," she said.

More strange creatures came to investigate as the dive continued. The first was a spookfish, with a long, conical snout, elongated brown body and a thin tail, so that it appeared to be pointed at both ends. This was followed by what Jessica identified as a fangtooth, six or seven inches in length with huge sabre-like fangs and the most ferocious expression Luke had even seen outside of a grudge match on the rugby field. Lurking just on the edge of their lights was a stoplight loosejaw, with two phosphorescent patches under each eye and no floor to its mouth, so that it looked like a grinning skull wearing particularly striking make-up.

Further down, they came upon the anglers: fish that appeared to be mostly head and jaws, and had a "rod" growing from a point between their eyes whose tip glowed with a bio-luminescent light, tempting smaller prey to approach the bear-trap jaws.

And then...

"There it is," said Jessica. "The ocean floor."

A featureless plain, seemingly composed of sand or mud, stretched away before them.

Luke spoke into the telephone handset. "Stop lowering."

Nick's voice came through clear, but as faint as though it were calling from the far side of the world rather than just over half a mile away. *"Stop lowering, aye."*

Little Em'ly stopped falling with a mild jerk, and hung motionless over the seabed.

"Bridge to submersible. Are you ready to begin the search, Mister Challenger?"

Luke swallowed hard. "Go ahead."

A faint rumbling noise came from infinitely far away. Jessica was startled. "What's that?"

"The *Challenger II*'s engines," said Luke, grateful that this silent world still held some surprises for her. "Low frequency sound travels a long way underwater."

Em'ly began to move, skimming over the seabed thirty feet below at walking pace. The water was full of particles. Some of these were tiny marine organisms, others were specks of detritus falling from the warmer seas above. It was like driving through snow. The minutes went past. The sea bottom was all but featureless and soon Luke found it hard to concentrate on the unchanging vista beyond *Little Em'ly*'s windows.

Occasionally the floodlights picked up living creatures. Phosphorescent viperfish undulated past and ghostly vampire squid flashed light organs on their arms and fins in alarm at their approach. A group of hideous blind hagfish, like long marine slugs, surrounded the remains of some less fortunate denizen of these dark waters, intent on their ghoulish feast. Delicate tripod fish sat on their three elongated fins, waiting for prey to pass incautiously close. Jessica pointed out giant isopods, similar to woodlice but a foot long, which scurried across the ocean floor on their unfathomable business; and sea-fleas the size of a man's fist, which she said were really a type of shrimp. Between delicate traceries of Venus's flower baskets, sea urchins and deep-sea cucumbers inched their way across vast expanses of mud and sand.

"Great place to visit," said Luke, "wouldn't want to live here." Into the telephone, he said, "The seabed's rising. Take us up."

"*Understood.*"

Em'ly rose until the seabed began to drop away, and Luke instructed the crane operator to level off, then to lower away again.

A few minutes later, the seabed vanished as a huge gash suddenly opened in the cliff face. "Underwater canyon." Jessica stared into the impenetrable black depths and shook her head. "May go all the way down to 20,000 feet or more. If the *Nautilus* is down there, we'll never find it."

The Geiger counter, which had hitherto produced only an occasional sound, clicked twice in rapid succession; then again. After a moment's hesitation, it settled down into a steady series of clicks. Luke glanced at its dial – the needle was jumping from its stop.

The opposite lip of the canyon appeared, and on its edge...

"My God." Jessica gripped Luke's arm so hard he almost cried out. "What's that?"

Luke said into the handset, "All stop. Hold this position."

Fulton's voice responded. "*All stop. Aye.*"

Em'ly slowed, then she came to rest, suspended over something right on the edge of the canyon. At first, Luke thought it was a strangely-shaped rock; then, as he looked more closely, he saw that beneath the marine growths that encrusted most of the object he could make out features that looked man-made: rails, deck-slats, an area of steel plating, what looked like a low, rakish conning tower, and, at the tapering end of what he could now see was a hull, propellers and a rudder.

"My God," Jessica said again, "there she is. I don't believe it. Nemo's position was spot-on. We've found her. First throw of the dice, and there she is." Her eyes shone with moisture in the dim reflection of *Em'ly*'s floodlights – she gave something like a sob and turned away from Luke.

Luke felt pretty emotional himself. His first reaction was one of relief at finding the *Nautilus* so quickly. This was accompanied by something close to veneration for the miraculous vessel that had defied the world and explored the depths of its oceans more than half a century ago. But shouldering aside both of these was sheer gut-wrenching excitement that the goal of their expedition was in sight.

He spoke into the telephone. "*Em'ly to Challenger II. We have found the Nautilus. I repeat we have found the Nautilus.*" To the background of cheering on the bridge, he added, "Send down the marker."

"*Marker coming down.*"

Luke put his hands awkwardly on Jessica's shoulders. "Are you okay?"

Jessica rubbed her eyes on her sleeve. "Sure. Sorry. It's just...it's there. It's really there. Great-Grandpa's story – he didn't make it up, it was true, all of it. And the ribbing Grandpa and Daddy took all their lives from folks who didn't believe them – it's just all too much. You know?"

"I know." Luke was taken aback – this was a side of Jessica he'd never seen before, that she took care not to let anyone see. He wasn't at all sure what to make of it. Fortunately, distraction arrived in the form of a weight, lowered from the surface, which landed on the seabed some thirty feet from the submarine and raised a cloud of silt. He drew Jessica's attention to it. "They've buoyed the *Nautilus*."

Jessica looked. "Yes." She took a deep breath and frowned. "You know, she's right on the edge of that canyon. It wouldn't take much to send her over. We're going to have to be very careful about how we attach the lifting cables – *what was that?*"

Luke caught the note of panic in her voice. "What? Where?"

"I saw something – a shadow – just beyond our lights – something big…"

"Another shark?"

"Maybe, but I don't think so…aaah!" Jessica screamed as *Little Em'ly* gave a sudden lurch, throwing her and Luke off balance. Something long and white appeared in the observation windows, then it was gone. "There's something out there, but I can't see…" She broke off, putting a hand to her mouth.

Luke gasped as an eye appeared in the starboard window – a gigantic eye, almost human in appearance. The eye withdrew to be replaced by a beak like a parrot's, which tapped at the glass as though the creature were trying to break in. It withdrew, and long arms or tentacles, covered with suckers, appeared.

"Giant squid." Jessica was trying hard to keep her voice level but she was plainly terrified. "One attacked the *Nautilus* while Great-Grandpa was aboard. Maybe this one's just curious – maybe it'll go away – oh!" She ended on a gasp, as the gondola shook again.

"Or maybe it won't," said Luke.

The telephone was squawking. "*Luke! Luke!*" Nick's voice was anxious. "*What the blazes are you doing down there? The crane's jumping around like crazy…*"

"Giant squid," Luke told him. "It's taken a fancy to *Little Em'ly* – either that, or it reckons we're prey."

The gondola was shaking continuously. Luke and Jessica wedged themselves against the curved sides as well as they could.

Nick's voice came again. *"Luke, that thing could tear Em'ly to pieces – we have to try to drive it off. We're going to send an electric current down the tow cable. You should be safe in the gondola as long as you don't touch any metal."*

Luke's fist tightened on the handset. "What about the gasoline in the tanks?"

"We're not sending a high tension spark, it should be okay."

"Should be?!"

"Remember, stay away from metal." The random motion of the cabin made it almost impossible to get back in their seats, so Luke and Jessica did the only thing possible – they pushed themselves away from the walls of the gondola and clung together in the middle of the rubber floor. *"Here it comes,"* said Nick, *"on a count of three: one, two, three..."*

There was a flurry of movement outside the windows, and the submersible's movement stopped.

"Power off," came Nick's voice. *"Any effect?"*

Luke disentangled himself, cautiously peered out of

the forward window – and flinched back as the squid, coming out of the darkness like an express train, slammed into *Em'ly* and shook her twice as violently as before.

He grabbed the handset. "Yes, it's had an effect – it's made the squid really angry!"

"We'll just have to try again with a bigger shock. Get ready…"

Anything else Nick had to say was lost as, with a jolt many times greater than anything they had already felt, *Little Em'ly* was suddenly in motion. Bubbles rushed past the observation ports. Luke and Jessica were flung to one side of the gondola by the sudden acceleration.

Luke gaped at the depth gauge – they were not only going fast, but down. He turned to Jessica. "Now what?"

Jessica lunged towards a window and stared fixedly out of it; Luke joined her in time to see the bulbous form of the squid come into view as it was dragged bodily away from *Little Em'ly*, clinging to the submersible only at the fullest reach of its long arms. The ghostly creature was writhing in gigantic jaws that dwarfed those of even the liopleurodon Luke had seen on the Lost World. The scene changed as the squid passed beyond the view from the small window. All Luke and Jessica could now see was what looked like a wall of grey, wrinkled, barnacle-encrusted skin; and then, suddenly, a close-up view of an eye – gigantic, old, wise and implacable.

"Sperm whale." Jessica's voice was despairing. "They feed on giant squid. This whale must have homed in on the one that's grabbed on to us..."

Nick's voice from the handset sounded frantic. *"Luke, what's happening? The whole afterdeck is swamped and cable's running off the drum like fishing line – there's not much more to—"*

There was another sharp jolt as the cables connecting *Little Em'ly* to her mother ship were ripped from their sockets. The handset fell silent. The cabin lights flickered as they automatically switched to battery power. The floodlights illuminating the scene outside the gondola died.

"I'm afraid we're now officially in trouble." Luke tried to keep the dread out of his voice. "We've lost contact with the *Challenger II*. There's nothing they can do for us up there. We're on our own."

18 STRANDED

Luke and Jessica watched as the depth gauge monitored their fall. 3,500 feet passed – then 4,000. The creaks and groans from the pressure on *Little Em'ly*'s hull were continuous.

"The whale must have carried us way out over the cliff and into the canyon, or the trench," said Luke. "It's not letting go of the squid and the squid's not letting go of us."

"The whale's an air breather," said Jessica. "It'll have to surface sometime."

"How long do they dive for?"

Jessica said nothing. Her eyes were unfocused and her breath came in ragged gasps. Her whole body seemed rigid with fear.

Luke took her arm. He kept his voice low and coaxing. "Come on, Jessica, this is important. How long?"

Jessica took a deep breath and said, "About forty to sixty minutes. That's according to Great-Grandpa's old notebooks, from when he was a harpooner."

"And how fast do they dive?" Luke was relieved to see Jessica's brow wrinkle in concentration. If the problem was doing nothing else, it was giving her something to think about, helping to overcome her fear. *And mine, too*, he admitted to himself.

"About 300 feet a minute," said Jessica, "judging by the speed they take line out from a boat following a harpoon strike."

Luke didn't approve of harpooning whales, but this didn't seem a good moment to debate the issue. He did a swift calculation in his head. "So this whale must have been diving for at least ten minutes to get to where we are, and we're going deeper, now..."

"I'd noticed," said Jessica tightly over the moaning of tortured metal.

"We're now at 4,500 feet." *Below Spotiswoode's estimation of our crush depth*, Luke thought but didn't say. He checked his watch. "It must be at least five minutes since it caught the squid. Fifteen minutes to dive, fifteen minutes to surface, and we've no way of knowing how long it was down here before it spotted the squid – at any rate, it can't stay down here too much longer."

Jessica's brow cleared. "You're right," she said. "Look!"

The depth gauge had finally stopped falling. It held steady for a while – then began to rise.

Giddy with relief, Luke and Jessica whooped and slapped each other on the back.

After a few moments of this, Luke said, "Let's not get carried away. We're a long way from being out of the woods yet."

He stared out of the window but could see little. Minutes passed. With only the gondola's emergency lights for illumination, the battle being fought outside was all but invisible. But the squid's arms, as they flexed against the thick quartz of the windows, seemed to be moving more slowly than at the moment of its capture. Maybe the creature was weakening. If only he could *see*...

Luke silently cursed himself. Of course he could see! *Little Em'ly* was carrying an emergency flashlight. He tore open the lid of a small locker, dragged it from a clutter of equipment dislodged by the squid's attack and, directing it out of the forward window, switched it on.

For a moment, the result was disappointing. Then the picture cleared, and Luke realized he had been staring into a cloud of ink – either the squid, in its agony, had released it, or the whale's teeth had punctured its ink sac. The ink plume cleared and Luke realized that during *Little Em'ly*'s ascent, cool blue twilight had replaced the utter darkness of the deep sea. Barely needing the torch, he and Jessica watched, spellbound, as the dying squid released its hold on their small vessel. Immediately, the buffeting of their passage stopped and the submersible slowly righted itself. At the same time the squid, twisting and writhing in its final agonies, wrapped its arms around the head of its gigantic predator – locked together in a dance of death, the combatants sank out of sight, falling with dreamlike slowness back into the silent depths.

"Do you think they'll kill each other?" asked Jessica in hushed tones.

Luke shook his head to recover his wits. "Do you know, just at the moment, I don't really care." He checked the depth gauge. "1,100 feet," he reported, "but we're going down again. We need to dump ballast." He reached over to the control panel and flipped switches.

The ballast consisted of steel pellets held in place by electromagnets. As Luke switched the magnets off, pellets began to drop out of the hoppers in which they were stored. *Little Em'ly*'s descent slowed. When the depth gauge steadied, Luke turned the magnets back on to stop the loss of pellets. The system had the added advantage of being fail-safe in operation – when the submersible's power ran out, the magnets would fail and dump the rest of the pellets so *Little Em'ly* would automatically rise to the surface.

"Luke, we're moving." Jessica sounded worried.

Luke checked the depth gauge. "No, we're steady at 1,200 feet."

"Not up and down. Along."

Luke joined Jessica in peering out of the windows.

The seabed was rising towards them, and it was clear they were skimming over it at something like five knots.

Luke whistled. "The whale must have carried us quite a way towards land for the water to be this shallow."

"And now we're caught in a current. How far are we from the *Challenger II*, do you reckon?"

"I don't know, but probably quite a way. We won't have any idea until we surface." Luke's hand went to the controls. He switched off the magnets to release more ballast.

At the same moment, Jessica cried, "Look!"

Startled, Luke joined her at the forward window, and saw a rocky slope rising from the seabed directly in their path. "What is it?"

"Seamount. Underwater mountain, what's left of an extinct volcano – and the current is carrying us straight towards it."

Luke made a dive for the controls, setting the electric motors to run full astern. A reassuring whirring filled the gondola – but only from the starboard side. Luke checked the instruments and cursed. "Our port engine's out – the squid must have damaged it. I'll have to compensate with the rudder."

It soon became clear that this wouldn't be enough. The current was carrying them along faster as they neared the seamount and *Little Em'ly*'s one working motor, running on battery power only, was not powerful enough to resist it.

Jessica stared at the looming wall of the seamount. "Can't you dump more ballast?"

"No – it flows out of the hoppers at a set rate, like sand in an egg-timer. There's nothing I can do to speed it up."

Jessica's hand clutched at his shoulder. "In that case, hold on tight..."

Little Em'ly struck the rising seabed, bows first, at

something over six knots. After that, all was confusion as the force of the current bowled the submersible across the slope of the seamount, rolling and pitching it from side to side and end-over-end until, with a final jarring shock, it stopped dead.

Luke rubbed his head where it had slammed into the gondola's unyielding steel wall. Jessica was curled up in a ball. He patted her shoulder. "You okay?" Jessica uncurled and nodded as if unsure. Luke began checking the instruments. After a few moments he breathed a sigh of relief. "It looks as if we've escaped serious damage. The force we hit, we could easily have ruptured a gasoline tank or something."

"That's good." Jessica hesitated before adding, "Luke…?"

"Yes?"

"Are we still dumping ballast?"

Luke checked the instruments. "Yes."

"They why aren't we rising?"

Startled, Luke peered out of the window. The wall of rock outside was unmoving. He set the starboard motor to full ahead. *Little Em'ly* jerked slightly, but failed to move. He tried to reverse *Em'ly*, with no better result. Luke shut down the motor and wriggled his way round to stare out of the port observation window, looking upwards as far as he could.

When he turned back to face Jessica, his expression was bleak. "We seem to be caught in a cleft in the rock. There's an overhang above us. The more ballast we lose, the more tightly we're being forced against it."

Jessica said, "You mean we're stuck?"

"Well and truly stuck."

"How much air do they have left?"

It was Spotiswoode who answered Captain Fulton's question. "They started with six hours and they've been down for two already."

"Four hours." Captain Fulton shook his head wearily. "What the hell *happened* down there? We were trying to drive the squid off, then all of a sudden…" He clicked his fingers. "The breaking strain on that cable is thirty tons! It couldn't just snap!"

"It could if it was tugged hard enough," said Nick, "and the way it was running off the drum before it broke, something was certainly tugging it good and hard! Could a squid drag it out that fast?"

"We know very little about giant squid," said Spotiswoode. "Nobody's ever seen a live one – excepting the crew of the *Nautilus*, if Verne's book is to be believed. The only way we know about them at all is from dead ones that get washed ashore, and fishermen's tales. We really don't have much idea what they're capable of."

"Well, there's no point in standing around here speculating. We'll have the answers when we find the submersible." Fulton looked around the bridge. "Suggestions?"

Spotiswoode immediately became businesslike. "The only sensible thing to do is start from their last known depth and position and search outward from there."

"Search, how?"

Spotiswoode scratched his head. "We can try our home-made ASDIC set, but I wouldn't expect it to find something *Em'ly*'s size at those depths..."

"The hydrophones, sir." Nick's voice was eager. "Lower them on the cable, hooked up to the umbilicus. They should pick up the noise of *Em'ly*'s motors."

"And if the motors aren't running?"

"I'm sure Luke will make a noise. Tapping on the hull...something. He knows we have the hydrophones, he'll expect us to use them."

The Captain considered. "Mister Spotiswoode?"

"I've no better suggestion, sir."

"All right – you'd better get on with it." Captain Fulton waited until Nick and Spotiswoode had left the bridge before adding quietly to himself, "And let's hope they're still alive down there."

* * *

Luke selected a spanner from the locker that had held the torch, and raised it to tap on the hull – three short taps, then three long, then another three short: SOS in Morse code.

In snappish tones, Jessica said, "What makes you think anyone's looking for us? They probably think we're dead. And even if they are, how do you expect anyone to hear that?"

"Hydrophones," said Luke. "The *Challenger II* is carrying them. They'll come looking for us, so we need to make a noise." With a confidence he did not feel, he added, "They'll find us, don't worry."

"They'll need to be quick, then. We only have air for three and a half hours – it's a big ocean, and they have no idea where to look." Jessica faced Luke, her expression serious but oddly calm. "Looks like we're going to die down here."

Luke had too much respect for Jessica to continue to offer false comfort. "It does rather seem that way, yes."

"Occupational hazard for a diver; everyone knows that, it's just you don't expect it to happen to you. What a lousy way to earn a living – one fifth of the profits, against all of the risk. If things go right, I'm on a measly twenty per cent share, but when they go wrong, I get to be a whole hundred per cent dead. I ask you, is that fair?"

Luke shrugged, and tapped out SOS again.

After hearing the message a dozen or so times, Jessica said, "I may have to brain you with that thing before we're much older. I'm sick of SOS. Can't you send some other message?"

"Certainly," said Luke. "Any requests?"

"How about, 'Shave and a haircut, two bits'?"

"Do you mean, 'Shave and a haircut, five bob'?" Luke tapped out the rhythm.

"That's it. In the interests of Anglo-American understanding, what's 'five bob' mean?"

"Five shillings. One dollar twenty-five cents."

"That's what they charge in London for a shave and a haircut? Two bits is a quarter – twenty-five cents. Your barbers are making a dollar clear profit on every mug who comes through the door."

"I could do 'Pop Goes the Weasel'. Or 'This Old Man'. Or how about 'Green Grow the Rushes, O'? You know..." Tapping out the rhythm as he did so, Luke said, "One is one, and all alone, and ever more shall be so..."

Jessica gave him an odd look. "Maybe you should go back to SOS," she said quietly. "SOS is fine."

Nick checked the gauge on the cable drum. "That's it – 3,000 feet. Hold it there."

The crane operator nodded. Nick raced to the bridge. "The hydrophones are in position, sir."

"Very well," said Fulton. "Standard search pattern. Engines ahead, one half."

The officer of the watch rang the order through on the engine telegraph. "Ahead one half, aye."

The engines rumbled. The propellers turned. The *Challenger II* began to move through the water.

Mere moments later, there was an eruption of foam a hundred yards away, on the starboard side of the ship. A conning tower emerged from the sea. It had *U-X1* painted on the side.

Spotiswoode groaned. "Roth."

A second conning tower appeared to port. This one had *I-40* emblazoned on it.

Nick's shoulders drooped. "And Mochizuki." He watched as hatches on both submarines opened, and gun crews hastily manned the deck-mounted weapons, training them on the *Challenger II* in unmistakable threat.

With an air of defeat, Captain Fulton said, "Stop engines."

The telegraph clanged. The engines stilled. Ship and submarines, silent and watchful, swayed gently in the waves.

19 AGREEMENT

"So it comes down to this." Korvettenkapitän Roth's voice was angry but controlled. "We know where the *Nautilus* lies, but your submersible is missing with Mr. Challenger and Miss Land aboard, and you do not know where."

"That's about the size of it," Fulton agreed heavily.

"Then we must find the submersible. Quickly."

Captain Mochizuki glared at the German commander. "I do not see why 'quickly'. I would not lift a finger to save Challenger."

"But I think you would extend yourself to a greater extent to save the submersible." Roth's voice dripped scorn. "I do not know your submarine's capabilities, but I doubt even the Imperial Japanese Navy has detection equipment capable of finding such a small vessel in so vast a search area by echolocation alone. Mr. Malone is right – our best chance is to search with hydrophones, which will only work if the crew of the submersible is making a noise, and they will only be able to make a noise as long as they are alive."

Nick held his breath. The atmosphere on the bridge of the *Challenger II* had been electric ever since her captors had arrived to take control. The ruse by which the ship had managed to escape from the lagoon under Roth's supervision had evidently strained relations between the German and Japanese allies to breaking point. He wondered whether Roth had gone too far now. But though the muscles in Mochizuki's jaw tightened, she gave no other signs of resenting the U-boat captain's sarcasm. After a brief silence, she said, "Very well. We will search for the submersible. All of us."

"Is that right?" said Fulton harshly. "And exactly why would you be willing to help us find *Little Em'ly*?"

Roth gave him a cold look. "Captain Fulton, you have already seriously inconvenienced our mission once; I would not advise you to do so a second time. And you know the answer to that question. My submarine is the most advanced in the German U-boat fleet, but neither it, nor Captain Mochizuki's, is capable of operating at the depth where the *Nautilus* is lying. If we are to recover her, we will need the submersible which you have so carelessly lost."

"Then if you want to steal *Em'ly* to recover the *Nautilus*, why should we help you?"

"Because, unlike the amiable Captain Mochizuki, you want Mr. Challenger and Miss Land back alive."

"He's right, sir." Nick's comment brought him the baleful attention of all three captains. His mouth dry, he forced himself to continue, "We don't have any choice, do we? The search area is much too big for us to cover ourselves. The subs have hydrophones, too. We can cover three times as much ground if we work together. Please, sir. It's the only chance Luke and Jessica have got." *Come on, you stiff-necked old fool,* he added silently. *If you carry on acting stubborn, Roth and Mochizuki will just take over the ship anyway. Let them have* Em'ly – *a lot can happen once we have Luke and Jessica back...*

Fulton and Spotiswoode exchanged glances. Spotiswoode gave the briefest of nods. The captain of the *Challenger II* said, "Very well. We search together."

"So. We will, of course, take precautions against your suddenly remembering an urgent appointment elsewhere." Fulton opened his mouth to protest – and then closed it again. Having been given the slip once, Roth was hardly likely to risk being caught out a second time. "A number of my men, under the direction of my second lieutenant, will join this ship. A similar number of Commander Yoshida's men will also come aboard. A person from your crew will join the complement of each submarine."

"I will take Malone," said Mochizuki instantly.

"I do not think so." Roth's smile was pleasant but his voice was like ice. "You will take Mr. Spotiswoode. I do not think Mr. Malone would be altogether safe in your custody."

Mochizuki bristled. "You forget yourself," she spat. "You would do well to remember that it was your incompetence that allowed this vessel to escape from the island. You have forfeited your right to dictate the course of this operation."

Roth's smile froze. "Your opinion is noted," he said softly. "The fact remains that I am in command until our masters dictate otherwise, and both you and Commander Yoshida are under orders to co-operate fully with my wishes. I hope that is clear."

The stand-off persisted for several seconds, and it

was Roth who broke it. "We are wasting time. The crew of the submersible now have less than three hours of air remaining. Captain Fulton, you will take the centre of the search formation. Our submarines, running at maximum operating depth, will sweep to left and right of your position. Mr. Malone, with me."

Jessica checked her watch again. "Two hours."

Luke nodded. "Right."

As the minutes ticked by, conversation between them had become halting and intermittent. For a while, they sat in silence, hearing nothing but the mysterious sounds of the sea.

At length, Jessica said in a low voice. "I'm glad you're down here with me."

Luke raised an eyebrow. "Thanks!"

"I didn't mean it that way. I wish we were neither of us here at all. I just meant, when the end comes...I'm glad I won't be alone. Having you here makes it better." Jessica sighed. "I know it's selfish." In barely more than a whisper, she added, "I like being with you. Ever since we met. When you're not being a stuffed shirt, anyways. Do you like being with me?"

Luke felt suddenly hot and uncomfortable. "Um – this isn't really the time..."

"Looks like it could be the only time we have," said Jessica bitterly.

"I suppose you're right." Luke cursed himself. He didn't want to hurt Jessica. And he did like her, in lots of ways. But even now, he wouldn't pretend to feelings he didn't have. "Well – er – I think you're great, but..."

"Yeah, that's me." Jessica gave a bark of mirthless laughter. "*Jessica Land: she was great, but...*' Put it on my memorial."

Silence fell again. Luke reached out hesitantly and squeezed Jessica's hand. She returned the pressure. He thought she was crying, but she had turned away from him, so he couldn't be sure. They sat in the cramped gondola, holding hands and staring at nothing.

After a minute or two, Luke picked up the spanner again and struck it against the hull: tap-tap-tap; tap... tap...tap...; tap-tap-tap.

Nick was in the control room of the U-X1. It wasn't at all what he had been expecting.

For a start, it was untidy. Fresh fruit and vegetables hung in nets between the wheels, valves and levers used to control the submarine. Bunches of bananas dangled above the chart table. Tins and cartons of food were tucked into every nook and cranny. Nick could appreciate that a submarine on a long patrol needed plenty of supplies, and space was limited, but he still found the chaotic storage methods disturbing, and contrary to the image he had in his mind of Teutonic order and efficiency.

But he had long ago ceased to worry about his surroundings. The search had been going on for well over two hours, and the hydrophone operator on the U-X1 had heard nothing.

Nick glanced at the clock above the chart table. Roth checked his watch and nodded grimly. "Twenty minutes of air left. Your friends are running out of time."

"*Kapitän,*" said the First Officer. "*Wir nähern uns einem Unterwasserberg.*"

"*Langsame Fahrt voraus.*" Roth turned to Nick. "It seems we are approaching a seamount. I have ordered the engines to slow ahead. I cannot risk damaging my submarine..."

"*Kapitän!*" The hydrophone operator put a hand to his headset. "*Hier ist was!*"

"We're picking something up." Roth snapped an order to the operator. "*Stellen Sie es auf den Lautsprecher.*"

A hiss of static came from the control room loudspeakers. Nick strained every nerve to listen – after a moment, he was rewarded. A rhythmic tapping came from the speakers, faint but unmistakable. SOS...SOS...

"They're alive," he breathed.

After a brief consultation with the hydrophone operator, Roth said, "The sound is coming from a position 800 metres dead ahead of us and 370 metres down. They must be somewhere on the slope of the seamount." Raising his voice he called, "*Periskop!*"

A tube, about six inches in diameter, rose from the deck. Roth snapped down the folding handles at its base, and looked through the complicated eyepieces between them. He turned the tube, moving his whole body around its centre of rotation. "Most submarines have two periscopes," he told Nick. "One for search, one for attack. This one has a third – an undersea device for locating mines and making visual contact with other submarines. It is equipped with special lenses and the latest night-vision devices, to allow us to see underwater and in low light – ahhhh!" Roth halted, swept the periscope back slightly, and gave a sigh of satisfaction. "*Alle Maschinen stoppen!*"

The engines stopped. In the silence, the insistent tapping of Luke's SOS could even be heard faintly through the submarine's hull.

"So. There they are." Without taking his eyes from the periscope, Roth added, "Their situation is not good. They appear to be stuck. See." He lowered the periscope for Nick, who peered through it eagerly.

At first he could make out nothing but vague shadows; but then his eyes adjusted to the strange tints of the night-vision view, and suddenly he could see, clearly though far away, the rounded lines of *Little Em'ly* with her gasoline tank above and observation gondola below. His heart leaped – but then seeing the tightness of the crevice in which the submersible was wedged, and the size of the overhanging rock above, it sank into his boots again.

He gave Roth a pleading look. "What can we do?"

"We could grapple for the submersible from the surface, but Mr. Challenger and Miss Land would be dead long before we could arrange that." Roth smiled grimly. "No doubt Captain Mochizuki would prefer that option; I, however, do not." He raised his voice. "*Halb achtern. Torpedorohre eins und zwei laden.*" The engines came to life. Turning back to Nick, Roth said, "I intend to fire a torpedo to strike ten metres above the ledge." Nick gawped at him. "The overhang should protect the submersible from the blast, but I hope it will then crumble, releasing your friends."

Nick found his voice. "That's insane!"

Roth looked almost happy – the Sea Wolf of legend, battling against overwhelming odds once more. "Insane? No. A gamble – and their only chance. Sometimes a gamble is all one has."

As Roth gave the range and depth for the shot and issued final orders to place the submarine in the ideal position to fire, Nick ran those final words through his mind again and again. A gamble, an only chance, a forlorn hope. Despite his fear, Nick knew that Roth's action was one that Luke himself would approve.

"Are we moving in closer?" he asked.

"No, further away. The torpedo cannot be set to arm itself in less than 300 metres." Roth listened intently as his crew reported the lengthening range. Then he said, *"Rohr eins, Feuer!"*

The air in the gondola was foul. Although it was cold down here, Luke was sweating from every pore, and a quick glance told him that Jessica was, too. The air smelled of the mud at the bottom of a pond and tasted like stale milk. Every breath was a torment, and he had to force himself to breathe normally while his brain, starved of oxygen, was sending out panic signals demanding that his lungs take huge gulps of air. Even though he knew it was hopeless, he continued mechanically to tap out his unvarying message: SOS... SOS...

Jessica was at the window, staring out through half-closed eyes. Suddenly she gave a convulsive jerk and grabbed at Luke's shirt. In a voice cracked with strain, she said, "There's something out there." Luke joined her to peer out of the window. "It's a sub!" Jessica gave a whoop and waved out of the window.

Luke felt light-headed – elated and let down all at the same time. "Roth, then, or Mochizuki. Nothing to celebrate."

"Don't look a gift horse in the mouth." Jessica snatched the spanner from Luke and beat out the SOS rhythm on the hull, adding her voice. "Hey! Over here! Come on, you guys – hey!" She continued to yell until, her voice rising and taking on a nose of panic, she cried, "They're going away! Hey, you lousy bums!" She beat out a regular tattoo. "Come back here!"

"Nothing they can do anyway," said Luke dully. "It's too deep for divers. They could be ten yards away, and they still might as well be on the far side of the moon." Jessica shook her head, unwilling to believe that rescue could be so close, and yet so impossible.

The distant rush of compressed air sounded faintly from outside the gondola. Luke sat up and let out an oath. Jessica stared at him. "What's eating you?"

"That sounded like a torpedo launch...but surely they wouldn't..." Over Jessica's shoulder, Luke caught sight of a slim, dark shape arrowing through the water towards them. "Hell's bells!" He made a lunge at Jessica and hauled her away from the window as the torpedo struck.

The noise from the blast was deafening. The gondola shook violently, pelting Luke and Jessica with loose objects. One of the control circuits shorted out, sparking weakly in the oxygen-poor air. The hull rang as it was struck by falling debris.

Luke felt as if he had a head full of cotton wool. He released Jessica and stared out of the window. "Are they trying to kill us?"

Jessica's voice sounded muffled, as though she was speaking from several rooms away. "Luke! The depth gauge!"

Luke checked the gauge – and laughter burst from him, uncontrollable, half-hysterical. The overhang that had been holding them down was gone, destroyed in the explosion. The rocks that had held them prisoner were tumbling down the slope of the seamount, to come to rest on the ocean floor. The last of the ballast had been dumped long ago: *Little Em'ly* was free, and rising.

Luke hugged Jessica, still laughing weakly. "Going up!"

The lightened submersible's ascent was so rapid that, on reaching the surface, she leaped almost completely from the water before settling back with a mountainous splash to wallow in the placid waves. A few seconds later, Luke cracked the hatch on *Em'ly*'s back. He and Jessica climbed unsteadily out and lay gasping on the tiny deck while waves lapped at their sweat-soaked clothes.

With a blast of foam and clouds of spray from its emptying ballast tanks, a submarine surfaced alongside. Before the deck had fully risen from the waves, Roth appeared on the conning tower. Cupping his hands around his mouth, he called, "Mr. Challenger! Miss Land! Welcome back to the land of the living. Come aboard, please. You are my prisoners."

20 THREAT

"**D**," said Luke.

"No." Nick added a rope dangling from the crossarm of the gallows he had already drawn on a page of his notebook.

Luke pondered briefly. "All right – P then."

"No." Nick drew a head at the end of the rope.

Luke and Nick were playing Hangman. They had been locked in their cabin on the *Challenger II* for two days. They had seen no one except the unsmiling German guards who brought them food, escorted them to the heads on demand and, against all precedent in any book they had even read or movie they had ever seen, had presented them with not one single opportunity to escape. When Nick had pretended to be ill, one of the guards had dosed him with castor oil, so that he genuinely *was* ill. And when he and Luke had set fire to their blankets, they had both been doused with water and made to sleep on bedding that was not only charred, but damp.

So they had spent a lot of time playing simple games in one of Nick's half-used exercise books, using a stump of pencil. Nick was ahead in Hangman by 116 games to ninety-eight, but behind in Battleships and Cruisers to the tune of six battleships, eight cruisers and fourteen destroyers.

"T?"

"Nope." Nick drew the hanged man's body.

"Oh come on. There's got to be a T. It's the second most used letter in the English language!"

"No T. Sorry."

"Let me see that!"

Nick held out the pad. Luke checked the letters he had guessed correctly:

_ o _ a _ e L. _ u _ l e _

Luke handed back the pad and growled, "W?"

Nick drew an arm.

"M?"

Another arm.

"Blast! Right then. S."

Nick drew a leg. "One guess left," he said happily.

"N," snapped Luke.

Nick whistled softly. "Very good." He showed Luke:

_ o _ a _ e L. _ u n l e _

Luke stared at it. "What sort of a surname is that? Bunlet? Funleg?"

"No 'T', remember," said Nick smugly. "One guess."

"Oh for pity's sake – F!"

"Hangman!" Nick drew in the remaining leg with an air of triumph. "117!"

"Well, who is it then?"

Nick filled in the missing letters.

Horace L. Hunley

"Never heard of him!" protested Luke. "We're supposed to be doing famous people. You just made him up."

"No I didn't," said Nick. "He's a famous person."

"What's he famous for?"

"He was an engineer."

"Oh, of course! I should have guessed."

"And also a Confederate Captain in the American Civil War. He helped design one of the earliest military submarines."

"Was it any good?"

"Not so's you'd notice – it sank three times during trials and killed over twenty Confederate sailors, including Hunley himself. So they named the sub after him."

"Very thoughtful."

"But then a feller called Lieutenant Dixon and eight volunteers attacked a frigate with it."

"With torpedoes?"

"Well, unfortunately, the self-propelled torpedo wasn't developed until a couple of years later. The *Hunley* was carrying a spar torpedo – basically a bomb on the end of a pole."

Luke stared at Nick. "You're kidding! Wasn't that suicidal?"

"As it happens, yes. Dixon's crew set it off under the USS *Housatonic* – she went down, but so did the sub. So the *Hunley* was the first submarine to sink an enemy ship, as well as the first to be sunk in action."

"You should suggest Mochizuki uses a spar torpedo

– she's crazy enough to do it." Luke reached out for the book. "Come on, then – Battleships and Cruisers. I'll be a whole ruddy fleet ahead of you before I'm done…"

The door swung open. A guard stood in the doorway. He was, as usual, unarmed. The armed guards were the ones at either end of the corridor, waiting for Luke and Nick to try any funny business with the first guard. But this time, the guards were not German. They were Japanese.

The guard made an unmistakable gesture, and said, "*Ima sugu koi!*"

Luke stood up and stretched. "I think he wants us to go with him."

"Your grasp of foreign languages is uncanny." Nick followed him out of the cabin.

Their escort led them through the accommodation decks and up the ladder to the bridge. There were no German guards in sight – just poker-faced Japanese stationed at every door. Captain Fulton and Chief Officer Marsden were there, as were Spotiswoode and Jessica. Sitting in the chair normally occupied by the officer of the watch, with an M-94 Nambu pistol held negligently in her lap, was Captain Kasumi Mochizuki.

She took off her tinted glasses and gazed at Luke, with no expression in her cold, dark eyes. Luke returned the stare.

After a long silence, Mochizuki said, "Luke Challenger. Your life is forfeit to me. I can take it at any time."

Luke said nothing. What was there to say?

"However, for the moment, I have a use for you. The work of raising the *Nautilus* is not going well..."

Captain Fulton drew himself up to his full height. "I protest against your unauthorized use of Challenger Industries equipment—"

Mochizuki said, "I am tired of your protests." She raised her pistol and shot Fulton through the heart. The Captain's eyes opened wide with surprise; he gave a barely audible grunt, and fell. The Master of the *Challenger II* was dead before he hit the floor.

Jessica screamed. Marsden took a step forward; a guard brought up the butt of his rifle. The Chief Officer staggered back, with blood running down his neck.

"You crazy—" Jessica never finished the sentence. As Luke sprang forward, Mochizuki seized her in a stranglehold and thrust the muzzle of the gun into her neck. "No dramatics from you, Luke Challenger!" Luke glanced around at the guards, whose weapons were now raised and ready to fire, and forced himself to relax. As he looked down at Fulton's lifeless body, the vicious act struck home in all its senseless cruelty; he had to use every ounce of self-control to stop himself from trembling.

Nick's eyes were wide and horrified. "There was no need for that."

"You killed him!" Spotiswoode, who had been shocked into silence by the terrible speed of the event, found his voice. "You killed him!"

"Do I have to kill you, too?"

"You can't! I did what you wanted – I repaired *Little Em'ly* for you."

"And now the submersible is fixed, you are of no further use to me. Must I repeat the question?"

Before Spotiswoode could reply, Roth stormed onto the bridge, accompanied by two of his men. "What is happening here? Who fired that shot?" He caught sight of Captain Fulton's body and turned to Mochizuki, eyes ablaze. "You did this! Why?"

Mochizuki gave him a lazy smile. "To encourage the others." She pressed the gun muzzle even more tightly against Jessica's throat.

The German captain looked around the bridge, at his own guards and the Japanese submariners who were standing with guns raised, clearly uncertain about whether they should be menacing their prisoners or each other. Signalling his men to lower their weapons, Roth said, "You exceed your authority, Captain. Where is Commander Yoshida?"

In languid tones, Mochizuki replied, "Commander

Yoshida is confined to his quarters. I have relieved him of command. He was showing signs of mental instability."

"What signs?"

"He wished to continue taking orders from you. I would call that *serious* mental instability."

Roth said tightly, "We will discuss this later. Release Miss Land."

Mochizuki ignored him and addressed herself to Luke. "As I was saying before the late Captain Fulton's unwise interruption, the work to recover the *Nautilus* is not going well. Neither my crew, nor that of Kapitän Roth, is familiar with the handling of your submersible. We are no nearer to raising Nemo's submarine than we were two days ago – indeed, in their efforts to attach lifting wires to the vessel, our pilots report that they have only succeeded in pushing it closer to the edge of the trench. Their incompetence has been punished.

"Luke Challenger, you have shown yourself adept at manoeuvring the submersible. Nicholas Malone, you will act as his co-pilot and devise a method of attaching the lifting cables. You will ensure that the *Nautilus* is ready to be raised no later than tomorrow at noon."

Luke's mind felt as hot and heavy as molten lead. He dragged his eyes away from Fulton's body with an effort and faced his killer. "You," he said thickly, "can go to hell."

Mochizuki smiled as if Luke had paid her a compliment. "I shot Captain Fulton to convince you of the seriousness of my intentions. I thought that Miss Jessica Land, having shown us the location of the *Nautilus,* had become expendable – but I have recently come to see that she still has her uses. You will comply with my directions, Luke Challenger, or she will be... disassembled. I use the word precisely. It is not a process that would find favour with the tender-hearted." She gave Roth a sardonic smile. "But I am an expert and my heart is not tender."

Jessica had turned very pale, but she said, "I guess this is where I say, 'Don't do it, Luke!'"

Luke gave no sign of having heard her. He looked into Mochizuki's fathomless eyes: a look eloquent of contempt and loathing. Then the muscles of his face stiffened, as if he had slipped a mask over it. He nodded once.

The Japanese woman snapped out a command. Two of her guards led Jessica away. Roth swore violently in German, turned on his heel and marched out, leaving Mochizuki alone with her prisoners, undisputed Master of the *Challenger II.*

* * *

Two hours later, Jessica's door opened and an expressionless Japanese guard ushered in Luke, Nick and Spotiswoode.

Jessica gave them an angry look. "Well, if it isn't the Three Stooges."

Her visitors exchanged glances. Luke asked, "Now what have we done?"

"Caved in to that Japanese hell-cat, that's what! Why did you do that?"

"To save your neck," said Luke bluntly. "She'd just shot Captain Fulton for no reason, remember."

"I'm not likely to forget it." Jessica's voice was unsteady. "That lousy bitch shot him just to make a point! I suppose he's still lying there..."

"No," said Luke quietly. "Roth sent some men with a stretcher. They took Captain Fulton away. Marsden went with them."

"And Mochizuki let them go?"

"She didn't seem to care." Jessica bit her lip. "I feel the same way about Mochizuki as you do," Luke told her. "I just didn't want what happened to the Captain to happen to you."

"Oh, thanks loads. How d'you think that makes me feel? The Germans and the Japanese get the secret of atomic power because big stwong Luke Challenger wants to pwotect ickle orphan Jessie. What's the point?

You know she's going to kill us all anyway!"

"But not today," said Luke. "That's the point."

Jessica turned to Spotiswoode. "You're supposed to be the adult around here – why did you fix *Little Em'ly* for them? Can't you see you're playing into their hands?"

"I repaired *Em'ly* to keep myself, and the rest of you, alive." Spotiswoode adjusted his glasses. "Grand gestures are all very fine, but usually not very practical. The thing about being a martyr is, you only get one shot at it, and if it doesn't work, then where are you?"

"Dead," snapped Jessica.

"Exactly. I heard an old Persian story, once." Jessica made a disgusted noise, which Spotiswoode ignored. "A mullah, a holy man, was preaching in the great square outside the Shah's palace. The Shah – the ruler, you know – didn't like what he was saying and sentenced the mullah to death. But the mullah said, 'Great Shah, if you spare me, within a year I will teach your favourite horse to sing.'

"The Shah laughed and promised the old man that if he succeeded, he should be set free. So the mullah was sent to the stables and spent the rest of the day singing to the horse."

Jessica snorted. "Sounds like another nut."

"That's what the grooms in the stable said. They all

laughed at him. 'You are a fool,' they said, 'for trying to trick the Shah. What have you gained by it?'"

Spotiswoode leaned forward, his face serious. "The mullah replied, 'I have gained a year, and a year is a long time. In that year, anything might happen. I might escape. I might die. The Shah might die.' He smiled. 'Or perhaps the horse will learn to sing.'"

"Or, to cut a long story short," said Luke, "'while there's life, there's hope'."

Jessica stared at them for a moment. Then she shook her head. "I still think you're crazy. What did you want to see me for, anyway? I bet Mochizuki didn't like it."

"She didn't." Luke didn't think it would serve any purpose to add that it had taken them an hour's frustrating argument to secure the interview. He held up Nick's notebook. "We need your help. Take a look at this."

Jessica took the notebook. "Battleships and Cruisers? Well, let's see now. I'd lob a shell into square D7 and see what—"

"Not that! The next page."

Jessica turned the page and found a reasonably accurate drawing of the *Nautilus* as they had found it lying on the seabed. She raised an eyebrow. "I'm impressed. You only got to see it for a couple of minutes."

"You've seen Nemo's diagrams," said Luke, "in the book you burned. Nick has an idea how we can raise the *Nautilus*, but we have to find lifting points where we won't just tear lumps out of the hull."

"That's right." Nick pointed at a curved spar with a serrated front edge that ran from the front of the conning tower to the bows of the submarine. "What's this?"

"Battering ram," said Jessica promptly. "*Nautilus* didn't carry torpedoes – if a ship attacked her, Nemo would just ram it. That thing would go through most hulls, wood or steel, like a hot knife through butter."

Spotiswoode shuddered delicately. "Charming."

"A lot of people were out to get him, remember."

Nick nodded. "That should do it. We need one more lifting point – what about here, the top spar over the propeller, that supports the rudder?"

Jessica shook her head. "Not strong enough, too far back. You'd risk ripping the whole stern off." She pointed. "Why not try the hatch just aft of the dorsal fin? Right here. There's a big locking wheel on top."

Nick looked dubious. "Will that be strong enough?"

"Should be. Hatches are always pretty well constructed on a submarine – if one comes open at sea, everyone dies."

Nick snapped the notebook shut. "That's it, then. Thanks, Jessica." As Spotiswoode knocked on the door to summon the guard, he added, "We'd better get on. We've got a lot of work ahead of us."

"So you boys get to play with your construction set while I'm stuck in here like some stupid princess in some dumb tower," complained Jessica.

"Oh, we won't be playing." Luke gave her a far from reassuring grin. "We'll be teaching the horse to sing."

21 SALVAGE

First light next morning found Luke and Nick standing on the afterdeck of the *Challenger II*, surrounded by armed and unsmiling Japanese guards and surveying the strange contraption that had appeared on the wire by which *Little Em'ly* would shortly be lowered into the sea. The apparatus that the combined efforts of Luke, Nick and Spotiswoode had produced to lift the *Nautilus* was a sort of yoke, from which two more wires dangled so that they were practically brushing the deck on either side of the submersible. At the end of each wire was an odd-looking hook: a four-bladed grapnel, but with each fluke terminating in a spring-loaded bar which, when closed, made the open C-shaped space between the fluke and the centre bar into a closed D.

Em'ly herself had changed. From a fitting just above the forward observation window she now sported a steel pole, long and slim like a spear, but instead of a point, it had an S-shaped double hook on the end.

"So, let's go through it again." Luke marshalled his thoughts and continued, "We're lowered down by the crane in the usual way. Then we release the lifting cable, but *not* the umbilicus..."

"Not unless it gets tangled in the wire," Nick put in. "That way, we have power going to the motors for longer, and we can communicate with the surface."

"Right. So, we release the cable; then we have to attach it to the *Nautilus* so that the *Challenger II* can raise her, while we dump ballast and make our own way back to the surface. We attach the cable with your hook-on-a-stick thingy ..." Luke pointed to *Little Em'ly*'s new appendage.

"It's that shape so you can push against the cable," explained Nick, "or pull it if you need to."

"I remember. And once we've grabbed the cable, we use *Em'ly*'s controls and motors to move the grapnels into position."

"That's it. Then we attach one grapnel round the

Nautilus's battering ram, as near as we can to the conning tower, and the other one to the locking wheel on the dorsal hatch. Once the first grapnel is in position, we give it a tug, the hook goes round the ram and the bar springs back like a snap-shackle so it can't fall off again while we're fixing the second grapnel to the locking wheel. Bingo! Piece of cake." Nick headed for the open hatch on *Em'ly*'s minute deck.

Luke followed. "What sort of cake are you thinking of?" he demanded. "The sort you can only make with the whites from dodo eggs? Getting those grapnels attached won't be a piece of cake, it'll be like threading a needle wearing boxing gloves. And don't forget that any false move we make could send the *Nautilus* over the cliff edge and into the canyon, where we'll never get hold of it."

"You worry too much." Nick disappeared through the hatch.

"Oh, do I?" Luke glanced up at the bridge where Captain Mochizuki was watching the preparations for the dive with her cold, unreadable eyes. He shuddered and followed Nick down the tunnel, closing the first hatch behind him. "I suppose you do remember that if we mess this up, we're all dead ducks? Don't forget, the German and Japanese pilots couldn't do it."

Nick grinned as Luke joined him in the observation

gondola. "Ah, but they didn't know about the Spotiswoode and Malone Patent Spring-Locking Grapnels! Don't worry, those babies will bring home the bacon."

Luke's stomach grumbled. "I'm missing breakfast for this," he complained as he sealed the inner hatch. "First cake, now bacon. Do you have to keep going on about food?"

"Not to worry. You can have breakfast on the way down."

"What sort of breakfast?"

Nick held up a hand of bananas and waggled it in front of Luke's face. "These! I begged them from Roth."

Bananas were Luke's least favourite fruit. "Oh, yum," he said drearily, "you think of everything." He reached for the telephone handset. "*Em'ly* to bridge: ready to go." With a wry smile at Nick, he added, "Wish us luck."

"*You have no need of luck.*" Mochizuki's voice was faint but clear. "*You know the penalty for failure.*"

"*Em'ly* to crane. Lower away."

Roth's voice replied, "*Understood, Mr. Challenger. Safe journey.*"

A lurch, and they were airborne. A splash, a rush of bubbles, and once more *Little Em'ly* was gliding down through the calm water, with the light fading above and the darkness of the ocean deeps gathering below.

"So Mochizuki is in charge on the bridge while Roth's

relegated to supervising the guy on the crane," mused Nick as they descended. "Doesn't that strike you as significant?"

Luke was testing the controls. "Roth isn't calling the shots on this operation any more," he said in an abstracted voice. "His authority must have taken a nosedive when we got away from him back at the island; but as long as Yoshida was taking instructions from him, he could still hold on to command.

"But now Mochizuki's shown her true colours: she wants to recover the *Nautilus* herself, she doesn't want Roth to have it, and she wants us dead. She's got Yoshida under lock and key, and I'm guessing Roth isn't sure what to do. He knows she won't back down, and if he tries pulling rank on her, he'll only succeed in starting a war between his sub and hers. I reckon he's playing along with her because he knows the Sons of Destiny will have his guts for garters if they don't bring back the *Nautilus*."

"Well, what about her? Won't the snake-and-spear brigade be a bit miffed when they find out she's locked up her own commanding officer and pulled the rug out from under Roth? They put him in charge of recovering the *Nautilus* after all, not her."

"Maybe she thinks if she brings them the *Nautilus*, they won't be too bothered about how she got it. Or maybe she just doesn't care. She's a dangerous cold-hearted killer, and stark raving mad into the bargain, in case you hadn't noticed."

"Oh, I'd noticed all right," said Nick. "It's the way she threatens to chop people up into little bits, and shoots them dead for no reason – those are definite clues." He glanced at the darkening water beyond the observation window. "Shouldn't we turn the lights on?"

"Not until we're lower. The pilots on the previous dives didn't report seeing any more giant squid, but there's no point in drawing attention to ourselves by using lights before we need them."

Nick shrugged and looked out of the port observation window. After a while, he said in a sing-song voice, "I spy, with my little eye, something beginning with 'S'."

Luke gave him an unfriendly stare. "It's 'Sea', isn't it?"

"Might not be," said Nick defensively. Then he sighed. "Oh, all right, it is. Not much else to look at, is there?"

"Watch the depth gauge."

"1,500 feet," Nick reported. "1,600...1,700..."

The crane had been set to pay out cable much faster than on Luke's first dive; even so, it was a full half-hour before they reached the seabed. Luke switched on the floodlights and ordered the crane to stop lowering; then his finger hovered over the button that would detach the lifting cable. "Ready for this?"

Nick's voice was calm, but beads of sweat dotted his

brow. "*Em'ly*'s a big girl now. She doesn't need her ma's apron strings any more."

"All right." Luke pressed the button. There was a clunk. The gondola jolted, and the submersible began to sink. *Little Em'ly* was now attached to the *Challenger II* only by the umbilicus that carried surface power and telephone communications. Luke would have to be careful not to overstretch the umbilicus for fear that it might break; and if something went wrong, the slim cable would not be strong enough to lift the submersible back onto the ship. Luke adjusted the ballast with care, and their slow drift downward stopped. He nodded to Nick, who took the handset.

Luke studied the situation. "The *Challenger II* must have drifted a little. Tell them to move slowly to the north-west." Nick relayed the order. Luke carefully matched speed with the detached cable as it swung towards the *Nautilus*. When it was directly over the downed submarine, he said, "All stop."

Nick spoke into the handset. "All stop." He joined Luke in staring out of the windows.

The spindle-shaped hull of the *Nautilus*, with its curved, shark's-tooth ram and fish tail, was still lying half on its side. But the metallic plates of its casing were now scratched and scuffed in places, and the submarine was closer to the edge of the undersea canyon than she had been.

"Mochizuki was right. They have dragged her." Luke's voice was worried. "Or she's slipped."

"Better get on with it before she slips any more, then," said Nick practically. Into the handset he added, "Lower away. Slowly."

The grapnels inched down. Luke made for the nearest one and, at the third try, caught it on the end of *Em'ly*'s projecting double hook. With infinite caution, he pushed the grapnel towards the selected lifting point where the *Nautilus*'s curved battering ram met the conning tower. Then he gave an exclamation of dismay. Nick immediately ordered the crane to stop lowering and asked, "What's up?"

"See for yourself!" Luke made a despairing gesture towards their target. "That ram thing is too thick – the grapnel won't go round it."

Nick thought for a moment. "No problem. Drop the grapnel down below the ram, go round the other side, hook it in so the cable goes through the gap, then all you have to do is clip the grapnel back onto the cable to form a loop."

Luke stared at him. "That's 'all I have to do', is it? And if you mention pieces of cake again, I'll dot you one."

By the time the cable was lying alongside the lifting point and the grapnel resting on the *Nautilus*'s sealife-encrusted hull, Luke had broken out in a cold sweat.

Taking care not to disturb the delicate balance of the arrangement, he backed *Little Em'ly* away and swung round to the other side of the *Nautilus*.

"Don't get the umbilicus wrapped around the cable now," Nick said in his ear.

Luke was too busy to spare his friend so much as a glare. Inch by inch, he manoeuvred the hook to pick up the cable.

"A touch more to the left," commented Nick. "Now forward – you're very close – right, right..."

Luke gritted his teeth. "You're not helping..." Hardly daring to breathe, he pulled *Em'ly* slowly back, and the cable slipped into the hook. "Got it!" He drew back further, pulling the cable through the gap between the ram and the hull. "Easy does it..."

"There's not enough slack." Nick spoke into the telephone again. "Lower more cable..."

With a jerk, the cable began to reel in. Luke and Nick exchanged an appalled glance – then Nick yelled into the handset, "No! No! Stop lifting! Stop!"

It was too late. The rising grapnel had caught on some projection on the *Nautilus*'s hull. The cable tightened, drawing *Little Em'ly* helplessly forward. The observation gondola hit the submarine's conning tower with a stunning jolt. The cable slipped out of *Em'ly*'s hook and the submersible was thrown backwards.

With a scream of tortured metal, and throwing up clouds of silt from the seabed, the *Nautilus* slid towards the canyon.

"No!" Luke could only stare in horror. "She's going over…!"

Nick groaned aloud. "Now she's properly sunk – and so are we!"

The cloud of silt made anything that was happening outside the windows completely invisible. Luke snatched up the telephone handset. "What happened?" he demanded.

Roth's voice was shaken. *"The crane operator… a mistake…"*

Luke was in no mood to listen to excuses. "Is there still a load on the cable?"

"Ja." In the moment of crisis, Roth's immaculate English was slipping. *"Yes – a big load."*

"And is the cable running off the drum?"

"No."

Luke dropped the handset and peered out of the observation window with bated breath. The silt was beginning to clear. His heart pounded as he saw that the *Nautilus* was poised halfway out over the canyon brink – but with a surge of relief, he realized that the submarine was slipping no further. As visibility cleared, he saw why: the grapnel had caught on the lip of metal that ran round the edge of the conning tower. The cable reached up, twanging taut, into the dark waters above. This fragile hold was all that was stopping Nemo's submarine from toppling into the abyss.

Nick bit his lip. "That could go any time."

"I know. We have to work fast." Luke swore.

Nick was practically tearing his hair. "This is impossible! Roth's crane operator fouls up but guess who'll get the blame if Mochizuki loses the *Nautilus*? We will! She expects us to succeed where her own men failed, and if we don't, she'll kill Jessica..."

"And dump us on the seabed and sink the *Challenger II*, I know. We can't afford to fail. But we'll never get the second grapnel to its lifting point, the way things are. The cable's far too short, especially with all the weight on the first hook."

"So what do we do?"

"Take a gamble. You said Roth was fond of them." As Nick gawped, Luke seized the telephone. "Now listen carefully. Crane: on my command, I want you to start lifting. Bridge: at the same time, I want the *Challenger* to steam north-east, dead slow. Have you got that?"

"*Bridge.*" Mochizuki's voice was low and menacing. "*You had better be certain of this, Challenger.*"

Luke's knuckles were white where he gripped the handset. "How badly do you want the *Nautilus*, Captain?

What am I getting from you? Threats, or co-operation? Are you ready?"

There was a short pause before the reply, *"Ready."*

"Crane – ready?"

"Ready."

Luke crossed his fingers. "All right. Lift."

With more shrieks and groans, the submarine began to move, raising more silt as it did so. The grapnel slipped – Nick gasped and Luke's breath caught in his throat as the *Nautilus* slipped back towards the canyon. But a heart-stopping moment later, the grapnel caught again. The submarine jerked like a hooked fish and hesitated for a split second: then it continued its slow rise and began to move away from the canyon lip. Luke remembered to breathe again. He waited until there was considerable distance between the *Nautilus* and the edge of the underwater cliff before he gave the order to stop engines.

"Lower away," he said, "slowly."

With the submarine once more resting on the seabed at a safe distance from the canyon edge, Nick and Luke could breathe more easily.

Even so, it took an hour, and many unsuccessful attempts, to clip the second grapnel to the locking wheel on the dorsal hatch. Once this was accomplished, Luke swung *Em'ly* around to inspect the first grapnel. The hook had wedged itself tightly over the lip of the conning tower, with the sprung bar partly closed behind it.

Nick shook his head. "I'm not happy with the way that's caught, but we'll never shift it down here. And that's the only set of grapnels – we could bodge something else up and try again..."

"I don't think Mochizuki's patience would run to that." Luke inspected the grapnel closely. Then he said, "It's held so far. You know what they say: nothing ventured, nothing gained." Nick nodded, and Luke picked up the telephone. "*Em'ly* to crane. Commence lift."

"*Commencing lift.*" Roth's voice had recovered its customary calm.

Nick wiped sweat from his brow. He turned a troubled face to Luke. "The minute the *Nautilus* touches the surface, Mochizuki and Roth will be all over her like a rash. We've just given them the secret of atomic power, tied up in a pink ribbon. I can't help wondering whether we've done the right thing."

"We haven't." Luke's expression was stony. "We've just done what we had to. But the year isn't up yet; there's still time for the horse to sing."

Trailing clouds of silt, Captain Nemo's fabled submarine rose majestically from the ocean floor to begin her long journey upwards, to the surface she had last visited over sixty years before.

22 NAUTILUS

"Whoever comes through that door next," said Nick grimly, "is going to wish we'd never been born."

When he and Luke had brought *Little Em'ly* to the surface the previous day, a ship's boat had been despatched to pick them up and tow the submersible back to the *Challenger II*. Luke and Nick hadn't been expecting to be showered with congratulations on their success, which was just as well because they weren't. On their return to the ship, they had caught barely a glimpse of Roth and Mochizuki gloating over the recovered *Nautilus* before they were unceremoniously bundled back into their cabin by gun-toting Japanese sailors, and the door locked behind them.

During the long hours that had passed since then, the knowledge that their enemies were so much nearer to achieving their goal had fuelled their determination to escape. Their sleeping quarters had been ruthlessly dismantled to create a variety of improvised weapons. They had ripped up bed sheets for use as gags and bindings. Pillows had been dumped so that the pillowcases could be bundled over the heads of incautious guards. Luke had removed half the slats from his bunk and bound them together to form a serviceable club. Nick had spent a dull but profitable hour dissolving a cake of soap into a bowl of water. "If we chuck this in the guards' eyes," he enthused, "it's really going to sting!"

The one drawback to their carefully laid escape plans had been that, in order for them to work, someone would have to come to the cabin, and no one had. In the excitement of raising the *Nautilus*, their German and Japanese captors seemed to have completely forgotten them. No one had brought them anything to eat or drink and their hammering on the door and demands to see an officer had been greeted by the forceful shouts of "*Urusai!*" which they had correctly interpreted as, "Shut up!"

It was now long after nightfall and their determination to free themselves at all costs had declined into a state of dull apathy. Nick was actually snoring when Luke heard the faint sound of bolts being drawn from outside the cabin door. A touch on his arm brought Nick instantly awake and reaching for his soapy anti-personnel device. Luke slipped to the hinged side of the door and stood poised, club raised, as the handle began to turn.

As the door opened, they sprang into action...a split second later, Luke managed to pull his blow and Nick to divert the stream of water onto the cabin wall rather than into the eyes of the interloper.

Jessica stood in the doorway, treating them both to baleful looks. "What are you two idiots playing at?" she hissed.

Luke returned her glare with interest. "We thought you were a guard! What on earth are you doing here?"

"He sent me to fetch you. He had an idea you might pull some crazy stunt like this if he sent his own men."

"He? Who's 'he'?"

"Roth. Shut up and listen. If you two make a lot of noise trying to escape, the whole thing blows up in our faces. So keep quiet and come with me." As Jessica stuck her head back out of the door, checking the corridor, Luke and Nick exchanged interrogative glances; when she slipped out through the door, they followed.

Two Germans were waiting at the end of the corridor, holding rifles and looking around nervously. Two Japanese guards lay sprawled in the corridor, snoring heavily. Half-eaten plates of food lying beside each gave a clue as to the cause of their sudden dereliction of duty. "Drugged," whispered Jessica. She gave them both a savage grin and beckoned urgently.

Stepping over the legs of their erstwhile captors, they followed her down the corridor and out into the clear night air. The Germans fell in behind them as an escort. Luke briefly considered making an attempt to disarm them; a sidelong glance at Nick was enough to tell him that his friend had been toying with the same idea. But in the light of Jessica's confidence that Roth had something up his sleeve, Luke caught Nick's eye and shook his head.

The small party moved as silently as possible down the accommodation ladder to the port side of the *Challenger II*, where the *Nautilus* lay, securely tethered to the ship. Luke was surprised that there were no Japanese guards on deck to challenge them – he assumed that these had been dealt with in the same way as those guarding his cabin. At any rate, the fugitives gained the ship's rail without mishap and took the gangway that had been rigged to give access to the shell-encrusted deck of the *Nautilus*.

One of the guards indicated the submarine's dorsal hatch with the muzzle of his rifle. "Down, please." Without hesitation, Jessica lowered herself through the open hatchway. Luke and Nick followed. The guards brought up the rear, the second one closing the hatch behind them with a muffled clang.

Luke took a deep breath. Since Roth and Mochizuki had caught up with the *Challenger II*, he'd never expected to set foot aboard the *Nautilus*. Yet here he was, treading the decks of the legendary vessel, Nemo's creation, the scourge of the seas. The ghosts of her long-dead crew whispered in the water that lapped against her hull and the musty air that sighed through her silent corridors.

The interior of the submarine smelled of sea-ooze, mould and an indefinable scent that caught at Luke's nose and scratched at the back of his throat like a cat demanding attention. The captives filed along a corridor whose walls were lined, not with the steel plates Luke was expecting, but with cracked and stained oak panelling. Cabins opened off to each side. All were dank and empty. At the end of the passage, they reached what was recognizably a watertight door. Their guards gestured them through this and closed it behind them.

They found themselves in what seemed to be a dining room. It stretched almost the full width of the vessel.

Light came from globes set in the ceiling and the floor was covered with carpet that had once been rich and expensive, but was now damp, faded and smelly. But on the oak shelves around the walls were secured glasses and plates that, though dusty, were clearly valuable, as were the oil paintings whose frames were placed either side of the doors at each end of the room.

The centre of the room was occupied by a solid-looking table in some dark wood, fastened to the tilting deck and surrounded by chairs upholstered in burgundy leather, with carved backs and arms. Korvettenkapitän Roth stood at the end of the table. He was gazing at the paintings as Jessica and the boys entered. "Magnificent," he murmured. "Titian, Giovanni Bellini, Raphael – a portrait of Pope Leo X, I think, and an undiscovered Leonardo da Vinci. Remarkable." Luke, who knew nothing about art, glanced at these masterpieces without interest. Roth, apparently recalling the urgency of the situation, turned to face his guests. "Please forgive me." He indicated the chairs. "Sit down."

As they did so, Roth leaned forward, hands palm down on the table. "I apologize for the unconventional means I used to bring you here, but I am sure you understand why it was unavoidable. It can hardly have escaped your notice that Captain Mochizuki no longer accepts my command. It therefore seemed to me that it was not safe to leave the three of you in her custody for a moment longer than necessary. I could make no move while the Captain was still aboard your ship. However, this evening I managed to convey to her certain hints that I intended later to board the I-40 and attempt to free Commander Yoshida. This served to send her back to her submarine, and a little sleight of hand in the galley ensured that the men she had left on board the *Challenger II* would take no further interest in the evening's events."

Luke said, "I take it you don't intend to free us."

"Regrettably, no. But, as I explained earlier to Miss Land, I judge that as my prisoners rather than Captain Mochizuki's, your chances of survival will be greatly increased."

"What about Spotiswoode?" demanded Luke. "And the crew?"

"Captain Mochizuki's thirst for vengeance is restricted to you and Mr. Malone, and she has shown herself prepared to use Miss Land as leverage to force you to obey her, but I judge the rest of the *Challenger*'s crew is in no immediate danger." Kapitän Roth steepled his fingers. "I could, of course, have taken you directly to the U-X1 – but I am aware that I am, by any reasonable measure, in your debt. I felt it only right that you should have at least a brief glimpse of the discovery you have made.

"So. Here she is. The *Nautilus*. As you see, surprisingly well preserved."

"I expected her to be full of water," said Luke.

Roth nodded. "So did we all. Evidently Nemo considered that just flooding the ballast tanks and not the whole submarine would suffice to scuttle her, and her remarkable construction did the rest. We have now succeeded in connecting power from the *Challenger II* so that the *Nautilus*'s electrical systems are working, and found them in good working order." Roth gestured towards the lights. "As you see. We have charged her batteries and pumped the water from her tanks. As long as they remain empty, even should she come adrift from the ship, she will not sink."

Nick could contain himself no longer. "Have you looked at her engines?"

Roth gave him a bleak smile. "Mr. Malone, you must not mistake your position here. You remain my prisoner. I bear you no ill will, but you have already shown yourself to be a talented and inventive engineer and I have no intention of allowing you any knowledge of the secrets this vessel contains. I will say only that I expect her engines to...repay further study. And, to set your minds at rest, I should add that radiation aboard, while higher than background levels, is well within safety limits.

"Nevertheless, you are here because there is something I think you should all see. Follow me, please." Roth rose from his seat and led the way to another watertight door at the opposite end of the room to the one by which they had entered.

The next room was a library with shelves of wood and brass and, below them, sofas covered in brown leather. The shelves were packed with books, their spines spotted with decay. Kapitän Roth hardly spared them a glance. He opened another watertight door and waved Luke, Nick and Jessica through.

On entering the room beyond, Luke could see little. As his eyes adjusted to the darkness he could begin to make out vague shapes of furniture: chairs and divans, a desk, display cases. Then Roth turned on the lights. "The saloon."

Jessica gave an involuntary gasp. Nick whistled. Luke gazed about him in awe.

This room was more than twice the size of the previous two – about thirty feet long, eighteen across at its widest point, and fifteen high. The ceiling was decorated with geometric patterns based on waves, shells and sea creatures. In the centre of the floor was a fountain. As Luke stared, it burst into life: water leaped and danced from the tails and mouths of the fish at its centre and fell into a giant clamshell.

Around the walls was a collection of painting and sculpture that even Luke could see would have done credit to London's National Gallery or Paris's Louvre Museum. Other cases held displays of fabulous marine organisms – corals and shells; starfish, urchins and bryozoans preserved in amber-like blocks; and in pride of place, surrounded by enormous pearls, the shell of a gigantic nautilus.

Roth, watching their reactions with a crooked smile, flicked more switches. The overhead lights went out and, with a fair amount of groaning, rectangular panels slid back on each side of the saloon to reveal sheets of glass or transparent crystal. On the starboard side, the window showed only the red-painted plates of the *Challenger II*'s hull; but to port, a shoal of silver-scaled bigeye jackfish, perhaps using the *Nautilus*'s hull to shelter from predators, swam back and forth as though in an aquarium.

"Captain Nemo's windows on his undersea world," said Roth. After a few moments, he operated switches to close the panels and turn the main lights back on. Luke's attention was drawn to the far end of the room. There stood a magnificent church organ, its collection of keys, stops, pedals and pipes as sculpted and intricate as a coral reef. And seated at the organ...

Luke caught his breath. Now he could identify the

scent that had caught his attention the moment he had set foot on this vessel, faint but unmistakable: the scent of death. "Captain Nemo," he whispered.

The body of the *Nautilus*'s creator was dressed in decaying robes. The mummified head was thrown back. Its eye sockets were empty. Skin as pale and delicate as tissue paper stretched tight over the bones of the skull, lips and gums mere scraps of parchment over the yellowing teeth. The withered hands still rested on the organ keys.

"It really is him, isn't it?" Jessica said in a voice over which she was not quite in control. "It seems a shame to disturb him." Nick, lost for words, nodded.

"However, disturb him we must." Roth's voice dispelled the hushed atmosphere. "I wish I could give you more time to explore, but it would not do for Captain Mochizuki to find you here. I must ask you to make your way to the U-X1. My men are waiting."

Nick glanced at Luke, and an unspoken message passed between them. Taking Jessica by the arm, Nick led her to the door at the end of the saloon and through it into the library.

When Luke made no move to follow, Roth said, "Mr. Challenger?"

Luke stood his ground. "There's something I don't understand, sir."

"How may I enlighten you?"

"Sir, I'm sure this will sound impertinent, but I have to ask. You seem like a reasonable man – a decent man. You're taking a risk by snatching us away from Mochizuki like this."

"Captain Mochizuki has her way of doing things," said Roth evenly, "I have mine."

"Yes. So why are you on the same side? I mean, Mochizuki, yes, the Sons of Destiny are right up her street. But for pity's sake, sir, what possessed you to work for them?"

For a while it seemed that Roth would not reply. Then he said, calmly, "Do you know how I first knew I wanted to be a submariner?" Without waiting for Luke to reply, he went on, "It was because of this man." He turned his gaze on the remains of Captain Nemo. "I read of his adventures, and those of the good Professor and Miss Land's great-grandfather, when I was nine years old." With half-closed eyes, he recited: "*The sea is everything. It is a pathless desert where a man is never alone, for it is infinitely alive. It is the last refuge from tyrants. Below its surface, their power wanes, their influence dwindles, their dominion ends. From the sea, the earth began, and to the sea it will one day return.*" Roth opened eyes that still held a faraway look, as though he were returning from a long journey. "Nemo's words," he said. "From that moment on, I longed to follow in his footsteps."

"If you believe what Nemo said about tyrants," said Luke bluntly, "how come you ended up working for the worst of the lot?"

"There are many types of tyranny, Mr. Challenger." Roth's voice was low but more charged with pain than Luke had ever heard it. "War is a tyranny, and when I went to war I soon learned that the sea provided no refuge. Good men died, on both sides. And good men killed them. I must have killed thousands; there is blood on my hands enough to stain an ocean red."

"That was in battle," said Luke.

"Yes, and I told myself many times that it was my duty to sink the ships of my enemies. But Captain Nemo broke away from the surface world to find peace in the sea, and I could not pretend that I had done that.

"Then the war ended. The allies could have made a fair settlement with Germany, but they chose instead to humiliate us. I had to surrender my submarine to the British. Then I returned home, to a country in ruins. Money was so worthless that people used banknotes to paper their walls and stuff their mattresses. The government was weak, corrupt.

"Then Hitler came, and I rejoiced, because at last I believed we had a strong leader, a man who would rebuild our nation – who would create a Navy and allow me to go to sea once more. But before long I saw our beloved *Führer* for what he is: a mad dog, driven by hatred and insane fantasies. A friend approached me – he knew of an organization that sought to control events behind the scenes, one that could harness the power that Hitler sought to wield. I allowed myself to be persuaded to join the Sons of Destiny."

Luke said carefully, "And have they turned out to be everything you hoped?"

Roth gave him a crooked smile. "You are a diplomat, Mr. Challenger. You might as well call me a foolish old man and have done with it; I could not disagree with you. But the die is cast. I accepted membership of the Sons of Destiny. By the time I saw them in their true colours, it was too late." He pulled up his sleeve to reveal a tattoo of a striking snake coiled around a spear. "I carry their mark upon me. It is not an organization from which one may easily resign."

"You could still walk away from them."

"My life would not be worth a moment's purchase. That is unimportant, but I have a family, and the Sons of Destiny are endlessly vindictive." Roth pulled his sleeve down again. "I have a mission, and I must complete it. I am sorry, Mr. Challenger. I cannot allow you to appeal to my better nature."

"I think I already have. But I'm sorry we must be

enemies." Luke stared the old Sea Wolf straight in the eye. "You know that I will stop you if I can."

Roth gave him a grim smile. "I would expect no less." He gestured towards the door. "Please."

Luke turned and strode through the silent rooms and corridors of the *Nautilus* into the custody of the waiting guards, and a new captivity.

23 DIVISION

"We're moving," said Jessica.

The U-X1's diesel engines had started several minutes ago. Luke now felt the vibration beneath his feet as the submarine's propeller shafts began to turn. He cursed and rattled the handcuffs by which his left wrist was attached to a strong steel pipe. "Where are we going, d'you suppose?"

Jessica gave him a weary look and shook her head.

Luke tugged at his handcuffs again. "Blast Roth! We let him bring us onto his submarine without a squeak of protest, and here we are trussed up like something in a butcher's window. Talk about turkeys voting for Christmas! We were better off locked in our cabins on the *Challenger II*."

"Except Mochizuki can't get her claws into us here," Nick pointed out. "Roth saved our bacon, all right. You can't expect him to give us the run of his boat, can you now?"

"Stop being reasonable," Luke told him. "It's getting my goat."

"Boys," said Jessica. "Let's not go stir-crazy. Play nicely, huh?"

Luke counted to ten. Finding that he was still seething with anger, he counted to ten again. He had reached seventy before he had calmed down enough to speak calmly. "Sorry," he said. "I'm tired of being cooped up. I can't see how we're ever going to stop the Sons of Destiny getting their hands on the *Nautilus*. And I want to know where we're going!"

"We are running for shelter." Kapitän Roth was clambering through the narrow watertight door that led from the aft torpedo room to the crew's quarters. He straightened up, brushing creases out of his uniform, and treated his prisoners to a sympathetic grimace. "Bad weather is forecast. The *Nautilus* is being towed alongside the *Challenger II* and we cannot risk the tow breaking in a rough sea. The *Nautilus* might be damaged – even, at worst, lost. So we are heading inshore. There, the *Challenger II* and her escorts shall anchor in sheltered water while we complete the preparations for long-distance towing. I'm sorry that your confinement must continue for a while yet."

"Oh, that's fine," said Nick. "We can stand up – nearly – or sit down, or lie on this nice hard deck – we could be really comfortable down here if only you could do something about the décor…"

Roth looked around the compartment, which, set as it was in the very stern of the submarine, tapered down to a point at the far end. His gaze took in the aft torpedo tubes and the sinister-looking torpedoes lying on their racks waiting to be loaded; the escape hatch set into the ceiling and the untidy nets of stores. "I'm afraid your living quarters lack amenities," he said gravely. "A submarine is not a hotel."

"A hotel?" complained Nick. "It's not even a bed and breakfast."

Roth gave them a thin smile. "I'm afraid I cannot open the exterior hatch while we are at sea, but once we have reached safe waters, I shall arrange for you to have fresh air. I regret that I cannot release you to take exercise – unless you are prepared to give me your word that you will not try to escape?" He looked at their set faces and said, "Obviously not. Please excuse me – I have my duties to attend to."

When he had gone, Luke said, "This could be our chance."

Nick gave him a blank look. "How do you figure that out?"

"They'll be busy with the *Nautilus* – resupplying, too, I shouldn't wonder. They've been at sea a long time. We'll be near land, and people. We can swim for it, maybe get to a radio…"

"Whoa, whoa." Nick held up his handcuffed wrist. "Aren't you forgetting something?"

"I know, I know, I'm just saying if we can get free, we'll be in a better position to stop the Sons of Destiny than we would be in the open ocean." When this was greeted with silence, Luke continued, "We have to try. We can't let Roth and Mochizuki tow the *Nautilus* off somewhere their tame scientists can crawl all over it. And what about Spotiswoode and the crew of the *Challenger*?"

"What about them?" asked Jessica. "Roth and Mochizuki have got the *Nautilus*, they don't need the *Challenger* or *Little Em'ly* any more."

"Oh, yes they do. They'll want to transport the *Nautilus* to some friendly port – friendly to them, that is – where they can examine it properly. That will mean transporting it over long distances, and how are they going to do that without the *Challenger II*? They can't tow the *Nautilus* behind one of the subs, their engines aren't powerful enough. They have to keep hold of the ship, and you don't suppose they'll just allow the crew to leave, do you? Roth might be prepared to do that, but Mochizuki won't."

Nick frowned. "Like you said – they're working for the Sons of Destiny so they've betrayed their own countries. If word of what they're up to reaches London, Berlin or Tokyo their goose is cooked."

"What do you think Roth will do?" asked Jessica.

"I don't know," said Luke. "I don't think he knows himself. I think he's putting off a decision he doesn't want to make."

"You mean," said Jessica quietly, "he might decide to kill us all?"

"Put yourself in his shoes. That's what Mochizuki will want. And it would be the safest way."

"There's a cheery thought..." Nick broke off as two German sailors came in carrying bowls of thin, pallid stew and hunks of bread for which the word "stale" was totally inadequate. "Ah," he concluded gloomily, "room service."

* * *

Luke glanced up at the exterior hatch as the locking bar on its underside spun round; a moment later, it opened with a metallic creak and he blinked in the sudden glare of daylight. A glimpse through half-closed eyelids revealed that Nick and Jessica were doing the same.

"Bright," Nick commented unnecessarily. "And warm," he added. He looked up at the small area of sky visible in the open hatchway. "Quite a lot of cloud though, and moving fast. Looks like Roth was right about bad weather coming in."

Luke struggled to reach the hatchway. If only he could see out, he might manage to spot a clue as to where they were, or see something that might help them escape. But his handcuffs brought him up short. Jessica was nearest the hatch, but even she could see no more than a patch of sky.

"Wouldn't you know it," said Nick bitterly. "Here we are, within reach of a tropical island paradise: golden sands, waving palms, lovely island girls…"

A young officer dropped down the hatch. He had supervised the men bringing them food from time to time, and Luke had taken an instant dislike to his flabby, sly-looking face and the way he leered at Jessica. He was leering now as he held up a roll of surgical tape. "We are bringing supplies aboard," he said blandly. "The islanders who are supplying us are not speaking English, but cries for help might make them – what is your word? – curious. So I gag you."

"Come and try it." Luke clenched his free hand into a fist.

The officer smiled faintly. "Please do not make this difficult." He gave a whistle, and a sailor armed with a rifle dropped through the hatch.

Luke was boiling with fury, but he could see no purpose in attacking the disagreeable officer – the armed man would have plenty of time to shoot Nick or Jessica while he was doing so. Glumly, he submitted to having surgical tape plastered across his mouth. It tasted bitter and smelled of antiseptic, and the officer wound it much tighter than was necessary. Though he made an efficient job of gagging Luke and Nick, he lingered over the process with Jessica, ogling her as he did so.

Having completed this task, he and the guard left. Shortly afterwards, Luke heard the sound of paddles and something bumped against the hull – seemingly a canoe or proa, because one of the submarine's crew came down through the hatch to be passed bunches and bundles of fresh fruit and vegetables – apples, bananas, guava and breadfruit among them – which he stacked against the walls, completely ignoring the captives. This process went on for some time, but when it ended, and the sailor departed the way he had come, no one arrived to remove the gags. Luke struggled to breathe normally as his anger rose.

Then he heard another sound – not the splashing of paddles, but the regular dip of oars. There was a clatter, signalling that the oars had been shipped. Then came a voice that made him clench his fists and brought the sweat to his brow.

"Kapitän Roth! Why did you not obey my summons to the *Challenger II*?"

Roth's distant reply was polite but uncompromising. "Captain Mochizuki. I am not aware that it is your power to summon me anywhere. I have already told you that I will negotiate further only with Commander Yoshida. And by the way, you do *not* have permission to come aboard my submarine. Do not approach any closer."

"Do not worry, Kapitän. I have no intention of attempting to seize your vessel. You may even keep Challenger, Malone and the Land girl – for now. But your refusal to talk jeopardizes our mission."

"I do beg your pardon, Captain. I have a strange premonition that if I set foot on a vessel under the control of your men, I would be very lucky indeed to leave it alive."

"You have my assurance—"

"I'm afraid I have little faith in your assurances. In any case, I have my instructions, with which Commander Yoshida was in full agreement before he was struck down by the sudden mental collapse that, according to you, has made him unfit for command. Those instructions are that the *Nautilus* will be towed to the Marshall Islands, where selected scientists from both our countries and others will work to discover the secrets of its propulsion, and report their findings to the High Command of the Sons of Destiny."

"Why the Marshall Islands?" demanded Mochizuki. "Why hide away on some naked rock in the middle of the Pacific when Japan is just as close? There, we would have a proper harbour and research facilities."

"Again, Captain, I'm afraid you must pardon my incurably suspicious nature. My intuition warns me that, if I were to agree to your kind proposal, the secrets of the *Nautilus*, while proving of great benefit to the Japanese wing of the Sons of Destiny, would mysteriously fail to be passed on to the other nations represented in our organization."

Captain Mochizuki's voice shook with suppressed anger. "And what if I took my submarine, and the *Challenger II* with the *Nautilus* in tow, and set course for Japan?"

"Then I should sink your submarine and, if necessary, the *Challenger II* also." There was steel in Roth's tone. "As my record indicates, I am expert at sinking... enemy shipping."

"You would risk the *Nautilus*?"

"Rather than let it fall into your hands? Yes, Captain. You will accept my men on board the *Challenger II*, and we will both escort her and the *Nautilus* to our agreed destination: otherwise, I am afraid that neither you, nor the *Nautilus*, nor your submarine will ever leave this bay."

Luke barely heard Mochizuki's hiss of rage, or her orders that sent her boat skimming back to the *Challenger II*. His mind was racing. Mochizuki and Roth didn't trust each other – he'd always known that, but now it was clear that they were practically at war! It would take only the slightest additional push to send them over the edge. He tugged at his handcuffs in frustration. If only he could get free...

"Enough of that!" The flabby-faced officer was back, with an armed escort. He looked sulky. "Kapitän Roth says your gags should now be removed." His eyes glinted. "However, he did not say *how* they should be removed." He eased Jessica's gag gently from her lips, and was rewarded with a melting smile. Then he grasped Luke's gag and tugged it viciously. The gag tore away, bringing the top layer of Luke's skin and a sizeable chunk of his hair with it. Luke gasped at the sudden pain, and drove his free fist into the German's stomach. As the man went down, his escort stepped forward, rifle raised, and clubbed Luke to the floor.

As he lay, dazed and bleeding freely from a scalp wound, Luke made every effort to hurl himself at the man and snatch his rifle. But his body would not obey him – his legs and arms felt as if they were made of string. By the time he had recovered sufficiently to scramble to his knees, the man had stepped back to a safe distance, from where he watched Luke's struggles with detachment.

The German officer, pale with fury, staggered to his feet. He stepped towards Luke, hand raised to deliver a vicious backhanded blow.

"No!" Jessica's voice rang through the compartment.

The officer turned to her, his expression a strange mixture of anger, scorn and curiosity. "No? What is he to you, *liebchen*?"

"Why, he...I..."

The officer approached Jessica, raising a hand to stroke her cheek. "You must understand, he struck me. That is mutiny. The penalty for mutiny is death."

"Oh..." Jessica's response was practically a whimper. Then she looked up at her captor. "Couldn't you...

forget that Luke laid hands on you?"

The officer smirked. "Why would I do that?"

"Maybe...if I was to tell where you could find something valuable on the *Nautilus*. Something *real* valuable."

The officer's eyes shone, but his reply was offhand. "Everything of value on board the *Nautilus* is to be seized by Captain Roth."

"Not this. Roth doesn't know about this. He hasn't read Nemo's journal. I have."

The officer raised a supercilious eyebrow. "Well? Go on."

"It's like this – you don't suppose Nemo spent so many years roaming the bottom of the sea without coming across shipwrecks, do you? Some of them, he put there himself. And where you get shipwrecks, what else do you get? I'll give you a clue. It's a rich kinda word, beginning with 'T'."

Luke stared at Jessica. Treasure? She's never mentioned *that* before...

"I see." The officer stared at Jessica for a long moment. Then he reached up with deliberation and closed and locked the exterior hatch. "What do you wish to tell me?"

Jessica shrugged. "If I told you my secret in front of other people, it wouldn't be a secret any more, would it?

It would be better if we could have a talk in...private."
She gave the officer a wink.

Luke and Nick exchanged bewildered glances. What on earth was Jessica up to?

The officer turned to his escort. "*Geben Sie mir den Schlüssel!*" The man hesitated for a moment; then he dipped his hand in a pocket and drew out a small key, which he passed across. The officer took it. "*Lassen Sie mich allein!*" he ordered. "*Sofort!*"

The guard glanced quickly from Luke to Nick. Evidently concluding that they did not pose a threat, he turned on his heel and left.

"You had better be telling me the truth," the officer told Jessica, undoing her handcuffs as he spoke. "If not, the consequences for you will be...unpleasant." Jessica gave him a nervous smile as he led her to the doorway to the next compartment of the submarine. As she stepped over the sill and lowered her head to duck through, she half-turned – and gave Luke and Nick an outrageous wink.

Nick gave Luke a questioning glance. Luke shrugged back, motioned Nick to silence and listened intently.

Jessica and the officer had disappeared. For some time, Luke could hear nothing but indistinct whispers. But then, through the open doorway came a high-pitched shriek; a succession of sobs; a long, bubbling moan...

Jessica slipped through the hatchway, looking as if she'd just returned from a particularly wholesome Sunday school picnic. She removed Nick's gag, and glanced from him to Luke and back again.

"Hi there, fellers." She held up a small silver key and waggled it playfully. "Well?" she continued brightly. "Are we busting out of this dump, or what?"

24 HOSTILITIES

Nick massaged his wrists while Jessica turned the key in Luke's handcuffs. "What now?" he asked.

"First-aid kit," said Jessica briskly. "You're bleeding." She headed through the hatch. Luke and Nick followed.

The next compartment was divided into cabins for the crew. Jessica searched them until she came across a box with a red cross on the lid.

Nick was peering into another cabin. Luke joined him. The young officer who had taken Jessica away was lying on a bunk in the foetal position. His face was deathly pale, and beads of sweat shone on his brow; his eyes, wide open, stood out of his head like bloodshot mushrooms. He was clutching himself in what a submariner might describe as his midsection, and giving little whimpers of agony.

Jessica took a small bottle of iodine from the box and dribbled a few drops onto Nick's bleeding wrist. "Ow!"

"Baby!"

Nick couldn't take his eyes off the German. "What did you do to him?"

"You don't want to know." Jessica took a bandage from the box and bound Nick's wrist.

"But where...I mean, how...?"

"I grew up in New Orleans," said Jessica matter-of-factly. "It's a tough town." She took the handcuffs and secured the moaning officer to the bunk. Her eyes glinted as she held up a roll of surgical tape. "Oh, and by the way," she went on as she applied a businesslike gag, "for getting your sorry butts out of here, my salvage fee just went up to thirty per cent."

"I'm not arguing," Luke told her.

"And what was all that about treasure?" Nick put in.

Jessica rolled her eyes. "There is no treasure, chucklehead. Leastways Nemo never mentioned any – he wasn't interested in that kind of thing."

Nick sighed. "Pity."

As Jessica and Nick completed the task of securing their prisoner, Luke took the officer's cap from the floor. Putting it on, he led the way back to the torpedo room and reached for the hatch. "Let's see where we are." He jammed the cap down low over his eyes, opened the hatch, and took a couple of steps up the ladder to peer out.

A quick survey showed him that the submarine was lying in a small bay. The sky was filled with scudding grey cloud and the crowns of palm trees were waving fretfully in the building wind. The lookouts on the conning tower were gazing at the *Challenger II*, which lay at anchor nearby with the *Nautilus* floating alongside. Gangs of men, both German and Japanese, swarmed over the salvaged vessel. Luke saw bright flashes appear at various points on the hull. These puzzled him until he realized that they must be from welding torches – either the men were repairing damaged hull plates, or they were installing strong points to attach cables for towing.

The U-X1 was moored with her bows towards the open sea where, outside the sheltered waters of the bay, spray streaked from the crests of the angry waves. The I-40, Mochizuki's submarine, was further inshore, floating quite close to rocks on the east side of the bay. A slow grin spread across Luke's face as he realized that the German submarine's stern was pointing almost directly at the bows of the Japanese vessel.

He ducked back inside and handed the cap to Nick. "Take a look," he said, "but be careful." Nick nodded and mounted the steps.

Jessica said, "I take it from that smug look that you have an idea."

"For your information, this is a look of steely resolve."

Jessica shook her head. "Smug is what it is. Well?"

Luke waited for Nick to duck down and close the hatch behind him. Then he said, "What do you suppose Mochizuki would do if this submarine fired a torpedo at her?"

"Do?" said Nick. "She'd do her nut! She'd think Roth was attacking her." He grinned. "If that's the plan, I like it." Then his face fell. "But the stern of this sub isn't pointing directly at the I-40."

"Good. I don't want to hit Mochizuki's sub. We're not murderers like her. But she and Roth are spoiling for a fight already..."

"And if she thinks Roth fired the torpedo, even if it's a near-miss, she's not going to listen when he says, 'Who? Me? Never!'"

Luke indicated the gleaming torpedoes on their racks. "Can you rig one of those to fire?"

Nick rubbed his palms together in anticipation. "Watch me!"

"We'll have to work fast. Someone's bound to come looking for toadface sooner or later."

Under Nick's supervision, Luke and Jessica used a chain-hoist that ran on overhead rails to lift a torpedo from its rack. They were sweating with exertion by the time the deadly missile was poised, ready to enter the torpedo tube.

Nick examined the arming mechanism. "I wish I could read German," he muttered, "but it's fairly obvious how this works."

"You'd better be right," Luke told him. "I'd rather this thing exploded outside the sub than inside."

"Don't worry – even after it's armed, it won't explode until it's run over a certain distance." Nick frowned with the effort of memory. "300 metres, Roth said. That's about 330 yards. How far away do you reckon those rocks are?"

"About 400 yards."

"Close, then. I'll set it for minimum distance and hope for the best." Nick fiddled for a moment. "There. Done! It's armed. Let's load it up."

As they hauled the heavy torpedo into position, Luke said, "As soon as this thing explodes, we swim for the *Challenger II*."

"We'll be spotted," said Nick. "They have guards on the conning tower. If they see us in the water, they're bound to start shooting."

"Only if they see us." Jessica pointed to a rack at the far end of the compartment. The aft torpedo room was also the emergency escape compartment and the racks held underwater breathing apparatus. "The gas cylinder is supposed to inflate a bladder to bring you to the surface as well as give you air to breathe. We want to stay down, so I'll have to fix the valves."

Luke grinned. "You're a genius."

"Better believe it. You boys load that torpedo."

After a final effort, they succeeded in manhandling the torpedo into the tube and Nick closed the watertight door to seal it. "Now, the firing mechanism," he said. "We have to flood the tube, open the outer door and *boosh!*" He stared at the array of valves and levers that controlled this operation, and swore softly. "Of course, it's all in German again. I can work it out, but it will take time."

"Maybe there's a quicker way." Luke picked up the key to the handcuffs and went through to the next compartment. A couple of minutes later he returned with their prisoner.

Luke tore the gag from the officer's mouth with as little consideration as the German had shown him earlier. He pointed at the control panel. "Which of those floods the tube?"

The officer drew himself up as proudly as his injuries would allow. "I would rather die than betray my fatherland!"

Without turning his head, Luke called, "Jessica!"

The man's eyes widened with terror. "Not her!" he screamed. "That valve! There!"

"He doesn't stand up well under pressure, does he?" Nick gaped at Jessica. "Seriously, what did you do to him?"

Jessica gave him a wry grin. "Seriously? Trust me, you *really* don't want to know."

Luke was already reaching for a set of breathing apparatus. "Let's get these on. Jessica, stand by the hatch. Open it as soon as the torpedo explodes – with any luck we'll be over the side while they're still watching the fireworks." He struggled into the unwieldy breathing gear and waited while Nick and Jessica followed suit.

"Now," Nick told the demoralized officer, "you're going to tell me which lever opens the outer door to the tube, and which fires the torpedo."

"Aren't you?" added Jessica sweetly.

With a terrified glance at her, the officer indicated the relevant controls. Nick opened the tube's outer door and waited expectantly.

Luke drew in a deep breath. "Here we go, then," he said. "Fire."

Nick pulled a lever. There was a rush of compressed air. "Torpedo away."

"I reckon about half a minute until it hits." Luke checked his watch. Breathlessly, they waited, counting the seconds.

At twenty-three seconds, there was a thunderous explosion. Luke grabbed for the ladder as the impact of the shock wave threatened to knock him off his feet. "Now!" he snapped. "Go!"

Jessica was already half out of the hatch and Nick was following her up the ladder when the hull rang to the impact of heavy objects. Luke was startled – had Mochizuki started shooting already? Then he realized that the sub was being pelted with debris from the explosion. Fervently hoping that their escape would not end in being brained by flying rocks, Luke reached the hatchway. Two trails of bubbles heading towards the *Challenger II* indicated that Nick and Jessica were already in the water.

A brief glance took in the scene of chaos. Rocks were still tumbling into the bay. Men were rushing to leave the *Nautilus* and boats were being speedily lowered from the *Challenger II*; threats, insults and shots were exchanged as the Japanese and German sailors guarding the vessel hurried to return to their submarines and join the fight. On the I-40, a gun crew was assembling round the submarine's deck cannon. As its barrel swung menacingly towards the U-X1, Luke pulled goggles down over his eyes and pitched forward to roll down the submarine's casing and into the sea.

The water was warm, but plunging into it was still a shock. Hastily, Luke opened the valve to the air cylinder. As soon as he had his breathing under control, he set off swimming towards the *Challenger II*. His progress was slow: the escape kit did not run to flippers, and he knew the air supply in the tank would be limited. He had entered the water on the side of the submarine nearest the ship, and had tried to swim in its direction, but after some minutes, he began to lose confidence that he was going the right way, and he did not dare surface to check his position.

After what seemed an age, Luke spotted something rising from the seabed: an anchor chain. He followed it upwards, and before long the barnacle-encrusted hull of the *Challenger II* was looming above him.

Nick and Jessica were already waiting when Luke dragged himself onto the ship's boarding platform. "What's happening?" he gasped as he shucked off the cumbersome breathing gear.

A puff of smoke erupted from the Japanese submarine's deck gun. A split second later, a fountain of spray erupted alongside the U-X1's conning tower. As the German submarine's gunners returned fire, Nick grinned. "Couldn't be better. Mochizuki and Roth are knocking seven barrels out of each other and most of the men they left on guard here seem to have gone across to join in the fun."

"All right." Luke scrambled to his feet. "Let's go and find the crew."

Their appearance at the top of the gangway was so unexpected that the fight was over almost before it had begun. An expert karate kick from Luke sent a Japanese guard tumbling over the ship's side. Nick swept a German guard's legs from under him – staggering backwards, off balance, the man was helped over the rail by Jessica and splashed into the water almost on top of his floundering companion. Nick snatched up the gun the man had dropped and followed Luke and Jessica into the accommodation deck.

Here, the corridors were full of yells and the sound of fists hammering on doors. Against this background, the remaining guard had no notice of Luke's approach. A downward chop to the neck sent him crashing to the floor.

Luke searched the man's belt and cursed. "No keys! The other guards must have taken them. Mochizuki's idea, I'll bet."

"Not a problem. I've always wanted to do this." Nick raised his rifle to aim at the lock of the first door. "Stand back in there!" He pulled the trigger.

A kick from Luke's boot completed the demolition of the door. Half a dozen members of the *Challenger II*'s crew spilled out, angry and looking for trouble, Chief Officer Marsden among them. While Nick gleefully shot the locks off the remaining doors, Luke quickly explained the situation.

Spotiswoode appeared, wild-eyed and with his spectacles askew. "What's happening?" he demanded. "Are we fighting?"

"Roth and Mochizuki are fighting each other," Nick told him. "If we get away quickly, we won't need to get involved."

"Oh." Spotiswoode sounded disappointed. But as he listened to Luke's explanation, his eyes gleamed. "I say! Sounds like you diddled 'em good and proper. Well done!"

As soon as Luke finished his account, the Chief Officer began issuing orders. "Thompson, O'Mally, Evans: get the engines started. Emergency procedure – five minutes. Lucas, Galbraith – get ready to slip anchor. Johnson, Cole, Kennedy – find whatever weapons you can and make sure there are no more of our Japanese or German friends on this ship: if you find any, chuck 'em over the side." He pointed to the groaning guard Luke had disabled. "This one, too. He looks like a dip in cold water will do him good. The rest of you, make ready for sea. We're getting out of here while the getting's good."

Only when his men had been despatched about their tasks did he turn back to Luke and his friends. "Good job," he said. "Thanks. Come to the bridge. Let's see how much trouble you three have managed to cause."

As soon as they arrived on the bridge, Luke could see that the amount of trouble was considerable. There were several gaping holes in the casing of both submarines where shots from the opposition's deck gun had hit home. The conning tower of the I-40 looked as though something had taken a bite out of it, one of the periscopes was missing and the radio aerial was dangling over the side. As Luke watched, a foaming wake appeared at the Japanese vessel's stern. He groaned aloud – if Mochizuki could get her submarine clear, she could overpower the *Challenger II* again anytime she chose. But then, a shot from the U-X1's deck gun sent up a plume of water at the I-40's stern, and the Japanese submarine slewed drunkenly to one side and stopped dead in the water.

Marsden gave a grin of satisfaction. "Got her rudder," he said with relish, "or her prop – maybe both, with luck. She won't be going anywhere for a while." He pointed at the battle-scarred U-X1. "And Roth's boat is so low in the water it must be partially flooded. Time to go." He reached for the speaking tube to the engine room. "All set down there?"

In answer, the engines rumbled into life. Marsden made for the side deck of the bridge and signalled to his anchor crew. One swung a sledgehammer and the chain rushed out, rattling. The Chief Officer was sacrificing the ship's one remaining anchor in the need for a quick departure.

Marsden rang "Full Ahead" on the engine telegraph. The propellers churned, and the ship, towing the *Nautilus* alongside, was under way. For a few precious moments, the combatants on the submarines seemed unaware of what was happening. By the time they realized that their captive was escaping, it was too late for effective action. The deck guns on both vessels swung to aim at the departing ship; three rounds went home. After that, the enemy shells did nothing but send up fountains of water, falling short as their quarry moved out of range.

On finding that one of the successful shots had caused a few splinter wounds, Jessica headed for the sick bay. Another round had torn through the (fortunately unoccupied) mess hall, causing widespread devastation; but it hardly mattered that there was nowhere for the crew to eat because the third shell had taken out most of the galley, so there was nothing to eat anyway. Luke and Nick helped the ship's cook spray the smouldering wreckage with seawater from a hosepipe.

"Lovely jam roly-poly and custard all over the bloomin' walls," moaned Cookie. "It's a tragedy, that's what it is!"

Luke sympathized with the man, but he couldn't help feeling that a ruined jam roly-poly (with or without custard) was a small price to pay for their freedom.

25 PURSUIT

Above Java Trench:
010° 18' S, 109° 54' E

Chief Officer – now, since he had assumed control of a vessel at sea, Acting-Captain – Marsden slammed the bridge door on the howling wind and shrugged off his oilskin jacket. "It's not getting any better out there," he remarked.

It was after midnight, more than twelve hours since they had escaped from the Sons of Destiny. There was no sign of pursuit, but the bad weather that had driven their enemies to seek shelter showed no signs of abating. Though nowhere near as violent as the storm that had nearly wrecked the *Challenger II* in the Pacific, the conditions were bad enough to cause concern for the master of a ship towing a priceless piece of salvage. The ropes that held the *Nautilus* to the ship's side creaked and groaned with every wave, chafing on the encrustations of the submarine's hull, and though rope fenders were supposed to prevent the vessels colliding, repeated clangs were evidence that the sea state was testing these to the limit.

Luke was peering through binoculars out of the broken windows at the rear of the wheelhouse; back over the afterdeck where *Little Em'ly* nestled, seemingly content to take a well-deserved rest after her exertions. He was scanning the horizon for any sign of their enemies.

Marsden glanced at him. "Better get some rest, Mister Challenger. I daresay you can't see a mile in these conditions, anyway."

"I can't," admitted Luke. "Too dark, too much rain. But even if I can spot them a mile off, we'll have a few minutes' warning. That could be vital."

"They're not following us," said Marsden. "Both subs were too badly damaged. In any case, even if one crew could get their sub under way, they'll expect us to go west, hugging the coast, and through the Sunda Strait heading for Jakarta or Singapore. The last thing they'll expect is for us to head back out here."

"As Captain Fulton once said, they don't call Roth the Sea Wolf for nothing." Luke lowered the binoculars and rubbed salt-reddened eyes that ached from hours of staring at crashing waves. "Captain, if Roth does manage to follow us, and catch up with us, what can we do to stop him getting his hands on the *Nautilus* again?"

"Precious little, I'm afraid. Roth could stand off at a distance and sink us with gunfire or torpedoes – I shouldn't think he'd do that as long as we might drag the *Nautilus* down with us, but there's nothing to stop him boarding us again. His men and the Japanese took most of our guns when they had control of the ship. We've a couple of rifles from the guards we overpowered, and three or four pistols; that's all."

Luke nodded unhappily. "That's what I thought." He didn't feel this was the moment to discuss the reason he had persuaded the reluctant Acting-Captain to steam directly away from Java, into the open ocean. Time for that if his worst fears were realized. He was sure that the I-40 was out of the picture. With damage to her rudder and propellers, he couldn't see Mochizuki persuading a crew whose commanding officer she had deposed to make an all-out effort to repair the Japanese submarine, even if repairs were possible. Roth was a different proposition. After their private conversation aboard the *Nautilus*, Luke felt that he understood

Kapitän Roth – he knew that if there was any way of repairing the U-X1, Roth would follow the *Challenger II* to the ends of the earth to reclaim his prize.

Luke suddenly felt very alone. Nick was on board the *Nautilus* with Jessica, Spotiswoode and the Professor from Berkeley, whose name, infuriatingly, he still couldn't remember. They were examining the vessel's engines as best they could in the conditions – Luke imagined that the pitching and rolling, which was bad enough on the *Challenger II*, must be giving them a pretty horrible time in the dank and stuffy atmosphere of the *Nautilus*.

Wearily, he raised the binoculars to his eyes and trained them on the horizon. After a moment, he gripped the instrument tightly, straining to penetrate the darkness and sheets of rain. Fifteen seconds passed, and he was sure of what he had seen. "There! Bearing three-two-zero, directly behind us."

Marsden was at his side in an instant, raising his own binoculars to his eyes. After a few seconds' intense scrutiny, he lowered them again. "Hellfire and damnation! It's the U-X1 all right! Doesn't that man ever give up?"

Now that the moment of crisis was upon them, Luke felt suddenly calm. All the anxieties of their flight were swept away. There was only one possible course of action now, and he was determined to follow it. Without taking his eyes from the submarine that was bearing down on them, its desks awash and its conning tower lashed by spray as it shouldered aside the churning sea, he said, "What's our depth, Captain?"

Marsden stared at him. "Our depth?" Luke nodded and Marsden checked the depth gauge. "3,000 fathoms – 18,000 feet. We must be over the Java Trench."

"Good. Please assemble an axe party."

"An axe party?"

Fighting down the urge to ask whether the bridge had suddenly developed an echo, Luke said, "Yes. To cut the ropes holding the *Nautilus*. There's been so much strain on them, you'll never loose them by hand. In any case, there won't be time." At last he took the binoculars from his eyes. "Roth will start firing warning shots any second. Ignore them. I'm going to the *Nautilus*. I'll get everyone off: then I'm going to scuttle her."

"Sink the *Nautilus*?" Marsden stared at Luke. "Mister Challenger, I don't think your father would approve..."

"He'd approve if the alternative was to let the Sons of Destiny get their hands on her again – because that is the alternative, Captain, and you know it. We're over one of the deepest ocean trenches on earth. If the *Nautilus* goes down here we'll never find her again – but nor will anyone else. I'll take full responsibility."

Marsden gazed at him in an agony of indecision. Then he nodded, slowly. "You're right, of course. Very well, Mister Challenger. The axe party will be ready to cast off the *Nautilus* when we have all the boarding party back on the ship."

"Thank you, Captain." Luke was already making for the door.

"Good luck, Mister Challenger."

Luke plunged through the door into the rain, and took the slippery accommodation ladder two steps at a time. He reached the ship's rail, where a scramble net had been hastily rigged to give access to the *Nautilus* – in the conditions it had been impossible to lower a gangway. Two members of the *Challenger II*'s crew were leaning on the rail, watching the wildly bucking submarine. One looked up anxiously as Luke approached. "You ain't thinking of going aboard her, are you, sir?" he asked. "The sea's so rough, I don't know how we're going to get them as is aboard her back to the ship, and that's a fact."

Quickly, Luke explained the situation. The man swore. "Ruddy German submarines – I had a bellyful of them in the Heligoland Bight back in 1918. Well, we've rigged a jackstay from the netting to the hatch, sir. Keep hold of that and you should be all right."

"Thanks." Luke swung a leg over the rail, and started the descent.

The *Nautilus* was rubbing against the side of the *Challenger II* like a large and boisterous puppy – one moment it was fifteen feet below Luke, a few seconds later he could have stepped directly onto the casing without dropping an inch. Clinging to the sodden rope of the net, he waited until the submarine's next rise, and leaped the gap between the ship's side and the *Nautilus*'s tiny deck. For a terrible moment he slid, feet scrabbling helplessly on the rain-lashed casing; but then his clutching fingers caught at the jackstay, the safety-line rigged to aid the perilous crossing, and he hauled himself onto the deck. With numbed fingers, he tugged at the locking wheel on the dorsal hatch. Moments later, he dropped into the relative safety of the *Nautilus*, dragging the hatch closed behind him.

He found Nick and the others in the engine room. Spotiswoode was being noisily seasick in the bilge, but Nick and the man from Berkeley were measuring everything in sight and calling out the results of their investigations to Jessica who, her shoulder jammed into a gap in the pipework, was writing them down.

The room echoed to the crash of the waves outside. Luke put his thumb and forefinger in his mouth and gave a strident whistle. "We have to go," he told the startled boarding party. "Roth's on the way. Grab whatever you can and get out."

"What do you mean?" Spotiswoode was green about the gills and looked about to faint, but he was still able to frame a sensible question. "Roth's here?" A sudden roar penetrated the casing and the deck shuddered: the first of Roth's warning shots Luke had predicted. Spotiswoode stared at Luke, wild-eyed. "What are you going to do?"

"Scuttle the *Nautilus*."

"What?" Nick was aghast. "Are you mad? After all the trouble we went to to get her? Even if you do, what's to stop Roth just taking over the ship and diving for her again?"

"We're directly over the Java Trench," Luke told him. "The *Nautilus* will sink 20,000 feet, straight down to the bottom. Let Roth try to get to her then."

"But..." The Berkeley man was practically wringing his hands. "There's so much to learn here – these engines could save us years of research and development!"

"Yeah," put in Jessica, "and what about my thirty per cent?"

The deck juddered again. Roth's second warning shot had fallen closer. Luke felt like tearing his hair out. There was no time for argument. He forced himself to speak calmly. "Listen, there's no help for it. Yes, the *Nautilus* could save us years of research – and if Roth gets hold of it, it could do the same for Hitler, with the Sons of Destiny egging him on. Do you want to live in a world where the first nuclear power is Nazi Germany?"

Nick shook his head helplessly. "But…"

"Jessica, remember what Nemo said in his last message? When he chose to go down with the *Nautilus*, it was because he didn't trust humanity to use the secrets of her engines without destroying itself." Jessica gave a reluctant nod. "Can anybody seriously argue that we're any more ready to deal with nuclear power now than we were then? How many millions died in the Great War? If war comes again, how many millions more will die – and how many tens of millions, hundreds of millions if nuclear weapons are used?" His voice dropped so that the others had to strain to hear. "I thought we – Britain and America – should have Nemo's secrets, but I was wrong. Maybe this way is best. With the *Nautilus* beyond reach, nobody gets them."

"Until we work the secret out for ourselves," said the man from Berkeley defiantly.

"There's nothing I can do about that. But I can stop the Sons of Destiny getting their hands on those secrets, here and now, and that's what I'm going to do."

The third warning shot to rock the *Nautilus* was terrifyingly loud in the silence that greeted this announcement. Unexpectedly, it was Spotiswoode who spoke first. "I'm afraid Luke's right. We could spend years trying to find out how these engines work, and we haven't got years. We haven't even got minutes. And we can't let Roth get hold of the *Nautilus* again. There's nothing else for it. Is Marsden ready to cut the moorings?" Luke, weak with relief that the argument was settled, could only nod. Spotiswoode drew himself up. "Good. The rest of you, go. I'll flood the tanks and send the *Nautilus* down..."

"No, you won't," said Luke hastily. "Sinking the *Nautilus* was my idea – I won't ask anyone else to take the risk..."

"Sure, and how would you know which valves to open?" Nick's voice was serious but a slight smile tweaked the corner of his mouth.

Luke gave him a glare. "All right," he said, "together."

Nick broke into a broad grin. "That's the way it's always been."

Jessica let rip a blood-curdling oath. "Thirty per cent," she moaned. "*Dammit!*" Then she tucked the notebook inside her jacket and shrugged. "Ah well – like my daddy always said, if at first you don't succeed, try again; then give up. No sense in being a damn fool about it."

"That was your da?" said Nick. "I thought it was W. C. Fields."

"My daddy said it first. You want to argue?" Jessica was already pushing Spotiswoode and the man from Berkeley towards the engine room door. "Git going!" she told them. She turned back to Luke and Nick. "Don't hang around."

As soon as they were gone, Nick said, "The buoyancy tank valves are in here – the saloon and the helmsman's position only have steering controls and instruments. Six valves." He pointed them out. "You take port, I'll take starboard."

Luke nodded. "Then a fast exit. And you go up the ladder first. Right?"

"If you insist. What about the main hatch? Are you going to leave that open?"

Luke thought about the treasures the *Nautilus* still held: the library, the porcelain and glassware in the dining room; the paintings and sculpture in the saloon, the collection of marine organisms, the mortal remains of Nemo himself still seated at the organ keyboard... He shook his head. "No."

"At 20,000 feet, the hull will collapse under the pressure anyway."

"If the *Nautilus* is to be destroyed, let the sea do it. That's what Nemo would have said."

"Right." Nick reached for the valves. "I reckon the others have had time to get clear. On a count of three: one, two, three..."

He and Luke spun the valves. There was an instant gurgling from outside the pressure hull as the submarine's ballast tanks began to fill.

Nick finished turning the last valve. "That's it. Let's

go. Will the last one to leave please turn out the lights."

They pelted for the ladder. The *Nautilus* was already beginning to settle, and water slopped through the hatch as they climbed, seemingly trying to force them back into the doomed vessel. Luke struggled through the hatch, and caught sight of Nick throwing himself at the scramble net as he slammed it shut and spun the wheel for the last time.

Then, on the submarine's next rise, he made a froglike leap for the net, caught it, and began to climb. At the same time, he heard the sound of axes as the crew of the *Challenger II* cut away the ropes holding the *Nautilus*.

He tumbled over the rail. He turned to see the U-X1 almost alongside – it was so close he could see Roth, staring in horrified disbelief as his precious prize slipped beneath the waves in its very final dive. He heard his anguished cry of "*Tauchen! Tauchen!*" and the raucous bellow of the klaxon as the U-boat prepared to follow.

Nick was at his shoulder, staring as the conning tower sank beneath the waves. "What's he trying to do?"

Luke shook his head. "I don't suppose even he knows. Maybe he thinks he can get underneath it and hold it up with the U-boat until his divers can blow the tanks."

"Not a hope!" said Jessica, leaning over the rail.

"He must have performed miracles to get here at all."

Luke passed a hand wearily through his rain-soaked rat's-tail hair. "One last gamble. That's the way he thinks."

Captain Marsden must have cut the engines. For several minutes the *Challenger II* rocked uneasily in the swell, its rail thronged with silent watchers.

Then there was a cry from the lookout on the bridge. The surface of the sea seemed to bulge – a vast bubble of air rose from the depths and burst, just for a moment calming the surging waves. Then a slick of oil appeared, and after that, the first pieces of wreckage.

Tears came to Luke's eyes. The pressure hull of the U-X1 had been crushed. Roth's last gamble had failed.

"I suppose his submarine must have been more badly damaged than he thought." The man from Berkeley shook his head sorrowfully. "And the *Nautilus* – gone for ever, and the secrets of atomic power with her." He sighed. "At least we got a look at the engines, and we have Miss Land's notes. That's a start. As for the rest, I guess it's back to the drawing board."

Luke glanced at him – and absurdly, in that unhappy moment, he remembered the man's name.

"That's right, Professor Oppenheimer." He watched as the relentless waves scattered the wreckage of the U-X1, and gave the scientist's shoulder a consoling pat. "That's right."

26 SUNSET

Sunda Strait:
005° 58' S, 105° 46' E

At evening the following day, the *Challenger II* was steaming between Java and Sumatra on its way to Singapore.

The ship had remained at the position where the U-X1 had gone down until dawn; finding no survivors, Marsden had finally called off the search. Since then, Nick, Spotiswoode and the ship's radio operator had between them managed to jury-rig a wireless set. This only worked intermittently, but even so, messages had been coming in thick and fast.

Luke glanced up from a pile of these as Nick stuck his head into the radio room. "How's it going?"

"Just peachy." Luke grabbed a handful of messages and waved them at him. "All these are from my father."

"Congratulating us on a job well done?"

"Ha, ha. He says here..." Luke scrutinized the message carefully. "*I might have known you'd muck the whole thing up.*"

"Ah, bless him. He's got such a forgiving nature."

Luke snorted. "Anyway, he's confirmed Marsden as Captain, and he's ordering the *Challenger II* back to England, once she's put in to Singapore for repairs."

Nick brightened. "Great! We can stay aboard all the way home..."

"No such luck. We're to take an Imperial Airways flight from Singapore to London. He says with any luck, we'll be back at school for the start of term."

"Rats!"

"There's a message from Nanny, too." Luke passed over the form with the message in the radio operator's hasty scrawl. It read:

Well done, Luke dear. It's a pity you couldn't hold onto the Nautilus, but you did the right thing to make sure those beastly Sons of Destiny couldn't get their hands on it. By the way, as soon as we got your message, Whitehall contacted the Australian Navy. One of their frigates found the I-40 high and dry in Pangandaran Bay. Apparently they'd run aground rather than let her sink and the crew claim they were out on a peaceful patrol when they suffered a most unfortunate accident. The Australians tactfully did not ask how any accident on board could possibly have resulted in gunfire damage all over the hull. They even promised to get a spare propeller to the submarine, and I daresay they will – eventually. In any case it will be at least two weeks before they have a tide high enough to refloat. One more thing might interest you – Commander Yoshida was back in charge of the boat, and there was no sign of Captain Mochizuki: indeed, the Commander was most adamant that she had never been on board.

"My eye!" said Nick crossly.

Now, Luke dear, do remember to wrap up warm for the flight. I hear the route goes via Northern India and Afghanistan, and this time of year it will be terribly cold in the Hindu Kush. Remember, Nanny knows best.

Luke threw down the messages. "Come on. Let's get out of this."

They wandered across the afterdeck to the stern rail, where they found Jessica and Spotiswoode enjoying the last of the sunshine.

"Ah, there you are." The Chief Marine Engineer of Challenger Industries was in a buoyant mood.

Luke treated him to a hard stare. "You sound disgustingly cheerful."

"Well, you have to take the philosophical view," said Spotiswoode expansively. "I mean, true, we didn't get everything we wanted from the *Nautilus* – but we definitely got an inkling of what to look out for. That Oppenheimer chappie reckons his team will crack the problem of atomic energy eventually – he thinks it'll take another ten years or so, but he's confident they'll get there in the end."

Luke nodded, keeping his thoughts to himself.

"And then again," continued Spotiswoode, "you have to admit that *Little Em'ly* has been a roaring success – outperformed all her specs." He took Nick by the arm. "In fact, I wanted to have a word with you about some modifications I'm planning for the next model..." The two of them wandered over to stare up at the submersible, gesticulating wildly, already deep in discussion about improvements to be incorporated in the *Challenger*

Self-Propelling Bathysphere Mark II...

Luke moved closer to Jessica. "I did manage to persuade my father to underwrite your next venture." He passed over a message form.

Jessica read the figure that Luke's father had promised and gave a low whistle. "That's real nice of Sir Andrew. But I guess I already took care of my thirty per cent." She undid the buttons on her loose-fitting jacket and held it open. Nestled inside was a small but exquisite oil painting.

Luke stared at it. "Isn't that the whatsit – the da Vinci – from the *Nautilus*'s saloon?"

"Sure. I thought it was a waste to leave it for the fishes. In any case, the sale of this should set me up nicely – and see Lou has all he needs to sort out his bar."

Luke shook his head in admiration. He and Jessica watched the wake in companionable silence as the sun dipped below the hills of Sumatra.

"So," said Luke eventually, "you're going to set up your own salvage company?"

Jessica shook her head. "Nope. I reckon I've done enough salvaging to last me a spell. I'm fixing to set up a diving school. Somewhere the water is warm. And clear. And most of all, *shallow*."

The sun disappeared. In the brief tropical twilight,

the wake stretched to the horizon; it was as though the ship were the only thing left in the whole world, and they were leaving the past behind.

But the future lay ahead – unknown, perhaps, but even in that peaceful moment Luke knew that in his future, the Sons of Destiny and Captain Kasumi Mochizuki would be waiting. Sometime.

Somewhere.

ABOUT THE AUTHORS

STEVE BARLOW was born in Cheshire and worked at various times as a teacher, actor, stage manager and puppeteer. Steve now lives in Somerset. He likes walking, sailing, reading, listening to music and shouting at politicians on the telly.

STEVE SKIDMORE was born in Birstall near Leicester and trained as a teacher of Drama, English and Film studies, before teaming up with Steve Barlow to become a full-time author. He lives in Leicester and is a great rugby fan.

The two Steves have had over one hundred and twenty books published. Their website is www.the2steves.net.

Look out for more of Luke Challenger's
death-defying adventures

RETURN TO THE
LOST WORLD

Someone is trying to kill Luke Challenger. And being
garrotted with cable car wires is not the way he wants
to end his young life! Luke and his friend Nick flee the
would-be assassins ino the deepest Brazilian jungle –
where they enter a lost world of real-life dinosaurs. But
the sinister Sons of Destiny are on Luke's tail. Why are
they hell-bent on destroying him?

ISBN 9781409520177

For more action-packed thrillers, check out
www.fiction.usborne.com